P9-DZO-678

JAN   2018

A
MAP
OF
THE
DARK

A MAP OF THE DARK

KAREN ELLIS

**MULHOLLAND
BOOKS**

Little, Brown and Company
New York Boston London

The characters and events in this book are fictitious. Any similarity to real persons, living or dead, is coincidental and not intended by the author.

Copyright © 2018 by Karen Ellis

Hachette Book Group supports the right to free expression and the value of copyright. The purpose of copyright is to encourage writers and artists to produce the creative works that enrich our culture.

The scanning, uploading, and distribution of this book without permission is a theft of the author's intellectual property. If you would like permission to use material from the book (other than for review purposes), please contact permissions@hbgusa.com. Thank you for your support of the author's rights.

Mulholland Books / Little, Brown and Company
Hachette Book Group
1290 Avenue of the Americas, New York, NY 10104
mulhollandbooks.com

First Edition: January 2018

Mulholland Books is an imprint of Little, Brown and Company, a division of Hachette Book Group, Inc. The Mulholland Books name and logo are trademarks of Hachette Book Group, Inc.

The publisher is not responsible for websites (or their content) that are not owned by the publisher.

The Hachette Speakers Bureau provides a wide range of authors for speaking events. To find out more, go to hachettespeakersbureau.com or call (866) 376-6591.

ISBN 978-0-316-50566-6
Library of Congress Control Number: 2017941134

10 9 8 7 6 5 4 3 2 1

LSC-H

Printed in the United States of America

A
MAP
OF
THE
DARK

For my father, Joel Spiegelman,
with love

PROLOGUE

She likes the feel of the ground underfoot and so she toes off her sneakers and carries them, swinging loosely from her fingertips. But after a couple of minutes she steps on something sharp and changes her mind. She drops her book bag in a pool of shifting shadows. Sits on it. Ties her left sneaker, then plants that foot on the ground and cantilevers over a bent knee to tie the other one. She feels tired. Tired from all the things on her agenda this week. All the schoolwork piling up. Yawning, she stands and continues walking slowly, vaguely, in the direction of her high school.

The whoosh of a car coming. And she remembers: *The biology test*. She prepared, so why is she nervous about it?

What is a quark? The smallest unit of matter; makes up protons.

What are molecules? Two or more atoms held together by chemical bonds.

What is an organelle? Part of a cell that has a specific function.

What are five types of organelles? Nucleus, mitochondrion, endoplasmic *something, something,* Golgi body.

Order from smallest to largest: Cell, tissue, organ, organ system, organism.

Again, what are five types of organelles?: Nucleus, mitochondrion, endoplasmic reticulum, *something, something.*

The third type comes to her but the fifth slips away, though she had it just a moment ago. The fourth one, she can't summon at all. She needs to do well on this test, but, honestly, why is it so important to know every detail about your body when it works just fine all on its very own?

Walking, slowing down, wondering where her life will lead her once she's free of school. Fanning open her fingers, she lets air circulate between her skin and today's rings: the purple glass one she bought at a flea market last year, and the brass braided one that always leaves behind a green circle. Several bracelets jangle on her left wrist. A clutch of necklaces hoop over the little tattoos that climb from shoulder to ear. Four earrings ladder from her right lobe; a long white feather swings from the left. The weight and movement of her jewelry reminds her of who she is. Who she *really* is, besides school and family and home and town and country and planet and universe.

A shadow moves and she's inspired to draw something on the sunlit patch of asphalt just ahead. She digs into her pocket for the nub of blue chalk she carries just in case. But then she hesitates.

A man is walking toward her. Tall. Brown hair swept back off his forehead, and a crooked nose that seems to get bigger as the distance between them shrinks. He nods at her. Her stomach gurgles. She keeps walking. No cars on the road at the moment. She wishes she'd managed to catch the bus.

"Excuse me." His voice is smooth, intent.

She pauses. "Yes?"

"Do you have the time?"

People always ask her that, maybe because, seeing so much jewelry, they assume she also wears a watch, which she doesn't. Why wear a watch when you can get the time off your phone? (Which is out of battery since, as usual, she forgot to charge it last night.)

Something in the man's eyes strikes her mute.

An impulse to run fires her nerves.

And then he shows her a gun.

SUNDAY

1

Roy's eyes are cloudy. He blinks and suddenly they're hazel again, like they used to be: green-streaked riverbeds of timeworn memory. Elsa gently squeezes his hand, hoping he'll say something, anything, as unexpectedly as his eyes gained color. He hasn't spoken all morning. He lies there, his short salty hair poking in every direction, staring at the charcoal screen of the turned-off television, taking in the latest news of his diagnosis. She feels the movement of an internal shadow, a pull toward grief, but resists it. Not yet. She's just about to lean in so she can feel the soft warmth of his breath and remind herself how he used to flutter his eyelashes against her cheek when she was a little girl—butterfly kisses—when her pocket vibrates with a call.

She releases his hand and it floats a moment before coming to rest on the crisp white hospital sheet.

Marco Coutts flashes on her screen. Her jaw clenches reflexively as she answers. Before she can speak, her boss says, "Yeah, Elsa, I'm really sorry to bother you on your day off."

Her whisper comes out like a hiss of steam. "You know I'm with my father."

"How's he doing?"

"Why are you calling?"

"A lot of red flags waving in Queens. A girl's missing, a teenager—"

A drumbeat forms in her chest: *Another one; here we go; please not today*. "What precinct?"

"Forest Hills. Some new guy caught the case."

Shitting his pants? is what she wants to ask, but her father is right there, eyes fixed open in his morphine fog of semi-consciousness, possibly listening. So she says, "Marco, I'm all the way up here in Sleepy Hollow. Can't you put Gonzales on it?"

"He's already out in the Bronx today. Anyway, Elsa, I like you better for this one. You have a special feel for the teenagers, always have."

The praise irks her. She says, "We really need more agents on-site," but her comment falls flat between them, a toneless reprise of an unsolvable problem. The Bureau doesn't have the budget to delegate more agents for the Child Abduction Rapid Deployment unit, which makes it tough to deploy rapidly in a city the size of New York, which is crazy, because these are kids. *Kids.* And each and every time one of them vanishes, an absence echoes through Elsa.

Marco breathes into a pocket of silence, hot, jagged, the way he does when he doesn't want to hear something. She can picture him in his neat office in DC, from which he remotely oversees far-flung CARD teams along the East Coast: Shelves behind his desk, framed photos of his wife and their new baby girl. Good people. But then she corrects the image; he wouldn't be in his office today, he'd be at home, because it's Sunday. As always, doing his best at a difficult job.

Elsa stands up and takes the call across the room to the window. Early-summer flowering trees border the hospital parking lot. A blue station wagon enters lazily and slots itself between white lines; the driver's door pops open but no one steps out. Elsa turns her back to the window, gaze landing on her father—his broken-doll fragility under the sheets, his sallow skin, his wheezing breath—and does a quick calculation. Phelps Memorial Hospital, where the ambulance had transferred him from the assisted-living facility to which he'd moved last winter, is an hour from the city. Her sister, Tara, is on the way from Manhattan and should be here soon. All the doctors and nurses agree that, though the cancer is moving faster now, he's still got time—"Two months," the oncologist said, then on second thought, "maybe three"—enough to be stabilized and released from the hospital to finish out his life, or his death, depending on how you saw it. Elsa could slip away and not miss anything and be back by tonight. Do everything, please everyone. Fail no one, ever again. Plus, if she returned to the city, it would offer an opportunity to get to the family house in Queens for a final visit.

It was strange, prescient almost, the way Roy decided to sell the house where he raised his family so soon before his diagnosis, as if his body were telling him, *Hurry, do this now, while you still have time and energy*. She hadn't believed he'd go through with it, but he did, just two days ago on Friday, with Tara as his proxy. It's really done. And he's really dying. Seeing him as weakened as he is today, she can no longer deny these facts. The shock of this, along with the loss of the house, has the effect of awakening her from a stupor of wishful thinking. She has to go back, even if she doesn't want to. When you grow up in the same house your whole life, it becomes a monolithic presence you can't escape fast enough, a shadow you need to outrun—and a shell that holds your secrets.

As she understands it, the new owners, in their hubris, intend to build a pool in the modest backyard immediately, wasting as little of the summer as possible. They plan to take possession of the house tomorrow, Monday, which leaves her with only today for an errand that suddenly feels important. A ribbon of sorrow twists around her. Yes, she'll be a good employee and run to the job her boss is assigning her; she'll be a good daughter and be back here tonight; and in between, she'll take a detour into her past.

Reaching down to scratch her thigh, hard, through the tough fabric of her jeans, she says to Marco, "Tell me about the girl—what makes you think she's been abducted?"

"You're a saint."

"You *know* I'm not."

"Her name's Ruby Haverstock. She's seventeen, almost eighteen, and her parents haven't heard from her since Friday night. She went to her job at a local café, left work on time, and that was that. The detective on the case—"

"You said he was new," she interrupts. "How new?"

"First day at the precinct was yesterday."

"Shh…oot"—transitioning the expletive into something nicer, for her father's sake. She glances over at him and he's looking at her now, drinking in the sight of her. She smiles at him, forcing back incipient tears. His dry lips open, just a little, and close again.

"My understanding is he transferred in from somewhere else in the city, not sure where," Marco says. "Alexei Cole, goes by Lex."

"First, second, or third? Because if he's a third-grade detective, Marco, you know as well as I do that this will take twice the time it should."

"First, I think. At least second. He isn't *new*-new. He's not panicking about the girl, not yet, but he could use some guidance. Let's reach out, Elsa, help him however we can."

"So what makes him so sure she didn't run away? Eighteen years old—"

"*Almost* eighteen. And I know what you mean, but I talked it over with Detective Cole, and, Elsa, I share his concern. He's done his due diligence. This is a good kid, never stepped out of line, never any real problems, college-bound. Something feels wrong here."

Roy's lips part again. Elsa's pulse jolts. If there's something he wants to say, she needs to hear it.

"Okay, Marco. Text me his info. I'll get right on it."

As soon as she slides her phone into her pocket, it pings with Marco's incoming text. She sits on the edge of her father's bed and leans in close. "What is it, Daddy?"

His lined, bony face contorts on a wave of complex emotion. *"Daddy,"* he echoes. It's true, she hasn't called him that in years. It just slipped out, and she's glad it did if it makes him happy.

"How are you feeling?"

He manages a twitch of his eyebrows, a familiar gesture

she reads instantly: *Don't ask the question unless you want the answer.*

"Are you thirsty?" Honing her inquiry to specifics. "Want some water?" She takes hold of his glass, straw bent at the ready, but he shakes his head.

"Your mother's almond…" His memory fades at the final word.

"Butterballs?" Her mother, Deb, has been dead twenty-four years. "You mean the cookies you love—the ones Tara makes sometimes?"

"I was thinking about them just before."

Elsa nods. Their mother called them almond butterballs, her cinnamon-laced version of Mexican wedding cookies or Russian tea cakes, depending on where you came from, rich nutty orbs doused in powdered sugar. Elsa can still picture Deb all those years ago, standing over a mixing bowl in her flour-dusted apron, struggling to tame the dense dough with a wooden spoon before giving up and plunging in her bare hands. The way the long muscles in her forearms would tweak with effort, her power resonating into the dough.

Roy says, "I'm trying to remember how they…" His words ease into a coughing fit. *Taste,* he wants to say. She's sure of it. Such a simple wish.

"I'd ask Tara to bring some, Dad, but she's already on the road. She's almost here. Mel too."

She waits for him to tell her that it's okay, he can do without the cookies. But he doesn't. His eyes go cloudy again, blank, and his gaze drifts to the ceiling.

"Dad?"

He struggles to refocus his attention on her face. Smiles. "Elsa. My Elsa."

"I'm heading to the city, for work, but I'll be back later, promise."

"Okay."

"While I'm there I'm going to swing by the house."

"They probably already changed the locks."

"I can slip in through a window."

The lines on his forehead compress. "Why? There's nothing left for us there. It's over."

But it isn't; not for her. Still, she gives him one of her acquiescent smiles, an old habit from their days of collusion when his passivity ruled. She's old enough now to see him with as much clarity as love, and she does love him, but she also recognizes that he let her down when she was a child, when his judgment might have counted.

He closes his eyes and retreats into silence. She waits. Leans close enough for him to feel the heat of her breath on his face, to remember what she remembers of their shared past. But his eyes don't open. After five minutes, ten, fifteen—she isn't sure, the way time has seemed to both race and blur from the moment she walked into the hospital this morning—she gathers herself. Standing at the door, she blows him a kiss, but he's sleeping, and it sails right past him.

2

A text message chirps for Elsa's attention: Where r u? Tara. At the hospital. Tugging at her big sister for support. She texts back:

Had to head back to the city for a few hours. Work.

Dad's not good.

I know. Won't be gone long—back asap.

Promise?

Promise.

Elsa's hand shakes as she puts away her phone. She thinks of her father, weakening, and a spot on her shoulder that she hasn't heard from in a while sizzles awake. She slips a finger under her shirt and rubs calm her skin. Closing her eyes a moment, she transitions into professional mode, her *better* skin without all the hypersensitivity. Ready now,

14

or ready enough, she turns off the ignition of her little red Beetle.

She looks over at the Forest Hills precinct across Austin Street: a once modernist, now dated pale green building with lots of small windows, some flapped open, some humming with air conditioners. Her gaze climbs to the fourth floor. She wonders which window contains Detective Lex Cole and if he really needs her or if this is a false alarm. He'd told her on the phone that she'd find him in the detectives' unit, room 403. Once she gets the meeting over with, she'll head to the house.

She steps out of her car into a bright morning sun, lugging the striped canvas shoulder bag that goes everywhere with her. Crossing the street, something knocks against her shoe: a baseball bounces back and hits the curb. A girl of nine or ten, wearing cutoffs and a navy Yankees T-shirt, comes running for the ball, ponytail flying. Elsa scoops it up and makes eye contact; pale blue irises around pinpoint pupils stare back.

"Never chase a ball into the street."

The girl slams to a halt, hair horsewhipping around her face.

Elsa tosses her the ball. "Here you go, kiddo."

"Thanks, ma'am." She runs in the opposite direction, throwing the ball in a high arc to someone Elsa can't see.

Ma'am. The honorific ripples through her uncomfortably. She sometimes can't fathom that she actually grew up, or understand how or even why. Or that in a matter of months she's going to be a forty-one-year-old orphan.

The elevator doors whine open and discharge her into the musty fourth-floor hallway, a series of closed doors concealing what sounds like raucous ghosts: unseen voices, electronic bleeps and hums, the crisp slap of something shutting. The door marked *403* with an old white-on-black imprinted Formica sign swings open onto a Sunday morning that could just as well be a Monday or Tuesday or Any-Day morning of law enforcement in the city that never sleeps. A dozen or so investigators work at their desks, alone or in pairs, competing to be heard over a familiar incessant din. Elsa immediately feels at home.

Across the room, at a desk bare except for a chipped black mug and an outdated desktop computer with a flickering screen, a youngish man in scuffed cowboy boots unfurls himself from his chair and waves her over. His russet hair cropped at the jaw strikes her as uncoplike verging on adolescent, but she decides on the spot, as she crosses the room, that anyone who veers from the norms in a profession defined by them must have confidence for a reason. He reminds her of a famous actor, she can't think of which one; not classically handsome but a good smile and charm enough to mask whatever might be lacking.

She extends her hand and he clasps it with both of his. His skin is dry, soothing.

"Special Agent Myers, I'm really grateful you came." His two front teeth have a noticeable gap, and he has an accent she didn't register over the phone. Eastern European, maybe Russian. Probably a subtlety in how his mouth forms words, the kind of visual cue that makes it so important to meet a person face-to-face. He hasn't shaved since at least yesterday.

"Elsa." She pulls away her hand, sloughs the heavy bag off her shoulder, and sets it on a chair.

"Lex. Can I get you some coffee? Tea?"

"Coffee would be great. Milk, no sugar. I'll get unloaded so we can go right to work."

By the time he returns with another chipped black mug—evidently the signature matched set of the Forest Hills precinct—her laptop is open and ready, tapped into the FBI's secure network she can access anywhere she goes.

"Wow, that's dedication." He sets her coffee on the desk and pulls up his chair.

"We can't afford to waste time, not when it's a kid."

"No, I mean that you bring your own laptop," he clarifies.

"Actually, it's not mine, personally. We're mobile units so they deck us out—we've got to be able to work anywhere. Only thing that doesn't travel in my bag is—" She crosses her legs and swings out an ankle to flash her Glock 22 pistol. "*This* never leaves my body."

A half smile lifts the right side of Lex's mouth as he slides a hand to his hip and pushes back his sports jacket to reveal *his* weapon.

Elsa grins. "No one, but no one, knows how to strike up a friendship like a pair of cops."

His laugh escapes in a loud bubble of sound that causes others to stop and look. He ignores the attention and sits down beside her.

"So"—she clicks a New Case tab and a screen segmented with blank fields pops open—"let's get all the details sorted out first."

"You know the basics," he says. "Ruby Haverstock, seventeen, eleventh grade. Public high school, academically solid, socially active but not a queen bee or anything like that."

17

"Home life?"

"Stable, from what I can tell. She's an only child. I spent a bit of time with her parents yesterday, Peter and Ginnie Haverstock, and they're worried out of their minds. Told me everything they know, even gave me Ruby's journal and laptop. No red flags—"

"That they know of."

He tilts his head. "Cynical, are we?"

"Experienced. Go on."

"She works at a café called Queens Beans, has the after-school-to-evening shift three times a week. Worked her full shift on Friday, then zippo. But"—he pulls his chair so close that she picks up a scent of astringent soap, the no-nonsense kind that cleans fast and doesn't cost much—"just before her shift ended, two things happened that concern me. One, she turns off the security camera. Two, she buzzes someone in."

"Who?"

"That's the thing—no one I've talked to can figure it out. And once her shift ends? A few minutes after she buzzes whoever in? Her phone, her credit card…she stops using them…no activity of any kind since eight twenty-three p.m. on Friday. Her CDR suddenly goes flat."

"That's worrisome," Elsa agrees, "but with teenagers, you never know." It used to be that you could count on call-detail records to be at least somewhat revealing, but lately, ever since new apps started offering ways for people to fly under the radar, Elsa has sometimes encountered a surprising void. "I have a teenage niece and all her friends are big users of self-destruct messaging apps—they send each other texts and photos that go away, *poof,* once they're opened."

"My warrant list had some—Snapchat, Kik, maybe another one." He turns to his computer and looks. "Yik Yak. Nothing back from any of them yet."

"Not surprised. Some of them are privacy evangelists; they don't care as much about predators using their apps as a hunting ground as they do about their users' confidentiality."

"I get that. It's a mixed bag—but what good are secrets if you're dead?"

"Exactly." Elsa picks up her phone to text Marco. "I'll ask my supervisor to add a few more apps to the list and kick them all up the ladder. Sometimes we can get a warrant expedited when it's a—"

"Kid," Lex jumps in. *Good,* she thinks, *this one learns fast.* She might not have to babysit him all day.

Marco replies: I'm on it.

Elsa notices the time on her phone: almost noon. She'd hoped to get back to Sleepy Hollow by late afternoon, evening at the latest. "Show me the security footage from Queens Beans."

Lex leans back to dig into his front pocket his jeans, she notices, are on the tight side and look worn at the knees— and pulls out a thumb drive. He's about to plug it into his desktop when she stops him.

"Mine, please. So I can download it."

"Sure." He slots the drive into the side of Elsa's laptop and scrolls down a week's worth of files. "It's a small shop with a drive-through window, about half a block off Queens Boulevard, at the back of a lot where there isn't much visibility." He clicks open the file for Friday night.

There is Ruby, wearing a backward-turned baseball cap

over her long dark hair, moving gracefully around the small area, making coffee drinks, smiling at customers, rolling her eyes into the camera when a woman takes a long time fishing money out of her wallet. Ruby is pretty without being cute. No makeup. A stack of bracelets that jangle every time she moves. Whenever the café is quiet, she consults her phone, scrolling expertly with her thumb, holding it with both hands when she texts, and smiling from time to time at messages she receives. The second she hears the bell, she slides her phone into her pocket and turns to the customer. Then someone speaks to her from off to the side, perhaps someone who's arrived on foot. Her expression fogs with something hard to read: irritation, alarm. She reaches under the counter and the tape suddenly stops. Panic curls through Elsa's stomach: That's it, the moment something happened that shouldn't have happened. The moment Ruby slipped, or was taken, out of sight.

Elsa asks, "Where's the exterior footage? Maybe we can see who it was."

"No cameras outside," Lex says.

"Seriously?"

"Guess they were more worried about employees stealing from the till than about who might drive up."

"Huh." Elsa doesn't like it.

"I've gone over and over the timeline with the parents," Lex says. "I talked to all four teachers she had classes with on Friday. I talked to the guy, Steve, who she relieved at Queens Beans at the start of her shift. I'd really like to talk to her best friend, Allie—kid's not calling me back."

"You tried texting her? My niece only responds to texts."

"Yes, but here's the thing—the Haverstocks said they've

talked to Allie and she hasn't seen or spoken to or heard from Ruby at all since Friday, when she stopped into the café for a quick visit."

"Did you try showing up at her house?"

"Should I?"

"Definitely. Other friends?"

"I called about seven kids her parents identified, and no one saw her after school on Friday. Still trying to reach her former boyfriend, Charlie, but he hasn't returned my calls either. Or my texts."

"How long did they date?"

"Five, six months."

"Ended when?"

"A few weeks ago."

She looks at him, his expression full of concern, and wonders why he didn't just go to the homes of these noncommunicative kids. Why he hesitated. And then it hits her, the actor Lex reminds her of: Al Pacino when he was young, the cool masculinity and the soulful eyes, but taller.

She asks, "This your first missing kid case?"

"Actually, yes."

"What's your normal beat?"

"Until last week, three years undercover for Vice."

Elsa worked undercover briefly, years ago, and hadn't liked the constant gnaw of personal risk. "You survived that, you'll survive this."

"This is more…emotional than I expected."

"You've got to learn to put a cap on that or your brain will stop working the way it needs to. And here's one more piece of advice, if you don't mind."

"Shoot."

"Dealing with kids, teenagers especially—well, you need to think a little differently than with adults. Try to listen between the lines when they talk. And allow your questions to come at them sideways. Does that make sense?"

"I think so."

"Their minds work differently, so yours also has to."

"Right."

"Lex, here's what I'm thinking. I understand why you're worried about Ruby. I am too. If she weren't almost eighteen, and if she hadn't turned off that security camera and buzzed someone in, and if you'd gotten ahold of that best friend and that ex-boyfriend and they were as clueless as Ruby's parents, then pulling the trigger on an Amber Alert yesterday would have been the right thing."

"I was tempted, but it seemed too soon."

"It was. But now, given the various factors, including that a whole day has gone by—it's time." Elsa texts Marco: initiate amber asap. "Within five minutes, every cop in the country will have eyes-out for Ruby."

"So it *is* bad."

"Maybe, maybe not," Elsa says. "We keep digging until we find out. Where's her computer?"

He reaches under the desk for a battered backpack, his own, and withdraws two things: a laptop covered in a rubbery purple skin, and one of those hardback blank books.

"That her journal?"

He nods. "I had them at home last night, went over everything. She seems like a good kid. Couple of things jumped out, though. From her journal, it looks like things didn't end

22

too well with Charlie, the ex. And this other boy, Paul, starts turning up a lot in these pages over the past two weeks."

"Oh?" She leans back, away from the laptop. "Know his last name?"

"Not yet, and nothing else specific, except that he has a skateboard. Paul who likes to skateboard. Must be hundreds of that boy in this city."

"May I?" Elsa reaches for the laptop and journal and slips them into her bag for later. "Come on, let's take a ride."

The drive to Forest Hills Gardens, where Charlie the ex-boyfriend lives, leads them into a cozy network of genteel blocks with stucco-and-brick Tudor houses fronted by manicured lawns.

"In high school," says Lex, in the passenger seat beside Elsa, "I had a couple of friends living around here. It was fancy then too."

She glances at him, curious. "Where did you settle after you came over?"

"Came over from where?"

"You tell me."

"It's that obvious?"

"Well, you have a slight accent."

The charming smile, tinged with humor. "I was eight when I stepped foot in New York for the first time, fresh off the boat from Russia," he says, reframing in sepia an immigration that probably occurred in Technicolor via plane. "Landed in Hell's Kitchen, back in the day when it *was* hell. Shit schools until high school. Bronx Science. Lots of those smart kids came from places like this."

"So you were a brainy kid," Elsa says. She too grew up in the city, but not Manhattan, and not Forest Hills. Her family lived modestly, way out in Ozone Park at the far end of Queens. She went to a decent high school, but not the best, and got through it. "Where'd you go to college?" Curious, suddenly, about this detective who needed her help so badly that she was summoned away from her father's hospital bed.

She waits for Lex's answer, which doesn't come. "I went to a state school—Purchase," she prods, "and I worked my way through. Now you have to tell me yours." She brakes for a red light and looks at him.

He holds her gaze when he says it—"Cornell"—as if assessing how the credential will affect her view of him. She doesn't blink, doesn't even smile or nod, nothing to make him think she's impressed. Because she isn't, yet. He's not the first Ivy League–educated cop she's come across, and it doesn't necessarily make you smart in the right ways for this job.

She says, "So you're a…"

"Pain in the ass?" An arch grin.

"No, I was going to say…what's the word I'm looking for? *Iconoclast*."

"Oh?"

"Either you come from a family of cops and you aimed higher before succumbing to the uniform, or you come from a family that expects everyone in it to go to schools like that and you shocked them by slumming it as police."

"Neither." He reaches into his pocket and pulls out a battered tube of breath mints. "Like one?"

She shakes her head. He pops one into his mouth and

peppermint tinges the air. The light turns green and she steers the car onto Charlie Hendryk's leafy block. They pull up to the curb in front of a brick pile with an alpine silhouette. A gardener kneeling in front of a bed of begonias doesn't bother glancing up from his work.

Lex cocks the door handle and a gust of warm air enters the car. "Look, we both know that the real show is what happens right now. With Ruby. Today. I requested you because I heard you were the best. Who gives a shit where anyone went to school?" He gets out and lets his door bang shut.

She follows him onto the curb. "You requested me? That's not what my boss told me."

"I don't know what he said, but yes, I asked for you. You have a reputation."

She assumes she does, given her record, but is unaccustomed to having it pointed out. Except by herself, when she wants something from Marco that he says she can't have.

The front door of the Hendryk house opens and a woman stands there, looking at them, her fitted jeans and low-cut T-shirt revealing an overly toned middle-aged musculature. Rich lady who spends her days at the gym. A tall, skinny boy with a rash of acne on both cheeks joins her.

Elsa glances at her watch—it's still early. "Come on, let's get this over with. If the ex-boyfriend isn't helpful, we'll go straight to the BFF's house, that girl—"

"Allie."

"Right. And then we can…" She stops abruptly, realizing how quickly she's been talking, a tic when she's anxious. And she sees the way he's looking at her, with such stillness in his eyes, reading her so well, her eagerness to get away.

"Full disclosure," he says calmly, and already she doesn't like this. "Supervisor Coutts mentioned that your dad's in the hospital. Obviously you want to get back."

Her insides gurgle up something sour she'd like to spit at Marco for saying *anything* about her personal life to a colleague she didn't know until today.

"The treatments alone can be pretty awful," Lex adds. "For cancer."

Fucking Marco.

"He isn't getting any treatment," Elsa says. "It's too advanced. Once he's stabilized he'll get hospice visits at his apartment." She raises an eyebrow and presses out a grin, but he refuses her bid to move the conversation to the safe ground of irony—the painful absurdity of reining in the symptoms of her father's cancer so he can be sent home to let it flourish and devour him.

"You're not taking a leave of…" *Absence,* Lex seems about to say, but cuts himself off, apparently realizing that it's none of his business. Which it isn't. Nothing in her private life is anyone's business but her own.

"You've been checking your watch all morning," he says, as if he knows what's pulling at her—how, on top of everything else, there's a detour she needs to make before driving back up to Sleepy Hollow. "Why don't you head back to the hospital to be with your dad? I can handle this. We can touch base later."

"I appreciate that, Lex, but I'm here now. Let's do this."

"I'm not asking you to walk away—I don't want you to. I *am* worried about Ruby, and I know you are too, but here's what I'm thinking. I'm grateful you came; you clarified the way forward. This, right now, is legwork that I can do alone. The minute I have a question, or if there's a change, I'll call you."

She watches his face, the way his skin molds over his cheekbones and flows into hollows that deepen when he speaks, not a twitch of uncertainty, the reassuring avuncular tone. She realizes that he doesn't want her to mother him or boss him or dole out more advice than absolutely necessary. Maybe he's not the kind of man who leaves his dirty socks on the floor until someone else picks them up. Maybe his competence is real and maybe she can resume her day off unless he needs her again.

"Okay." She jangles her car keys, opens the door to get back in. "As long as you keep me updated. You've got my number."

She settles herself into the driver's seat and watches him walk toward the house, the open door, the mother and the son, and almost jumps out of the car to run and join him despite their agreement. His argument that she should peel off until he needs her again is logical, humane even she's moved by his sensitivity in understanding what's going on with her father—but a kid is missing, and stepping back feels wrong.

About to push open the door, she remembers how her sister once accused her of being "codependent, controlling." A harsh thing to say, Elsa thought at the time (and definitely a case of the pot calling the kettle black), but probably accurate. Detective Lex Cole is a grown man and a seasoned investigator; the truth is, he doesn't need her supervision, not at this stage.

He turns, catches her eye, waves.

She wills herself to stick with their plan, starts the motor, and drives away.

It's fifteen minutes from Forest Hills to Ozone Park and the house where Elsa grew up. The Whitelaw Street clapboard with its gambrel roof and arched entrance is in need of fresh paint, and the bushes separating it from the sidewalk have grown spiky and full, showing the neglect of Roy's absence. Her late mother's once-lush garden was long ago reduced to grass that her father could easily maintain by mowing it every other week, grass now decimated by thirst and heat. How quickly an empty house returns to the wild, Elsa thinks, annoyed that a car is blocking the driveway, forcing her to continue around the corner to find parking on the next block.

She walks the long way, in the opposite direction, unable to resist the chance to stop in at the corner store and see if Mr. Abramowitz is still there. He ran it every day of the week all through her childhood, and as soon as she started going back and forth to school on her own, she would stop by in the afternoons. Mr. A. would chat with her and anyone else who happened to be there. The red sign read DELI but it was unlike any city delicatessen she ever knew, then or now. Along with the usual sliced meats and hot drinks were toys and flowers and random electronic accessories, books and coffee mugs and bags of the potpourri that Mrs. A. used to make at the back of the store. Mr. A. hated the smell of the potpourri and would cover it by burning incense. The place had a unique smell, an olfactory dissonance made stranger by the chalky odor from the white seams of boric acid that ran between the floors and walls in the never-ending battle against cockroaches. Elsa hasn't stepped foot in the corner deli for almost twenty years.

The door swings open with the same old *ding,* and the air is still lush with the weird patchouli of this place. The shelves are packed with familiar miscellany. Even the linoleum floor is as it was decades ago, only more stained and cracked. She expects to see either Mr. or Mrs. A. behind the counter, locked in time, but of course neither one is there. They had to be in their sixties when Elsa graduated high school. Instead, a young Korean man smiles and nods in greeting.

"I used to come here when I was a kid," Elsa says.

The man smiles and nods again.

"Mr. and Mrs. Abramowitz?" she tries.

"Ah, yes, we buy from them. Three, four years." *Ago,* he means. The business must have been thriving, since the new owners don't seem to have changed anything. That, or they're too cheap to restock until the shelves have emptied on their own.

Elsa peruses the offerings tiered at the front of the counter and reflexively chooses her favorite childhood treat, a small bag of corn chips. The door dings and eases closed behind her. Walking toward home, she rips open the package, pops a chip into her mouth, and is overpowered by the foul taste of rancid oil. She spits into a napkin and tosses it all into the nearest garbage can, suddenly uneasy about the presumptions that both kept her away for so long and brought her back now.

All the windows are dark. She walks up the driveway along the left of the house to the rear of the lot, where she and

Tara used to abandon their bicycles on their sides, race past Deb's gardens, and run through the back door directly into the kitchen. If their mother, who was a teacher, was home before them they would likely find her starting an early dinner, organizing ingredients, often sautéing onions in oil and infusing the downstairs with a rich aroma. Elsa was rarely hungry for her mother's cooking, though, and would escape upstairs to her room. It was Tara who would linger.

She crosses the overgrown back lawn and tries her key in the kitchen door, not surprised that it no longer works. The yellow curtain, now faded, that her mother had hung on the glass half of the door is still there, obstructing any view in. Elsa goes around to the side of the house, hoping that her father never fixed the gimpy old window lock that used to allow her and Tara to climb in late at night when they were teenagers. She slides her fingers under the bottom of the wooden frame, pushes up, and hears the telltale pop. The window eases open—and Elsa is shocked by what she sees.

The interior of the living room has been effectively demolished. The dining room and the kitchen, also demoed—there's nothing left of the room where her mother was killed. Bookshelves and kitchen cabinets are gone, doors ripped off their hinges; the wallpaper is hanging in shreds. The new owners have come in early. Without a permit from the buildings department they shouldn't have done any work, and they couldn't have gotten a permit this fast, but apparently they didn't let it stop them. Elsa's insides rumble. A lump rises into her throat as she mounts the stairs.

On the second floor, where the three bedrooms bloom off a single short hallway, nothing has yet been touched.

The brown wall-to-wall carpeting, worn thin in places.

The single bathroom the family used to take turns using.

The master bedroom, now empty, looks too small for her parents' queen-size bed and double dresser.

Tara's room; smaller than Elsa's, because she was younger. The pale pink color she chose when she was little still evident where posters were ripped down, otherwise faded to almost white.

At the far end of the hall, Elsa's room. Blue. In place of the paper lantern that used to cast light from the middle of the ceiling, a bare bulb now dangles from a cord. On the wall above where her desk once stood, a bright rectangle surrounded by faded paint reminds her of the name sign she made in art class when she was nine: ELSA in hand-carved wood letters glued to a board, each letter a different color— red, orange, green, purple. Her closet door hangs open, spilling shadows; she can smell the sharp mustiness of the enclosed space from across the room. She kicks the door shut. The familiar snap as the latch closes triggers a feeling of dread. She turns away.

3

Elsa has to blink away tears to clear her vision, she's laughing so hard at the David Sedaris download that has entertained her en route back to Sleepy Hollow. Interstate 87 flows steadily northward. In the silence following the comedy, the preoccupations she's depended on Sedaris to help her avoid come tumbling into the front of her mind.

The lingering taste of that rancid corn chip, and her disappointment at never having said good-bye to Mr. and Mrs. A.

The state of the house. Agitation twists; she still doesn't feel finished there.

And Ruby, especially Ruby. She can't stop picturing how carefree the girl looked in the moments before she vanished.

How improbable and painful it is that someone at the center of one's life would suddenly not be there anymore.

The different ways people go missing all the time. From their own lives. From their families.

Her father. Dying. How one day soon he'll also be gone. The reality of that, coming at her like a hungry demon.

Memories of her mother's murder, when Elsa was sixteen, still raw as the cookie dough seamed under her fingernails (because she *had* to make those cookies for her father, she couldn't refuse him). The hollowness of the kitchen in the moments when Deb lay, suddenly, dead. The headline that appeared every day—"Home Invasion in Queens"—until it finally petered out and became an annual rite in which the cold case was revisited in print, although eventually even that ended.

Elsa had planned to stop at a Mexican bakery and buy some almond cookies to bring to the hospital, but after leaving Whitelaw Street it gnawed at her, her father's wish to taste his late wife's recipe one last time. And so she made another detour, home to Brooklyn, and stopped at the grocery store to pick up the ingredients her phone had snared online: flour, butter, raw almonds, vanilla, powdered sugar. Cinnamon, also, since her mother and, later, Tara always added that. Elsa already had salt. Just salt. She never baked; that was Tara's thing. Their mother had been an excellent baker. Elsa couldn't stand the taste or even the smell of the butterballs but this was something she could do for her father, one last thing.

So she'd heated up her oven and poured almonds onto her kitchen counter and pounded them with a hammer until they were nearly dust. Tara always pulverized them in a food processor but Elsa didn't have domestic tools like that because she didn't need them; she worked, mostly just worked, pretty much all the time. As she kneaded the thick dough with her hands, she heard an echo of her mother's voice: *Elsa! Do you think you can hide from me?* The salty-sweet buttery smell grew nauseating as Elsa rolled ten little orbs in the palms of her sticky hands and arranged them on the piece of aluminum foil that would serve as a cookie sheet. In the bathroom, she retched into the toilet, but nothing came up. While the cookies baked, she threw away the remaining dough and tossed the dirty bowls into the sink. Then she dusted those ten little almond time bombs with powdered sugar, zipped them into a plastic bag, put them in the trunk of her car where the smell couldn't reach her, and headed upstate.

Driving now, thoughts spinning.

Afternoon, flying past.

The air, growing chillier.

Solitude, that gaping throat, swallowing her.

She turns on the radio and listens to a report about the search for Ruby: how on a quiet street in Queens, friends and neighbors are gathering; how social media is spreading the word and now strangers are arriving to help, followed in short order by the *real* media, the tech-muscled press corps; how, with the news triggered by the Amber Alert going viral, the search party is growing exponentially from a makeshift headquarters at the family home. It troubles Elsa to think that, as she speeds away from Ruby's disappearance, others speed toward it. Now that she's involved in the case, she feels guilty about the extent to which she's allowed herself to become distracted by her personal concerns. But she isn't going far, she won't be gone long, and her phone is always with her. Even so, maybe Lex Cole is right. Maybe she should take a leave of absence. Be there for her father. Conduct her personal quests on her own time, not stuck into the margins of a case. Yes, she probably should. But the thought of it makes her mind go numb and she reaches the same conclusion: not yet.

Eventually she finds herself alone on the road. She accelerates past the poky speed limit of fifty-five until she's sailing at eighty. She can not-think better in the quiet of this fast pace. She opens her window all the way, the fresh air invigorating against what little of her skin is exposed. Drives faster. Eighty-five. Ninety. When the car begins to shake, she slows to seventy-five and holds it there the rest of the way.

The wide hallway on the fifth-floor oncology ward is empty except for an unfamiliar nurse wheeling her well-stocked cart out of a patient's room on the right side. Elsa makes a point of not looking in; here, every open door is a view into someone's possibly terminal illness, a cliff overlooking a personal abyss, and the breach of privacy feels almost obscene. When she's halfway down the hall, a movement draws her attention to one of the utilitarian rooms on the left— the kitchen, where someone is foraging in the common refrigerator.

The fridge door swings closed, and there is her younger sister, Tara.

"You look terrible," Elsa greets her.

"Thanks." The sisters embrace. But it's true: Tara—who is profitably divorced, doesn't work, and is the mother of sixteen-year-old Mel—looks pale, her highlighted hair matted, purple bags under her eyes. Her gray cashmere sweater is buttoned all the way up against the chill hospital air, an extra layer that Elsa doesn't need with her long sleeves.

Elsa asks, "How's Dad doing?"

"Not great. He just woke up and he's hungry."

"Did he eat his meals?"

"Nope. I'm looking for a snack."

Elsa pulls the bag of cookies out of her purse. "Look no more."

"You made those? You?"

"Dad asked for some, and you were already on the road, so…"

"Will wonders never cease."

"Mel here?"

Tara sighs. "She was, but I dropped her back at the hotel so she could have an early night. Guess what I found out yesterday? She has to start summer school—tomorrow."

"What?"

"She failed Algebra Two. I can't believe it. How am I going to deal with this right now? I can't be in two places at once."

"They didn't give you much notice."

"Mel knew this was coming, she just didn't tell me, and my mind was on Dad. And of course Lars is out of town, so—"

"Don't worry." Elsa slings an arm around Tara's shoulders. "Mel can stay with me as long as she needs to, okay?"

"You're a lifesaver, sister." Tara manages a weary smile. "They're letting her take a night course that only meets a couple times a week. It's part of a pilot program some of the independent schools are trying out with a handful of kids, letting them take night classes instead of having them do full-time summer school. So at least she can come and go between here and the city. Which is something. Can you spend the night?"

"Unless I get summoned back to the case Marco stuck me on today."

"Shit. Really?"

"Let's go see Dad."

The light is off and the shade is drawn, immersing the private room in a dim haze. Roy half sits, cockeyed and frail, against a stack of pillows.

"Look what I brought you." Elsa plucks a tissue from the bedside box and places two cookies on it. She swivels the tray in front of her father and then leans in for a kiss. His cheek feels thin and cool.

"Did you make these?"

"That's exactly what Tara asked. Do you guys actually think I'm not capable of baking cookies?"

"You're capable of doing whatever you want." Exactly what he'd argued years ago when he hoped she'd choose just about any profession other than cop. He couldn't understand why she wanted to do it so badly—no one on either side of her family had ever been police—and she was unable to explain it to him adequately. She'd felt restless. Something important yet vague needed doing and she wanted to do it. Or maybe it was just another impulse toward control; the uniform of her early years, the gun, buttoned up tight and always prepared.

Roy's spindly fingers lift a butterball to his mouth and powdered sugar rains onto his blanket, his neck, his chin. He closes his eyes while he takes the first bite. Elsa watches his eyelids quiver and wonders what this means to him, exactly. Is he imagining her—Deb, his wife, the mother of his children? Tumbling backward into remembrances of a life that packed love in right beside some serious wallops? What is it like to face death? To stand on the brink of what will be your final days?

She recalls her mother on *her* last day, still vibrantly alive until the very moment that death took her. The panic in her eyes. The disbelief. Elsa inhales a sharp breath to plug the memory and turns away to see her sister slinging her big purse over her shoulder.

Tara says, "Call me if you need me to come back, okay?"

"You're leaving?"

"Since you're here now. And Mel's alone at the hotel. Do you mind?"

Elsa looks at Roy, still savoring that first taste, and realizes that no, she doesn't mind. In fact, she prefers it. What if this turns out to be their last chance to be alone together? Every opportunity has to be seized.

"If you don't hear from me," Elsa tells her sister, "go ahead and sleep in tomorrow."

"I won't be able to, but thanks." Tara pauses in the doorway to blow them both a kiss.

Elsa pulls a chair close to the bed, and Roy gestures at the remaining cookie, offering it to her, but then checks himself. "You've never cared for these."

"Nope."

"Thank you." His hand crawls through the air until she catches it in hers. She squeezes lightly, not wanting to crush him. "You didn't have to, you know."

"You asked."

"All my desires these days are rhetorical." He smiles.

"Well, they don't all have to be, Dad. This was easy."

"There's something I need to say to you." He struggles to right himself against his stack of pillows. Elsa leans in to rearrange them behind his head. "I'm sorry."

She listens.

"I don't think there's a parent alive who doesn't have mistakes he regrets."

An uncomfortable feeling tries to push itself to the surface and she forces it back. "Dad." She doesn't know what to say, not at this point, when it's effectively too late to change anything. "You did what you could. What you had to."

"It's just..." He blinks. "You've spent your whole life trying to outrun your childhood. You can stop now. Especially with the house sold, there's no need to look back. Let it go."

"The new owners already started demolition." Anxiety rising, she struggles to control the pitch of her voice.

"So soon?"

"The entire downstairs is basically gone."

Heat blossoms on his cheeks, color spreading back to his ears, up to his pale receding hairline. "This is what I mean, Elsa. When I'm gone, all of it goes with me. All those difficult memories. There's no need to go back there now."

"But Dad—"

"I always took care of you, didn't I?"

"Yes."

"I want you to do something for me—I want you to let all that go."

"Don't worry about me, Dad." An old refrain, taking his hand to dance the dance of their enduring complicity in believing, or wanting to believe, that you can move forward without the past dragging you back. Her skin blazes. She folds her arms across her chest to keep herself together.

The tendons on the front of his neck tighten and his eyes start to water.

"Dad, are you in pain? Do you need morphine? I'll call the nurse."

"Don't need to ask for it anymore. They hooked me up this afternoon so now I just push this right here." His finger hovers over a button attached to a wire that snakes over the bedrail. The flesh on his hand has sunken and his skin is liver-spotted where it wasn't a week ago and Elsa suppresses an urge to cry.

After Roy hits himself up and drifts off to sleep, or wherever the drug takes him, Elsa checks her silenced phone for messages and finds a voice mail from Lex, left almost an hour ago.

"Spoke with Charlie Hendryk, the former boyfriend, and his mother. They were surprised and upset about Ruby. Charlie hasn't seen her since Thursday at school, but that was only in passing, and they haven't talked in weeks. Still can't get ahold of Ruby's best friend but I'll keep trying."

Lex's tone, implying *We can check that off the list now,* bothers her. Part of her wishes she'd obeyed her impulse to stay for that interview, but the other part of her—sitting here with her father, whom she loves, *loves,* and already misses—knows she had no choice. Not really. She arranges two pillows on the large reclining chair so she can angle her attention toward Roy in case he wakes. Then she settles in with Ruby's laptop and journal.

Ruby stored a lot of homework on her hard drive. A lot of goofy saved images. And a racy selfie: topless, she stares straight into a bathroom mirror with one arm crooked behind her head, lips parted suggestively in the manner of a lingerie ad. Then Elsa finds a photo of a teenage boy, taken the same day as Ruby's picture. The boy, also shirtless, is tall and sinewy, wearing tight, low-cut jeans that expose his hipbones and a trail of fine hair rising from inside his pants. He stands in front of the same wall where Ruby's photo was taken and stares into the camera with a teasing grin that peeks out from behind a cascade of long hair. She remembers what Lex said about a new boy on the scene—Paul. Scrolling through Ruby's Facebook friends, she finds him, that hair whipping around his head as he flies on a skateboard: *Paul King of the Wolfpack; age 107; residence, Jupiter*. A feeling bubbles up: Ruby had an edge to her, something her parents weren't aware of.

She closes the laptop, glances at her father—still asleep—and picks up Ruby's journal.

In neat, rounded script, the girl vents about her parents, especially her mother, mostly hating on her mother's curiosity about her whereabouts. And she thinks that her father drinks too much but works at convincing herself that it isn't a problem. She lets him teach her things in some kind of workshop, and that makes him happy, but it doesn't really interest her. She spends a lot of time with Allie, who "can be a real bitch" but is also her "best friend in the universe." For a time, there are quite a few entries about Charlie, how "cute" and "sweet" and "nice" he is, until he morphs into someone who's "ugly under the surface" and "secretive" and "manipulative." Her entries about their breakup describe how she ended it, how he was hurt. And then, lately, she starts writing about the new boy. The most recent entry was on Wednesday, two days before she disappeared.

Remembering how she herself abruptly stopped writing in her diary after her mother's death, Elsa wonders if Ruby will ever have a chance to, or choose to, fill in more pages after whatever is happening to her is over. The potential outcomes cascade through Elsa's imagination until she closes the notebook and glances at her phone, nestled in a fold of blanket, still on silent.

Lex has called again and left another message: "We've been getting a lot of calls about supposed Ruby sightings but so far only from crazies. I'll let you know if and when there's anything of substance." Elsa smirks to herself in the gathering twilight. The first wave of callers is always made up of the true-crime enthusiasts eager to dip into the action of someone else's catastrophe.

Her mind flashes to a memory of the day her mother died. She can still see the gaggle of strangers who showed up on their lawn, waiting for—what? Insider information? As if anyone would let a bunch of rubberneckers be privy to what went on in a family, behind closed doors.

A spot just below her knee itches fiercely. Unwitnessed by her sleeping father, she reaches under her pants leg and scratches her skin, hard.

4

You don't bother flattening yourself out under the covers; there's no point pretending you aren't here. You listen to the pounding footsteps like a herd of elephants coming at you even though it's just one powerful woman taking the stairs in thumping, room-rattling leaps and bounds. The bed vibrates. Across the room, you hear something fall with a sharp slap on your desk (later, when it's over, you'll find the orange L of your homemade ELSA sign on top of your math workbook). No light seeps into the dark cavern of under-covers, and you imagine stars, lots and lots of pinpoint stars like you're lying in an open field at night, cool air bathing your skin, eyes wide to a universe speckled with million-mile-distant stars and the sky, this sky, belongs to you alone. You can soak in the beautiful distance and it will never, ever touch you. You are safe, out in the open, chilly and alone and happy.

Your sister isn't home from her friend's house yet.

Your father is still at work.

They don't know this is happening to you.

The footsteps thunder and shake closer and louder and you press your hands between your face and the covers to make some breathing space. You open your eyes. You see a sheet tangled with a blanket. You close your eyes and you see the sky.

You manage to keep your eyes closed when the covers are ripped off—*whoosh!*—creating a breeze. But still, you sweat. You hear her but don't see her because you don't want to look.

You hate her face when she gets like this, like a stretched-out Halloween mask.

She scares you when she gets like this.

You shouldn't have been so horrible, saying what you said, making her need to do this: "Why should I always be the one to take out the garbage? Tara's younger, it should be her job. At least sometimes."

When will you learn?

Your sky shatters at the first whack of leather on skin. Your leg blazes hot and you pull your knees under your clenched jaw and ball yourself up and roll toward the wall. Heat slices your back, your shoulder.

You are grateful; it's just the belt, not the buckle this time.

Finally you do what she needs you to do; you obey and roll into position, butt-up. She whacks in groups of five. Two groups for a total of ten. The first few whacks don't count because you weren't in position, so it was your fault because you did it wrong. You did it wrong and so she taught you a lesson but apparently you are unteachable because you never seem to learn.

Her breathing slows. She stands by the side of your bed. You know she wants you to look at her and tell her that you're sorry and you love her because now she's starting to feel bad but you won't do it. Your eyes stay shut and you wait and wait and finally she goes away, quietly, all calm after her storm.

When you feel it's safe, you pull your covers back up and over, re-creating your universe, and you open your eyes but in the aftermath your vision is blurry from crying and you can't conjure up any worthwhile distractions.

And so you wait; it's what you always do. For your sister to get home. For your father to get home. And then, later, over dinner, you will talk about your days but neither you nor your mother will mention this because it's unspeakable. There are no words.

5

Elsa, restless while Roy is lost to sleep, puts down Ruby's journal and steps into the hallway to return Lex's call. The girl's voice is stuck in her head now, her chatty jottings, her video self going suddenly blank.

"Anything?" she asks him.

"Just what I told you in my message."

"The girl, Allie—you talked to her?"

"I've been trying, trust me. I went by her house and no one was home, I've been calling, texting...nothing."

Regret flares as Elsa wonders if, had she stayed, they would have found Allie, talked to her, plucked out the important detail, located Ruby, brought her home safely, closed the case. If she hadn't left him to handle this without her, they wouldn't be having this frustrating conversation in which nothing has advanced since they reviewed the case that morning.

"The kid's elusive." Lex's words interrupt her magical thinking that her presence would have made a significant difference—as if some potent combination of mastery and best intentions could summon girls out of thin air. "But I'm not giving up."

"Well, it sounds like you're doing what you can. Call me the minute anything changes, okay? Otherwise let's touch base first thing in the morning."

Back in the room with her sleeping father, Elsa tries not to answer that familiar hankering after *control,* or *Control* with a big *C,* in which she stops bad things from happening by pulling the covers up over herself and seeing something better than what is actually there—a gentle starry sky instead of an angry mother. Or by other means that have presented themselves as useful over the years. One in particular.

She sinks into the middle-of-the-night hospital quiet and stops resisting. Her hand finds her Swiss Army knife, settled in its place at the bottom of her bag, and together the old friends retreat to the bathroom. She strips to her underwear and bra. Beneath the harsh fluorescent overhead, barefoot on the sticky tile floor, she places the folded-up knife on the edge of the sink—a temptation to defy—turns away from the mirror, and begins.

She scratches every neon-pulsing scar on her legs, hips, stomach, arms. The pictograms of her failures heat to the hard edges of her fingernails, the crude blade-drawn outlines of sometimes something—a closed eye with lashes, a bird able to fly away, a marble capable of rolling away unseen, the number 7 because she once thought it lucky—and often nothing, just scratches, cuts tallied on her skin. She's a patchwork quilt by now. It has ruined her love life; she can't date, and when she tries, it's invariably a disaster. She's been *sober* for years, chaste, untouched by anything sharp enough to rupture skin (if you don't count scratching), but it doesn't matter. The scars are always there, a web of permanent reminders. And sometimes her skin hurts, *hurts,* and other times the scars burn for attention. Elsa's skin calls to her the way a drink calls to an alcoholic, promising relief, delivering shame.

The crude reckoning on her thigh, her first-ever cut, produces a drop of blood and, mortified, she stops. No. She won't. She gets dressed, whisks the unopened knife back into her bag, and stores it in a drawer of her father's nightstand, out of easy reach. She lies on the reclining chair, arms by her sides, and takes deep breaths as the heat evaporates off her skin. Eventually she falls asleep and dreams of a girl, herself, Ruby: emerging out of a fog, almost graspable, and then fading to nothing.

MONDAY

6

I can't wait until you're older and *you* can do the driving," Elsa says, but Mel, staring out the passenger window as they travel back to the city, appears to have her mind on other things. Summer school, maybe; the unfairness of being ripped away from her grandfather's sickbed for something as inane as a math class. Glancing at her niece, Elsa is struck by how much Mel resembles Ruby Haverstock: the oval face, dark brows, and milky-blue eyes. Mel's hair is longer and straighter than Ruby's, which waves to the bottom of her neck.

Morning advances in quick swipes of speeding highway. Elsa does her best to ignore her guilt for leaving her father. But with no credible sign of Ruby, the media-monster has burgeoned overnight into a voracious enterprise, and she needs to get back. She needs to focus on locating the missing girl, something she has always been good at, *and* she needs to divert herself from her preoccupation with the sold house, *and* she needs to outrun the nagging sense of things slipping away from her. She'd frightened herself last night, almost naked

51

in the hospital bathroom with her favorite blade so close; she frightened herself and now she needs to get back to work. Work is the ballast that has always righted her when her equilibrium starts to slide. Work, and the *right now*. Holding a tight focus on the needs of a child is the best medicine Elsa has ever found for her inner restlessness, better than scratching an itch—obliterating it. At least she's looking, she reminds herself, knowing that sometimes no one does.

Mel sucks down the last of her smoothie and squeezes the oversize plastic cup into the car's holder. She picks up the blueberry muffin she's held nestled in her lap and peels off the paper, surprising Elsa with a delayed answer: "*You* can't wait? *I* can't wait until I'm really free."

That makes Elsa smile. "You know, they say freedom's a state of mind."

"It's gonna be fucking amazing when I turn eighteen!" Laughing, Mel kicks the underside of the dashboard. "Sorry I cursed."

"Curse away, I don't care. And, listen, if you're going to be free, you've got to learn not to apologize."

"Good advice. Please tell my mom." She begins to pluck out the blueberries with her chipped multicolored manicure, collecting them in the muffin paper.

"I thought you liked blueberries."

"Saving the best for last."

They laugh, and Elsa drives, and soon the city announces itself along a looming corridor of graffitied buildings, impatient traffic, and ill-tended roads. Meanwhile, Elsa's thoughts can't stop returning to Ruby, especially now, being with a girl about the same age.

She asks her niece, "Have you ever considered running away?"

"You think I should?" Mel's tone half alarmed, half intrigued.

"No! What I mean is, why do you think a teenager, someone without any obvious major problems, might want to run away?"

"Are you talking about that missing girl from Queens? I saw something about it on TV last night at the hotel. If you think she ran away, why'd you put out an Amber Alert? Isn't that for when someone's kidnapped?" Mel pops the remaining piece of muffin into her mouth.

"What makes you think I'm working that case?"

"Because it's New York City and you're, you know, always working *that case*."

"I shouldn't have brought it up."

"I guess most kids probably run away because of *their parents*." A squirm in Mel's voice, as if *that* should be obvious. "Parents can be pretty judgmental, if you haven't noticed. Anyway, Auntie Elsa, did it ever occur to you that sometimes people run *to* something? Not away."

"Good point." Elsa is well aware that it's quite possible, even probable, that Ruby is up to something her parents don't know about.

"The news showed a picture of her," Mel says. "She looked nice."

"Looks."

"What are the odds of someone who's kidnapped actually getting found? I mean, alive."

The question startles Elsa. The real answer is *bad,* but she isn't about to recite the ugly statistics to Mel: The first hour is crucial, and after three days it's reasonable to give up hope. But there are always exceptions. "We try not to assume the worst, because we know that sometimes people just walk away from their lives, especially older teenagers and adults."

She waits for Mel to say something along the lines of *Bullshit!* But she doesn't. Instead, she lifts her muffin paper and funnels the mound of blueberries into her mouth.

"So," Elsa says, "I'm going to have to work today. Okay if I drop you at my apartment?"

"Not sure what I'll do by myself in Brooklyn all day. Could I just go home for now and meet up with you later at your place? I have your keys."

Elsa considers it. At sixteen, Mel is used to being on her own in the Upper East Side penthouse she shares with her mother. She probably wants to see if any of her friends are around. "I guess it's okay."

"Cool."

They pull up in front of Tara's building on Eighty-Seventh Street and the doorman scoots out to open the car door for Mel.

"Hi, José!"

"Hiya, *chiquita*."

Mel grabs her knapsack from the backseat, blows Elsa a kiss, and heads into the building. Sitting at the curb, Elsa waits until every last bare-legged, shiny-haired, eager-eyed inch of her niece is out of sight before dialing her phone.

"I'm back in town," she says to Lex by way of greeting. "Any developments?"

"Nothing. How was the hospital?"

"I've been thinking"—avoiding the question—"that I'd like to talk to Charlie Hendryk myself."

A pulse of hesitation—Lex has already interviewed the kid, and no one appreciates the suggestion that his work needs to be redone—before he answers with "Good idea." Capitulating to her seniority, she assumes, or maybe just his way of welcoming her back.

She says, "Could you find out where he is right now? I'm going to make a quick run downtown to my office, then I'll be in touch."

"Sounds like a plan."

She knows, though—first in her gut and then in her mind—that she won't be going directly to Federal Plaza. Another investigation calls; another kind of itch.

Before she even arrives at the house, her car windows open to the warm summer air, she hears the sounds of pounding. Cracking. Breaking. A din of radio music beneath men's voices.

A pickup truck is parked in the driveway and the front door is open. Windows, wide, bleeding sound.

Elsa pulls up at the curb and sees someone, two people, maybe three, moving through the upstairs of the family house. A voice. A crash. A cloud of dust as a wall presumably comes down inside. It appears that the demo has moved to the second floor, and she feels a twist like rough-edged metal turning in her stomach.

A shiny black SUV swerves around her car and pulls in behind the pickup. At the wheel is a woman with cropped bleached hair and bright red lipstick. She strides across the lawn in her pretty sundress and leather sandals and polished toenails, then pauses to look at Elsa. Who looks back. So it's true; even way out here, on the urban edge of basically nowhere, gentrification is seeping in. To think, *a pool.*

"You must be the new owner," Elsa says.

The woman doesn't smile. "Can I help you?"

"No." Definitely not. Elsa can't imagine a single way this woman could possibly help her.

She starts her engine, drives to the end of the block, turns off Whitelaw Street onto Albert Road. Chastises herself for giving in to impatience; she doesn't think clearly when she allows anxiety to guide her. What did she expect, going home in the daytime (not *home* anymore), when common sense suggests she should only return in the dark when no one's looking? She should have done what she'd told Lex she was doing and gone into the office. Maybe she still will, if only to erase her lie.

The ceiling fan *tick-tick-tick*s its steady rotations above the bullpen of pushed-together desks, a vast chopped-up space with sealed windows overlooking the snaky gray East River on one side and the towers of lower Manhattan on the other. The morning has devolved into waiting: for Lex to report that he's located Charlie; for the interlopers to vacate (if temporarily) the family house long enough for Elsa to get back in; for Marco to return to their call from the on-hold void he'd left her in. Finally, she gives up trying to ignore the rhythmic beats of the fan, wheels away from her desk, crosses the room, with her phone still in her hand, and switches it off. Like when a refrigerator hum suddenly stops, a delicious hush unfurls across the eleventh floor.

"Do you mind?" Matt Gonzales looks at her with his up-too-late-last-night bloodshot eyes. "And you in long sleeves—aren't you hot?"

"Not really."

A sheen of sweat materializes on his forehead.

Elsa switches the fan back on.

On her colleague's desk, as casual as a flung-open magazine, sits a file on a missing child with a picture: a boy photographed against a backdrop of a bookcase, with side-combed hair, freckles, and a milk-carton smile. Elsa is sure she's seen him a thousand times before and wonders why some parents insist on sending school photos when something personal and specific would be much more helpful. Even so, despite the generic quality of the picture, the boy's eyes call to her. They always do. Green, clear, bright, impossibly innocent.

She asks "How'd it go yesterday?" assuming the photo is from his Bronx case.

Gonzales looks momentarily baffled, and then shrugs. "Yesterday was great. Took my son to Yankee Stadium." Elsa knows that his son is twelve years old and crazy for baseball, but that isn't what strikes her about his answer.

"I thought Marco put you on a case yesterday—you were supposed to be first in rotation."

He chortles. "Guess Marco pulled a fast one on you."

She already knows that Lex Cole requested her because he'd told her so, but why did Marco have to add a lie to an omission? Marco's voice resurfaces on the other end of their call. She lifts the phone back up to her ear. "Okay, Elsa, I had to kick 'em in the pants but they're putting the reports through now. Keep an eye on your e-mail and you should start to see things within a few minutes." A victory, given that until now none of the administrators of the implode-on-demand messaging apps have ponied up with the records for Ruby.

"Thanks."

"Talk later."

"Marco, wait. Tell me again why you put me on this case."

A beat. She wants him to know that she knows, and she wants him to regret lying to her—and to never do it again. And he answers, "You were requested."

"Oh. That's funny. I thought it was because Gonzales wasn't available."

"I don't believe he was."

"Right, because he was at a *baseball game*. Versus me visiting my *dying father*."

Marco sighs. "All right, I'm really sorry, I am, but I didn't want to take all day twisting your arm and I wanted you on this one."

"Why didn't you just tell me someone asked for me?"

"Because I didn't think you'd believe me."

"My ego's not that much in the toilet, is it?"

"Let's just say you can be modest to a fault. Okay? So I came at it another way. Got you on board, didn't I?" A hint of humor in his tone is infectious, and without meaning to she can't help forgiving him.

"Fine. But next time, do me a favor and don't bullshit me."

"You got it."

Back at her desk, the fan gyrating noisily above her head, Elsa clicks and clicks and clicks on her e-mail until a new batch floods in. Marco was right; all at once, each of the texting apps has finally responded to the warrants.

Kik and Yik Yak yield nothing—neither does Whisper, Ask, Omegle, Down, or Poof. If Ruby uses those apps at all, the texts that have already been read have self-destructed. But two unopened messages from her are sitting on Snapchat's server, both addressed to Paul, the boy she'd mentioned in recent journal entries. Ruby had sent him a close-up photo of one of her eyes with the pupil pinprick-small, as if she were staring into a light. He never retrieved the message. Half an hour later, about fifteen minutes before she turned off the security camera at Queens Beans, she sent Paul another unopened message: 10. C u. Bring.

Elsa glances up between the tall buildings and notes the cotton-batting sky. Rain is coming. She thinks of Allie, who still hasn't responded to any of their calls or texts. She's beginning to see what Ruby meant in her journal about her best friend being a real bitch sometimes, but then she catches herself. There has to be a reason for all this silence.

She picks up her phone to check in with Lex, but before she has a chance, a text from him pops onto her screen: Found Charlie. Pier 62 Skatepark, Chelsea Piers. I'll wait for you there.

Paul likes to skateboard, she recalls. He alone?

Nope.

On my way.

The park is busy with people in shorts and T-shirts or summer dresses, lapping up ice cream and scarfing down hot dogs and bottles of water. A pack of boys on skateboards swoop up and down and around the undulating curves of a concrete bowl, their bodies arcing into the movement. Standing beside Lex, watching from a distance, Elsa is amazed by the grace of these young men. She recognizes one as Charlie Hendryk, gangly, with close-cut dark hair, but in the blur of frenetic movement she can't tell if Paul is among them.

The sun beats down on Elsa in her slacks and long sleeves, a sheen of heat pillowing between skin and fabric. Not since she was a child has she exposed herself to sun or prying eyes, and though she's used to the discomfort of what's become her eccentric-in-summertime mode of dressing, she is never unaware of the difficult position her compulsion has put her in. By the end of June, which is when she generally gets around to switching from her winter wardrobe, she'll change to white linen and a broad sun hat, a costume suggesting an aversion to sun, not to visibility.

Lex asks Elsa, "Why aren't they in school?"

"Regents week." The end-of-school-year week devoted to state testing for public high-school students; different subjects were tested at different times, so the kids popped in and out of school.

"Ah, right."

He lifts a hand to cover a yawn, and suddenly she smells the deli's exclusive patchouli as if it wafted out of his clothes with the movement of his arm. She steps closer to him and the scent grows stronger. She presses her nose into her own sleeve to take a whiff and there it is, woven into the fabric of the same shirt she wore yesterday. She'd failed to bring a change of clothes to the hospital last night.

He grins. "Laundry day?"

"No. I thought you smelled like something, but it was me."

The grin broadens; he tilts his head as if about to deliver a comeback, but then he doesn't.

Surprised by her disappointment—she wants to hear what he has to say—she relegates herself to silence as well. Embarrassment sets in. The intensity of her visits to the family house hits her now, how her personal worries have risen to the front of her consciousness and threaten to skew the investigation, tempt her to see everything through the lens of her own story. It's one of the biggest mistakes an investigator can make; she learned early not to allow her private mind and her professional mind to merge. She tells herself that the confluence of her father's illness, the sale of the house, and the mysterious disappearance of yet another child is making her too sensitive. It isn't the first time that her tendency to overthink has edged her a little off track. She tells herself to stop it, stop it right now, and plant her focus back on Ruby. On personally questioning the ex-boyfriend. On the hope that one of these skateboarders is the boy Ruby was trying to reach just before she disappeared.

The strange moment dissipates when three younger boys glide over to the bowl and wait for a signal to join in, which never comes. When one of them dives in anyway, he's summarily chased out by a boy with long hair flying around his face. Rebuffed, the interlopers move to another bowl. Charlie and his friends yowl at one another and shake their fists.

Elsa notes, "They're a tight group."

"United front."

The boy who chased away the gatecrashers now flies above the edge of the bowl and simultaneously yanks off his T-shirt, throwing it down before diving back into the anarchy of male bodies. Elsa is startled to see that his back is covered by a tattoo of a dog, and the dog is wearing a crown.

Unless, of course, the dog is a wolf.

Paul King of the Wolfpack. Not a hundred and seven, but maybe seventeen.

Elsa says, "See that boy who just took off his shirt?"

"With the big tattoo?"

"I think that's Ruby's new boyfriend."

Elsa and Lex approach the bowl and stand with their feet right at the edge, calmly watching the boys until Charlie notices them and signals his friends to slow down. One by one, they fly up and out, land hard, and snap their boards up into their hands. They cluster, the six of them, while Charlie approaches alone. Tall and lanky. A mess of short brown hair.

"Hello, Officer."

"Detective," Lex corrects him. "This is my colleague Special Agent Myers. She's with the FBI."

"Elsa." Smiling, offering a hand. "Mind if we have a chat?"

The boy's eyes, filigreed with fresh bloodshot, glance at Lex. "Is Ruby still not home?"

"That's right," Elsa says. "I know you already talked with Detective Cole, but I have a few questions too. Forgive me if we go over some of the same ground."

"I can't believe this." Charlie glances behind him at his friends, all watching closely.

Elsa asks, "When was the last time you saw her?"

The way his expression clouds, something jumps in her chest. "Friday, I think it was. At school."

Elsa doesn't flinch. She clearly recalls Lex telling her that Charlie reported seeing Ruby last on Thursday.

And then, as if reading her, Charlie corrects himself: "No, Thursday. It was Thursday, in the cafeteria. I mean,

I see her around at school all the time. We're in the same grade. So."

"Okay if I ask a personal question?"

He shakes his head, but answers, "Sure, it's okay."

"I know that you and Ruby used to go out, and that you broke up. But were you interested in getting back together with her?" Beside her, Lex shifts his stance. He probably hadn't thought to ask this question yesterday when he spoke with Charlie; in Elsa's experience, the guy cops almost never do.

A flush rises on the boy's acne-scarred cheeks. "Maybe."

"Did you try?"

He nods, looking at the ground.

"When?"

"A couple of weeks ago. I really like Ruby. I tried to get her back, it's true, but she wasn't interested, so I gave up. That's it. I can't believe she's missing. I'll do anything I can to help find her."

"We know you will," Elsa tells him, because kids always deserve the benefit of the doubt. At first, anyway.

Lex asks, "What about your friends? Any of them know her?"

Charlie turns around. "Yo, Paul, get over here!"

The boy with the wolf tattoo lumbers over with a comically awkward gait, a surprise considering his mastery of a skateboard and a camera lens. Up close, he looks very young, barely sprouting facial hair.

Paul says, "Hello, ma'am and sir?"

"They're looking for Ruby," Charlie tells his friend.

Elsa asks, "Mind if we talk to Paul alone?"

They wait until Charlie rejoins their friends, out of earshot.

"Paul," Elsa begins, "were you and Ruby planning to get together on Friday night?"

"Yeah, like, she was supposed to meet me?" A waver in Paul's voice. "At, like, ten o'clock? And, like, she didn't show?"

"You give her a call?" Lex probes. "Find out where she was?"

"I dunno, maybe. Like, I can't remember."

"Text? Anything?"

Paul shrugs his thin shoulders. "I didn't hear from her, so, like, I figured she wasn't going to make it."

"Were you and Ruby"—Elsa almost says *dating* and corrects herself—"hooking up?"

Again, Paul shrugs. Apparently, he doesn't know that either.

She leans in and informs him, "You didn't open two Snapchats from her."

"Wait, you saw our Snapchats?" Paul's jaw actually drops, as if this intrusion into his privacy is the real problem at the moment.

"Was she supposed to bring something at ten o'clock, or were you?"

"I dunno what you're talking about."

Elsa forces a deep breath. "How old are you?"

"Sixteen."

The same age as Mel. No wonder teenage girls generally prefer older boys. Elsa has to wonder what Ruby, who has nearly two years on Paul, sees in him.

"What was she going to bring you, Paul?"

"Nothing."

"What were you going to bring her, then?"

This time there's a slight pause. "Nothing."

"How well do you and Ruby know each other?"

He shrugs again. "I don't know."

"Is she your girlfriend?"

"We weren't, like, hooking up, to answer your question."

"What were you doing?"

"Nothing. Just hanging out."

"Alone?"

"Not really."

"Does she skateboard too?"

"I dunno."

There are no girls in their group today, and Elsa guesses that this is an exclusively boys-only activity—*wolfpacking* together. She can't bring herself to believe that Paul is the leader of this posse. Is Charlie?

The pack reassembles, and Elsa and Lex hand each of the boys their cards with instructions to get in touch if they hear anything about Ruby's whereabouts. As soon as the investigators turn their backs and walk away, the boys on their skateboards crash and whoop back into the bowl.

"They don't seem to give a shit," Elsa says.

"No, they do. They're just boys, bad at talking."

"I'll say."

"Thing that struck me is that Charlie seems to be putting on an act with these kids, trying to be cool. At home yesterday, in front of his mother, he was smart and articulate. I don't know why he's hanging around with those losers."

They watch in silence for another few seconds as the boys circle one another in the bowl. Lex leans closer to Elsa as if joining her in seeing the same thing, the patchouli smell rising again, that powerful, unmistakable smell of the deli. Her thoughts reverse to yesterday, the half-wrecked house, and apprehension rekindles with an urge to run back yet again, but her mind takes over and quashes the impulse. She can still see the pursed red lips of the new owner, assessing her suspiciously—the recollection sends a flare of shame through her. It isn't the Myers family home anymore. Elsa has no right to lurk there. Her father's words echo like a skipped stone: *Let it go, let it go, let it go*. Move forward. Don't look back.

7

The Haverstocks' postage-stamp lawn is half mowed, the wild part strewn with spent dandelions, as if the job was postponed a long time and then hastily abandoned. To the left, beside the house, a white tent over chaos. People everywhere. A barrel with plastic water bottles sweating under the noon sun. Just beyond the tent and its dark swath of shade, a pair of reporters stand in the brightness interviewing a middle-aged couple.

"That the parents?" Elsa asks Lex. She parks at the curb behind a television van with an enormous antenna sprouting from its roof. She's been here before, many times; not here but *here,* in the roiling belly of a community trying to reel back in one of its children. Someone lost or taken or just gone. Sometimes it succeeds, sometimes it doesn't, but for Elsa this is always the moment when the strain of not-knowing kicks in. A reviled and familiar helplessness prickles across her skin.

"Yup. Peter and Ginnie Haverstock."

The father, tall and stomachy, has one arm fastened around his wife's shoulders. Her lips tremble as she speaks, her skin pale, untended black bangs stringy on her forehead.

Elsa and Lex get out of the car and cross the lawn. Under the tent, a long table is a free-for-all of food. Dunkin' Donuts has donated takeout coffee and dozens upon dozens of doughnuts, and people have brought homemade meals. Another table is stacked with photocopies and manned by a woman in a white visor wearing a stick-on name tag.

"Welcome to the circus," Elsa mutters to Lex, slipping into a useless digression in her mind: What would her life have been like if this many people had swarmed to the house in Ozone Park in search of her, only to find her huddled in a locked closet? She imagines the relief, the celebration, but wonders if outsiders could really comprehend how lost a child can be inside her own house. At some point you're beyond saving; no one can show you how to unswallow all that darkness.

"They're trying to help."

"Yeah, I guess they are."

"Even I'm not that cynical, and I worked Vice."

"Lex." She looks at him. "I wish you wouldn't do that."

"Do what?"

"Interpret me. That's the second time you've called me cynical."

"But aren't you?"

"You're doing it again."

"Sorry." He grins, not sorry at all. The kind of person who picks up on everything, lets nothing go. Who has a lot of friends because it wouldn't occur to him not to. Who doesn't understand, or accept, that some people—her, for instance—value their boundaries.

"I'm realistic," she tells him. "That's not the same as cynical."

"Elsa"—warmly—"I didn't mean it as an insult. We're cops—who *isn't* cynical? In fact, I think it gives you an edge. It probably makes you better at what you do."

She stops listening to him when Ruby walks through the front door of the house and onto the lawn, wiping her palms on her jeans as if she just washed her hands and couldn't find a towel. Elsa can't move. No one else seems to notice and then, as quickly as Ruby appeared, she morphs into another girl.

Elsa mutters, "What the—"

"Who's that?" Lex follows Elsa's gaze.

Stepping forward, Elsa asks, "What are you doing here?"

Mel's smile fades as she registers Elsa's dismay. "*Sorry,* Auntie Elsa, I got home and went online and saw this and I couldn't resist. Isn't it okay? I mean, they want volunteers. I thought maybe I could help."

"No," Elsa says, "it isn't okay."

Lex offers Mel a friendly handshake. "Detective Lex Cole, working with your aunt. Pleasure to meet you."

"Hi." Mel shakes his hand, then turns to Elsa. "Why not?"

"Because this isn't a world you need to see. This is my world. Your world is a better place."

"Do you realize how crazy that sounds?"

Elsa looks to Lex for some adult reinforcement—if he really does want to be her friend, here's a chance to prove it—but instead he uses the moment to steal away from the family drama. Mutters, "Thinking maybe Allie's around some-where, thinking maybe I'll have that chat," then loses himself in the crowd.

Elsa asks Mel, "Does your mother know you're here?"

Mel's expression reads, *Seriously?* But she attempts a more reasonable response. "Mom's preoccupied. You're my grown-up today and now *you* know I'm here. I was about to call you."

"Really?"

"Yes."

"I don't know, Mel. I'm not comfortable with this."

"Who's Allie?"

Silence thickens between them. Mel's curiosity and stub-bornness are just two of the things Elsa loves about her niece. But not here; not today. "I want you to go back home," Elsa says. "Now."

Mel hesitates. "Just so you know, I love you. A lot."

Elsa watches with a fleeting sensation of victory as Mel crosses the lawn as if to leave, but then she veers under the tent instead. Exasperated, Elsa follows, but doesn't catch up until Mel is already standing in front of the table where the white-visored volunteer—ROSEMARY scripted on her name tag—is distributing flyers to the troops.

Rosemary hands Mel an inch-thick ream of MISSING signs emblazoned with a recent photo of Ruby smiling cheerfully, looking right at the camera. Rapt, Mel reads over the details.

Elsa considers her options: She can stop this here and now and order Mel home, where she'll stew in resentment; she can tell her niece to stay by her side while she tries to investigate, which will land anywhere and everywhere on a range from inappropriate to unprofessional; or she can default to being the understanding aunt she's always been and allow this caring young woman to follow her instinct. When she reaches Mel, she hears her saying, "I want to help find Ruby," with such feeling that Elsa lands on option three.

"Of course you do," Rosemary says in the sweet tone of a retired kindergarten teacher trying to help in any way she can. "You could post those signs. I'll give you a map. How does that sound?"

"Awesome."

Mel glances at Elsa, who halfheartedly nods permission, and off she goes.

Resigned for now to the power of her niece's enthusiasm, Elsa sweeps her gaze across the bustling lawn. Lex is nowhere in sight. A few of the neighbors' houses have been engulfed in the effort to find Ruby, doors hanging open to the heat, people marching in and out. Everyone focused on a task: posting signs, like Mel, or serving food, or logging volunteers, or queuing to join the next group to depart on the ever-widening canvass of this neighborhood and beyond.

She looks at Ginnie and Peter Haverstock, crossing the lawn toward their front door, dragging long shadows. Their desperation frightens her and will continue to frighten her until she can solve this for them. She knows herself. Still, she needs to meet them, so she steps into the squall with her trademark gleaming-armor-of-false-stoicism.

She comes up behind them. "Mr. and Mrs. Haverstock?"

They turn to face her, and she's startled by their bloodshot eyes.

"I'm from the FBI, Special Agent Elsa Myers. I'm working with Detective Cole."

"The Amber Alert." Ginnie wastes no time getting to the point, her voice a stew of accusation and fear. "It didn't work."

Elsa says, reassuringly, "It can take time," though she feels like a liar. When Amber Alerts work, results are usually quick. Silence tends to evolve into bad news. "I know the wait is awful. Is there anything you can think of to tell me that you might have forgotten before?"

The father opens the front door. "*Please* come in." A shimmer of anxiety in his invitation; she hears the *plea* in his *please*.

The Haverstocks usher her directly into a modest living room. The windows are closed and the air is blessedly cool. Peter settles into a worn green corduroy chair beside a small table littered with objects: a folded newspaper, a TV remote, a bottle of upmarket beer, and a framed photograph of the family of three that looks like it was put down in haste. Elsa imagines that he's been gazing at the picture for reassurance; a loving father, lost in a fog of uncertainty. She thinks, suddenly, of Roy, and feels a twist of unease. Feels time slipping away from her. Forces her attention back to Ginnie Haverstock, sitting beside her on the couch, talking.

"Next week is Ruby's eighteenth birthday. She doesn't want a party. She has plans with her friends, but …"

Into the troubled silence, Elsa inserts the question that bothers her the most in all this: "Are you sure you can't think of any reason she would have disabled the security camera at Queens Beans Friday night?"

Mrs. Haverstock leans forward, the skin on the front of her neck pinching. "It doesn't make any sense to us. That's what worries me, along with her being gone—she isn't a devious kind of kid. She's a good girl, never does anything to disappoint us, always tries her best."

Elsa turns to Peter. "You must be proud of her too."

"Do my best to keep her in line," he says with an effortful half smile.

She asks, carefully, "How were things when she left for school Friday morning?"

"Fine." Peter's hands unfold, blossom almost. "I was in my workshop when she left. The garage door was up and I waved at her and she waved back. It was the last time I saw her."

"She was out pretty fast, as usual," Ginnie adds. "Ruby keeps busy. She doesn't waste a minute. She always lets me know if she won't be coming straight home from work, which is why I was surprised when I didn't see her by nine o'clock. She takes the bus home. Follows a pretty regular schedule."

"How was her day at school?" Elsa asks.

"I spoke with her in the afternoon," Ginnie answers, "and she sounded fine."

"Eleventh grade?"

"Yes. We have plans to visit colleges as soon as school lets out next week—the day after her birthday, as a matter of fact." Ginnie's smile incites a cascade of dry lines, turning her face into an abstract of dread. "She's our only child and we've been saving up for years."

"Mind if I ask what you folks do for a living?"

"I'm a medical research assistant; I work at Rockefeller University. My husband is an adjunct professor of statistics at Queens College, and he also has a business on the side."

Elsa asks, "Oh?"

"Three-D printing," Peter explains.

"The workshop you mentioned? Where you were when you last saw her?"

Peter nods. "I'll show you, if you want."

As they all pass through the living room, Elsa's gaze lingers on a collection of family photos atop an upright piano pressed between overstuffed bookcases. Ruby as a baby, a toddler, a little girl, a teenager. Lots of smiles.

Inside the attached garage, Mr. Haverstock's enterprise has displaced any possibility of housing a car. One whole wall is lined with metal shelves stacked with spools of plastic filament in a rainbow of colors. Leaning against one end of the shelf, flattened boxes are stacked vertically, according to size. In the center of the space sits a stainless-steel workbench holding a glass-fronted black cube that looks like a cross between a microwave and an old TV. With the garage door closed, the air in here is uncomfortably hot.

Peter walks across the garage and pulls aside a stained white sheet covering another shelf. "This is the kind of stuff I make."

It runs the gamut: a gray six-inch bust of a man in glasses; a blue statuette of a boy swinging a baseball bat; a DNA helix in primary colors; a shoe-box-size rectangle that, on closer look, is a model of a modular house; a pair of silver-webbed shoes; a gun.

"It isn't real," Peter tells her, noting her attention to the gun.

"It also isn't legal."

Color drains from his face. "I know—but the client's paying really well, and I didn't think it would do any harm." The absurdity of that last statement momentarily sucks the air out of the room. Ginnie averts her eyes. Elsa can't take hers off Peter's embarrassed expression.

Elsa asks, "Who's the client?"

"An executive who travels a lot. Said she'd feel safer."

She. Elsa gets it. But of course the assumption is dead wrong; statistically, the gun will make the client's life more endangered if she has the bad luck to run into trouble.

"Well," Elsa says, "she's mistaken, but that's not why I'm here. Just do me a favor, Mr. Haverstock, and don't make any more phony guns for people, okay? It's bad business, and frankly, it's part of the problem, not the solution."

"I get it. And I won't—I promise."

She stoops to glance under the workbench where an unfinished piece of furniture appears to crouch like a hiding animal. "Making a...chair?"

"That's the idea. I like to challenge myself, try stuff I haven't done before. This one's been tough." Adding: "Ruby sometimes helps me out in here. I've been teaching her a thing or two about how to use the printer. She enjoys it."

"She really does," Ginnie agrees.

Elsa asks, "Does she have any other hobbies?"

"She likes to knit, and she's a reader—historical thrillers are her favorite."

Both parents smile wistfully. Ruby is clearly a beloved child.

Elsa reaches into her purse, hoping for an old tissue to wipe the sweat dripping down her forehead. Finding nothing, she uses the palm of her hand.

"Sorry about the heat," Ginnie says. "I'll go switch on the garage AC."

As soon as his wife is gone, Peter leans close enough for Elsa to feel the sticky dampness of his breath against her face and whispers, "I need to talk to you about something."

"Okay."

"It's about that gun. Something I thought you should probably know."

The skin on the back of her neck shivers at the first curls of air-conditioning seeping from an overhead duct.

His pupils dilate, black pools on the yellowish eyes of a drinker. "The first one I made for the client, well, it disappeared."

"Stolen?"

"Not exactly."

"When?"

"Last week, Wednesday."

"What do you mean by 'not exactly'?"

"I asked Ruby and she admitted she took it because Charlie, the ex, was bothering her. She says she thought if he saw the gun, he'd get the message to leave her alone."

"Bothering her how?"

"She wouldn't give me specifics. Teenagers are secretive, you know?"

"And the gun—you let her keep it?"

"It isn't real."

"It looks real."

"Maybe I made a mistake, but at the time it seemed okay. I mean, she's a pretty girl. She could use some protection."

Elsa contains a quick reaction: she knows from personal experience that you don't have to be pretty to need protection. "Anything else you want to tell me while we're alone?"

"I'm sorry I didn't mention this to Detective Cole before. I didn't want Ginnie to know—it would scare her—"

And piss her off, Elsa thinks.

"But it's been bothering me. At first I was sure it didn't mean anything, but now I don't know what to think."

"So, did Ruby ever show Charlie the gun?"

"I don't know." Peter's face blazes crimson. "We never had a chance to talk about it again. I've checked her room, her locker at school, everywhere I can think of, and it's nowhere."

Shielding her eyes from the bright sun, Elsa searches the front lawn, the tent, the backyard for Lex, annoyance growing the longer he fails to answer her calls and respond to her texts. She needs to consult with him about the fact that Ruby stole a fake gun from her father's workshop two days before she vanished. Clearly, something was going on with the girl that doesn't align with the happy-family, good-student picture presented by her life's surfaces.

Under the tent, Elsa grabs a bottle of water from the barrel of melting ice and notices that Rosemary's information table is being supervised by someone else: a tall young man with combed-back brown hair and a notably crooked nose. *Not young,* Elsa corrects her first impression as she nears the table, *but youngish.* Thirty, maybe thirty-five. His name tag reads TEDDY. The left side of his shirt collar sags under the weight of a photo-button showing the adorable smiling face of a little girl, two lavender bows holding curly hair off her forehead— another missing child, Elsa assumes, thinking she doesn't want to hear the roll call of this guy's various rescue attempts. She's seen his kind before, perennial volunteers who show up at every possible search party, traveling real distances to help out but also to bask in the drama. She has a litany of her own never-found girls and boys, and replaying them is like a helpless dream where you're caught inside a hall of mirrors in which innocence inverts, those little smiles becoming helpless screams. She deflects the thought by looking at a well-worn copy of *The Invisible Man* beside a stack of flyers on the table. She uncaps the bottle of water and takes a long, cooling drink.

Tuned to her, he says, "Great book. Read it?"

"No," she says, "but I did read *Invisible Man* in high school, the one by Ralph Ellison." She'd had to write an essay on it but hadn't minded, as it was her favorite book that year.

"I read that too but I like the H. G. Wells better—it's science fiction. I like science fiction—I mean, if I had to choose a genre. My sisters told me always to bring a book, you know, in case things got boring. But this hasn't slowed down, not for a minute."

It's a strange remark, Elsa thinks—the idea that a search party could grow dull.

Teddy picks up a stack of MISSING signs and tops it off with a little-girl button identical to his own, plucked from his front pants pocket. "Here to volunteer?"

"No." She holds her hand up in refusal of the signs, the button with that sweet little girl. And then she asks, defying the emotional discipline that begs her not to: "Who is that?"

Teddy smiles. "My daughter."

"When was she…"—regret now for her assumption about the button when it seems that he himself is a parent whose life now revolves around his own lost child—"when did it happen?"

"She's fine." Teddy smiles. "I come to these so I can protect her, you know, *'gather ye forces while ye may.'"*

"Isn't it 'rosebuds'—*carpe diem,* 'seize the day'?"

"Is it?"

Well, Elsa thinks, *no one likes to be corrected, even if they're wrong.* She's just glad to know his little girl isn't anyone's victim, even if she's got a peculiar father.

"What can I do for you, madam?" he asks.

"I'm looking for someone—two people, actually. I can't tell if the network's spotty out here or if they're just not responding."

He turns over a sign and picks up a pen. "I'm happy to take down an analog message if you want."

Analog message; did he actually say that without irony? She wonders if, along with being a science fiction buff, he builds gizmos to test the air for signals. "My niece," Elsa says, "is sixteen, and she has—" About to offer details, she cuts herself off. The place is swarming with teenage girls with long dark hair, and now that she thinks of it, she can't remember what colors Mel is wearing. "I'm also looking for Detective Cole. He may have stopped in here."

"He did, just a little while ago. If he comes back I can tell him you were looking for him."

"Special Agent Myers—just say Elsa."

But Teddy notes it all, *Special Agent Elsa Myers,* in chicken-scratch handwriting. He asks, "FBI?"

She nods. "Thanks."

Before she has a chance to turn away, he leans over the table and attaches his spare daughter-button to her shirt, a knuckle pressing into her shoulder for leverage to close the pin. She wonders if he can feel how fast her heart is beating at the unexpectedness of this strange gesture, the fact that he's touching her, actually touching her.

"Extra protection," he says, "for my rosebud."

Elsa wanders out from under the tent, calming herself, refusing to make too much of that oddball—search parties always attract a handful of socially inept volunteers, people who don't get invited to real parties so they show up to any gathering that will have them—and veers in the direction of the street. She removes the button from her shirt and tosses it into her bag. Dials Lex's cell again and this time, finally, he answers.

"Where are you?" she asks.

"Station house," he says. "I thought I told you."

"You didn't. Listen, I spent some time with Ruby's parents, and we need to talk—Ruby had a fake gun."

"Shit."

"I'm on my way over. I just have to track down my niece..." As soon as Elsa says it, she spots Mel across the road in the company of a teenage girl. "See you in a few."

Mel and the girl walk with their heads tilted together, chatting. The instinct that Mel shouldn't be here returns with force.

Shading her eyes with her hand, Elsa says, "There you are."

The girl, whose limp blond hair angles across her face in

such a way as to reveal only half of it, looks out suspiciously with a crisp blue eye: *Who is this random person, and why is she talking to us?*

Mel says, "Hi, Auntie Elsa."

"Oh," says the girl. "She's your *aunt*."

"Yeah, but she's an FBI agent," Mel tells her, "and she's, like, one of the people in charge of the investigation. Special Agent Myers." The name rolls off her tongue with a borrowed authority.

Distrust quivers across the girl's features and suddenly Elsa recognizes her from Ruby's Facebook page.

"Please, call me Elsa." She offers a hand, which the girl shakes hesitantly. "You're a friend of Ruby's."

Mel smiles. "This is Allie."

Resisting an urge to say, *Yes, I realize that,* Elsa says, "Ah, the elusive Allie."

"The what?"

"We've been trying to reach you. Didn't you get our messages?"

"Who's *we*?"

"Me and my partner, Detective Cole."

"I never listen to my messages."

"He even stopped by your house."

"When?"

"Yesterday. No one was home."

Allie shrugs and seems on the verge of an eye-roll but stops herself, blinking away the impulse to dismiss this probing adult.

Elsa says, "I understand you saw Ruby on Friday night. At work."

"I was the *last one* to see her," Allie clarifies.

Lowering her voice, Elsa asks, "Allie, did Ruby say anything to you about the fake gun she took from her father's workshop last week?"

They look uncomfortably into each other's eyes a moment. "Gun?" Allie says. *"No."*

Elsa's pulse spikes, a subtlety in the emphasis of that *no*. She wants to get the girl alone and is about to suggest it when Allie's phone emits a repetitive boinging sound. She steps aside to read the message. When she's done, she looks at Elsa. "I'm so scared about Ruby, I really want to help … but if I don't hurry I'll be late for my math Regents. Should I skip it, do you think?"

"You can't think of anything else Ruby said that might be useful to us?"

"Honestly," Allie says, *"trust me,* if I knew *anything,* I would tell you."

"Okay." Elsa nods, though it isn't okay; the minute people start spouting *honestly*s and *trust me*s, red flags wave. "Go ahead, but I'd like to touch base with you later." She hands Allie her card. "Call me."

"I will. *Promise.*" Allie walks away quickly, thumb-scrolling the face of her phone.

"Did that seem weird to you?" Elsa asks Mel. "Kind of… abrupt?" As they pass the tent, she notices Teddy watching them.

"Did Ruby really have a gun?"

And he's listening too, Elsa thinks. "Shh. Keep your voice down."

"Did she?"

"It's plastic."

"Yeah, but still."

"I would have liked to talk with Allie a little longer."

"She has a test—don't take it *personally*." The way Mel says it—in defense of the girl, conspirators in a newly plotted friendship—sends a frazzle of discomfort through Elsa.

"Listen, Mellie, I need to work without distractions. I'm hoping we can get back up to Sleepy Hollow tomorrow and I have a lot to do first."

"The hospital"—Mel's face clouds—"is so depressing."

Impatience crackles, and Elsa orders, "Come on, we're going."

"Wait—why?" Mel follows her aunt in the direction of the car. "That detective said you guys were looking for Allie. I found her for you. I was only trying to help."

"Mel." Elsa raises her voice, finally out of earshot of Teddy and the tent and the other searchers. "This is an investigation—I can't have my family members getting involved." Elsa unlocks the car with a remote *bleep*.

"Why not?"

Another car pulls to a stop to wait for the parking space. Too upset to answer, knowing that *Because* isn't going to cut it, Elsa defaults to an authoritative "Get in."

Mel is silent all the way into Manhattan. This time, when José opens the car door, Elsa says firmly, "Stay inside until class. I mean it." Feeling that if Mel is locked inside, she'll be safe. Knowing that isn't necessarily true. Elsa's skin itches but she denies herself the satisfaction of scratching. Instead, she holds her breath, watching as Mel disappears behind the brilliantly reflective glass doors—an apparition that is fully there and then suddenly gone.

8

So what do we make of this gun thing?" Lex swings a
cowboy boot onto the edge of the station-house conference table and leans over to inspect a seam that's
coming apart.

"Lex, that's disgusting." Elsa pulls the half sandwich he
saved for her, tuna, away from the dirty sole of his boot.

"Sorry." He lands his foot on the floor. "Didn't sleep a
whole lot last night, lost my manners."

Elsa folds the sandwich into its wax paper wrapping. She
isn't hungry. "Clearly Ruby was up to something. The Amber yielded nothing, and now this."

"You know who I'm pissed at right now?"

Elsa nods.

"The father," he says, "for not telling me this up front."

"Yup."

"What was he thinking?"

"He wasn't, apparently. He was feeling. Lex, people seize
up when they're scared. It's human nature."

"Sure. But we're talking about his daughter."

"Yeah, I know. I'm pretty pissed at him too."

"So, Ruby had a gun—why? And she turned off the security tape at work—why? And then she disappeared." Tapping his boot on the floor to the rhythm of questions unpaired with answers, tiny echoes bouncing off the hard walls.

Elsa's phone bleeps with a text from Marco letting them know that a liaison from BAU-3—the section of the Behavioral Analysis Unit that deals specifically with children—is available to consult on the case. Calling in the BAU can mean leaps forward, but it can also bring more delays, and until now Elsa hasn't been ready to initiate that crapshoot. She tells Lex, "Marco wants us to talk to someone at the BAU. At this point, I think he's right."

"Psychologist?"

"More or less, but with Quantico mojo behind them."

"Probably a good idea."

Elsa answers Marco, tells him to go ahead and arrange it. In minutes, the call comes through.

"Hello." The analyst's tone is rich with confidence. "Just to start by introducing myself, I'm Dr. Joan Gottesman Bailey but please call me either Dr. Bailey or, preferably, Joan. I understand that you've got a missing seventeen-year-old, and you're looking just for phone consultation at this point?"

Elsa answers, "Correct."

"Well, a teenager that old could easily still turn up, of course."

"Exactly."

"She's been gone how long? Catch me up."

Elsa begins at the beginning, retelling a story that becomes less knowable the more familiar it gets.

"Okay," Joan says, "let me get on this," and already Elsa can hear the faraway click of typing as she taps, presumably, into the powerful database of the NCAVC—the National Center for the Analysis of Violent Crime. Elsa feels a murky combination of encouragement and fatigue, her thoughts swinging briefly to her father and an urge to call him, followed closely by a savage itch on her shoulder. When she reaches under her collar to scratch, Lex's attention shifts to her and she pulls her hand away from her skin. He stares at her with a disturbing intensity, finishing up his own phone call.

"What?" she asks.

"That was MasterCard. Ruby's credit card was used this morning—in Vermont, outside Bennington."

9

Coins of sunshine flash through the branches until leaves grow so dense they block out nearly all the light. The deeper in they go, the darker it gets. Her wrists are bound tight, like she's praying. Her parents raised her as an atheist and she never thought of it before but there are different kinds of prayers. Anything can be one, if you want it to.

What is a quark?

The smallest unit of matter; makes up protons.

What are molecules?

Two or more atoms held together by chemical bonds.

What is an organelle?

Part of a cell that has a specific function.

What are five types of organelles?

Nucleus, mitochondrion, *something something, something,* Golgi body.

The rope chafes with every step and then with a pop she feels the skin on her right wrist break apart. Pain burns raw.

He's got her cuffs tied to another rope that's attached to his belt, so if she tries to get away he'll feel a pull. He walks in front of her, fast, tugging her along in short jerky steps.

She stopped pleading an hour ago. Now she quietly goes where he goes, wherever that is. He's crazy. And strong. He actually used the word *love* before and she thought about becoming a nun if she lived. Or a monk if they took girls. Or just someone who lived alone and kept away from everyone. Her mother would try to stop her from "thinking that way" and help her forget the nightmare that was past. But it isn't past yet; it's happening now. This is her life right now. This is what is happening to her today.

She summons a feeling of her mother reaching for her to pull her out of this, and thinking about her mother makes her see a future, a tiny glimmer up ahead, as in the real world, the world outside of this. But in the now world, the right-here world, her last view of daylight is swallowed into a false sunset. And she feels a heaviness. A sadness. And she does not want to go on.

But then the side of her neck twitches with the little marching band of her tattoos, her Smurfy dwarfs mobilizing themselves for a meeting of the board. She invented them by accident, drawing on her bedroom wall when she was eight, angry at her parents, pencil in hand. Gradually their world grew and she called it Hopewall, a town and a world of its own, population currently one hundred and twelve.

They just keep reproducing. And they are busy, always up to something.

Their leaders are the original members of the clan: Carrie and Velma and Arnold (no one is named Arnold anymore) and Jesus, pronounced Hey-Zeus. Which is why when she got her first tat on her fifteenth birthday—just her and two friends and a tattoo artist who didn't care about parental consent, not that her parents have an issue with tattoos; "Choose your battles," her mother always says—she brought a drawing of them with her to the mall. The tattooist did a pretty good job, etching the miniature creations in a daisy chain climbing her neck. Now her little quartet, her board of directors, travels everywhere with her, all expenses paid. They always seem to know when a plan veers off course and are ready to volunteer for anything at a moment's notice.

Sensing trouble, they leap off her neck and shimmer into view on the ground in front of her, waving, calling, cajoling, urging her forward.

"Do not give up!" Velma orders.

"You go, girl," Jesus prods, "*you go.*"

Carrie scowls. "This isn't cheerleading."

Arnold marches quietly among them; he's scared too.

Velma, always practical, suggests: "Use your time to study!"

Order from smallest to largest:

Cell, tissue, organ, organ system, organism.

She wiggles her fingers until her remaining ring, the purple one, shimmies down over her knuckle and then past her other knuckle and falls to the ground with a soundless plop that she decides only she can hear.

If a ring drops in a forest and no one is there but you and him, does it make a sound?

10

The sign says PARKING ONLY WHILE SHOPPING AT GREENBERG'S. The lumberyard's outbuildings sprawl around the lot, green barnlike structures sheltering pallets of hewn wood planks, shelves stocked with vats of compound and paint and sundry other construction materials. Astride one building, a forklift is parked behind a flatbed truck, which is parked behind a cherry picker, an able convoy awaiting purpose in the sweet Vermont air. Elsa pulls in and takes the spot closest to the door marked OFFICE.

"Doesn't look like the kind of place a teenage girl would go shopping," Elsa observes from behind the wheel.

"Nope." Lex kicks up a storm of dust when he slams shut the passenger door.

Across the road, an empty lot is filled with starved, yellow grass. It looks as if it hasn't rained in a while, though the sky is so mottled with gray-white clouds that she suspects the drought won't last much longer.

They cross the lot to the office door. Inside a small room

stacked with paperwork is an industrial desk with a sign reading BOSS/SECRETARY/GREENBERG HISSELF. No one is there. Something moves inside a garbage can filled with crumpled paper, and then a mouse catapults out.

"Mr. Greenberg?" Lex asks, chuckling.

Elsa makes way for the mouse to leave through the front door, feeling proud of herself, *lover of all life,* when a large steel-toed work boot crushes it. It doesn't make a sound. The person belonging to the boot kicks the remains outside before they can get a look at it, which is fine by Elsa. She's seen plenty of bodies over the years—dead, almost dead, dead a long time—but something about an oversize person destroying an undersized creature for no reason gives her pause.

"Wow," she mutters.

To the six-foot-plus, two-hundred-fifty-pound red-haired man standing in front of them, Lex says, "Detective Lex Cole, New York Police Department, sorry to barge in unexpected."

"Cops?" the guy asks. "You're always welcome here. Mice, not so much. I'm Greenberg. What can I do you for?"

Elsa introduces herself, earning an eyebrow hike that would be comical if it weren't so offensive, the disrespectful *Lady detective* scowl every female investigator suffers from time to time. She ignores it. "You sold something this morning, about eight thirty, for exactly"—she consults her phone, where she'd jotted the number on her notepad app—"twenty-one dollars and sixty-seven cents. We're wondering who you sold it to."

Greenberg says, "Huh."

They stand back to give him space as he comes around to

the front of the desk, where he presses himself into the chair and flicks on his desktop monitor. After a minute, he looks up from the digital receipt. "Yup. Eight thirty-two a.m., for the amount you said, to one Ruby Haverstock. Shit. Wait a minute." His eyes flicker. "*Damn*. I made that sale myself, a dozen pine boards and a pound of nails, but it was a dude comes in here from time to time. 'Cept these days, you never really know if someone decided to make a change—guy, girl, whatever."

"You don't pay attention to the name on the credit card when you make a sale?" Elsa asks, stating the obvious in question form solely because she wants to see his reaction.

"Usually I do, ma'am. But this morning we were busy, and I was waiting on the coffeepot to finish. Wasn't too clear, I guess. Damn. Damn."

"Okay." She stops him. "You're not in trouble, Mr. Greenberg. We just want to know who used the card."

"Don't know his name, just his face."

"Can you make that bigger?"

Enlarged, the digital receipt shows a loop and a slash, a signature that could be anyone's.

"Do you by any chance keep security cameras on-site?"

"You bet we do." He slap-types angrily until he finds what he wants. "Been robbed too many times not to keep our eyes open. You wouldn't believe the junkies we got up here, and we carry copper wire, so you know what we're up against."

"Bane of every construction outfit all across the country, I hear," Lex says.

"*Oh* yeah." Greenberg types. "Okay, okay, here we go." He squints at the screen, furiously tapping the keyboard's down arrow. "Eight fifteen to eight forty-five this morning, that sound about right?"

"Just to save time," Elsa says, "let's narrow that to eight twenty-five to eight forty. Unless the buyer browsed?"

"Nope. He came, he ordered, he paid, he went."

Elsa and Lex stand behind Greenberg and watch some extremely boring television for four minutes, and then a dented white van drives into the camera's frame. Parks. Someone inside pauses to sip from a large cardboard cup and adjusts his aviator sunglasses in the rearview mirror before he steps out of the van. He carries the cup with him, finishes what's in it, and tosses it into the trash. Elsa makes a mental note to retrieve it on their way out.

For a moment he looks familiar, and then he doesn't. On the tall side, jeans, black T-shirt, a couple days of stubble, longish messy brown hair. Elsa asks, "Can you please replay that?"

Greenberg obliges, and she watches the man reverse back into the driver's seat and step out and reverse back in and step back out. Then he walks ten paces across the parking lot, speed-walks ten paces backward, and proceeds slow-motion until he disappears under the eaves of one of the warehouse buildings.

"You," Lex tells Greenberg, "are an artist with that thing."

"Yeah, well, back in the day I wanted to be a TV editor. Lived in the city for two years, but the work didn't come, so here I am. Sign should read Greenberg and Son, as I'm the son."

"Father still around?"

"Nah. I'm the son and the father and the holy ghost, if you must know—"

Elsa interrupts. "Keep going until he's back on camera."

The man reappears, heading toward the office. She squints, trying to read the man's face, body language, anything to clue her in to this tickle of recognition. But the harder she tries, the faster the feeling dissipates.

"You know him?" Lex asks.

She looks at her temporary partner, directly into his eyes: hazel like her father's, with a dizzying complexity between the greens and browns. Answers, "No."

Greenberg fast-forwards to the scene of the man leaving: he passively watches his lumber loaded in, hoists himself back into the van, drives away. And then the license plate, New York State, with the number clear as a bell.

While Lex drives Elsa's car, she works her laptop, dipping in and out of Internet on the mountainous roads. Each time she picks up a network, she abruptly loses it, but finally she manages enough of a connection to land somewhere useful.

"'Ishmael Edward Locke,'" she reads from the Bureau's central database, "no criminal record, lives at two hundred Jess Maxon Road in Petersburgh."

"New York?"

"Yup. Just across the Vermont border." She plugs the address into her phone's GPS, sways as Lex turns the car around, redirecting. Something twists inside Elsa: the sickened, energized feeling of a hunt when it really begins. "He has the credit card she carries with her, Lex."

"Maybe she dropped it somewhere. Maybe he found it."

"When? We know she used it during her shift at Queens Beans—ordered in a falafel and paid with her card."

"But Elsa, if he has her, why would he risk using her card?"

"Stupidity. Error. Greed."

"Twenty-one dollars and sixty-seven cents' worth of greed?"

"Right. Probably not that. Using her card would have been a mistake. He could have put it next to his, pulled out the wrong one, some idiot move like that."

"Did you find out how long to Albany?"

"About thirty miles from Locke's address." She's already alerted the FBI's upstate lab that they've got a high-priority forensics job coming their way in regard to a missing child: the white cardboard coffee cup Locke threw away in Greenberg's parking lot. The sour smell of someone else's old coffee still lingers in her nose; she'd leaned into the garbage, plucked the cup off a splayed banana peel fresh enough to still be partially yellow.

By the time Elsa and Lex turn off the main road, Marco is working on an emergency search-and-seizure warrant in case they need it.

The pavement devolves into a rutted single lane barely wide enough for an average car. Tucked into a clearing of hardened earth crusted with dead grass is Locke's land; on it, what appears to be a handmade cabin, a one-room structure somewhere between rickety and charming. A dusty black sedan is parked off to the side.

Elsa mutters, "Interesting."

"So he has two cars," Lex says. "Or maybe the van was rented."

"Take a closer look."

Lex's gaze lingers on the car before he turns to Elsa. "I don't see it."

"It's an S plate—part of the Sam Unit. State PD Special Investigations."

At the sound of their car doors crashing shut, someone appears from around the side of the house: a portly man with a ring of salty hair, his eyes dark slices in a potato-mash face.

"Help you folks?" He isn't wearing a uniform, but the cop edge to his tone is unmistakable.

"Special Agent Myers and Detective Cole." They show their IDs.

"Ah, welcome." He offers a hand, and they shake. "Detective Sang McCracken. You can call me Sang or you can call me Mick, but don't call me Cracker."

Lex outright laughs, a large, full laugh that makes Elsa smile.

McCracken says, "I heard the feds came up from the city."

"Heard how?" Elsa asks.

"You put out an APB on one of our landowners. Plus, we got a leaky border with Vermont—two small counties pressed together, you can just imagine."

"In other words," Lex says, "Greenberg told you."

"Yup. Thought we could help you out. How was your drive?"

"Easy," Elsa says. "Find anything?"

"No visible evidence Mr. Locke had any girl here lately."

Walking up the four stairs onto the slip of a front porch, Elsa notices the soft bulge of rot. She steps carefully. Behind her, Lex tests each plank before lowering his weight. They follow McCracken inside.

"Guy isn't much of a decorator," McCracken observes.

To say the least. The interior is constructed of rough-hewn boards. The floor whines and squeaks when Elsa walks inside, as if it's been built on nothing. The few pieces of furniture exactly match the unfinished quality of the walls: bumpy and raw, shaped by force but not smooth or refined. There's a small table and a single chair, a couch with no cushions, and a double bed with a thin mattress covered by a moth-eaten wool blanket. A wooden chest sits at the foot of the bed. Small shelves built into the walls hold partially burned candles in glass lanterns. An old gas refrigerator stands in the corner in a makeshift kitchen that includes a wooden sink with a hand pump for water.

Elsa has to cock the squealing handle four times to draw the first drop. "This hasn't been used in a while—strange, if he was just here."

Lex opens the freezer. "Stinks." He slams it shut.

Elsa catches a whiff of the rotten egg smell and holds her breath until it passes. She opens a drawer under the counter: a few mismatched utensils, a flashlight, extra batteries, several candles, and a box of utility matches. A large breadbox sits on the counter; she opens it. Crammed inside are a bag of potato chips, a jar of peanuts, and a sleeve of crackers. In a cupboard beneath the sink she finds half a dozen gallons of bottled water.

They wander the room, which takes all of five minutes. She uses her foot to open a chest at the base of the bed. Moths flutter out, dozens of them. The blanket folded inside is crawling with larvae.

She says, "I don't think he's opened this lately."

"Summer squatter," McCracken says. "Looks like the cabin's been sitting all winter."

Elsa kicks shut the infested chest. As she crosses toward the door, the floor's hollow whine reminds her: "I wonder if there's a crawl space under the cabin—let's take a look."

They all go outside and inspect the perimeter of the house, which sits cheek by jowl with the rutted earth, joined by a narrow seam of concrete—built without a foundation, just plunked down on the earth.

"No sign of the lumber and nails he bought this morning," Lex notes.

She turns and gazes into the woods, which seem to grow denser, quieter, the longer she looks at them. "How deep does it go?"

"Hundreds of miles, cut through by roads, but there are some deep pockets of forest in there," McCracken says. "I've got people in there searching. Seemed wise not to wait, considering. We're also canvassing rest areas from here to the city, see if he made any stops, if he had anyone with him. We're looking for him, and so is every neighboring state. If he's out there, we'll bring him in, let him tell his side of things."

"Well," Elsa says, "you know how to reach us. We've got to book it to Albany, little gift for the lab—picked up his takeout cup at Greenberg's."

McCracken's eyebrows dart up. "I can have someone run it over for you, if that would help."

"That would be great," Lex responds before Elsa has a chance to demur. She doesn't like this, the way he took charge, and the old feeling that the best way to get things done right and fast is to do it herself rears up. But before she can offer a plausible reason for them to make the trip themselves, Lex is in her car, fetching the evidence bag, sealed at the top with red tape stamped DO NOT OPEN * EVIDENCE * TO BE OPENED BY AUTHORIZED PERSONNEL ONLY. He hands it to the upstate detective, telling him, "Thanks, that's a big help."

They return to their respective cars with promises to keep each other posted.

The temperature up here is cooler than in the city, and Elsa and Lex keep their windows down, allowing in soft breezes and the musical sawing of grasshoppers. She consults her watch, sees that it's late afternoon, and wonders where the day went.

The construction workers will have left the house on Whitelaw Street already. By the time she and Lex reach Manhattan, it will be dark. She feels a tremor of anticipation at the thought that she could go back, if she wants to, that she doesn't have to keep fighting the urge.

Lex's voice abruptly returns her to the moment. "Head to the city?"

Through the windshield, a verdant mass of trees. She has a sudden sense that it's already too late for Ruby, but she doesn't want to say that. Not yet. She turns the car around and pulls away from Locke's cabin.

11

Lex asks, "Didn't you say your dad's hospital is in Sleepy Hollow?"

"Did I?" Elsa's fingers tighten on the steering wheel. She glances at the passenger seat, at Lex, whose attention is fixed on the green exit sign hurtling closer as they drive south. Without intending to, she decelerates.

"You did. We can take a detour if you want."

An image of Roy, ill, fading, materializes in Elsa's mind followed by a sharp tug toward him. Of course she wants to stop; any opportunity to see him now shouldn't be wasted.

Adept at self-denial, she says, "We probably shouldn't take the time."

"Elsa, we're doing everything we possibly can and we're far from the only ones looking for Ruby," he argues. "We can spare twenty minutes."

"You're right." She veers onto the exit so suddenly that Lex sways to the side, and she surprises herself with a feeling of satisfaction at having literally moved him.

As soon as they're on the local roads, he asks, "What kind of cancer does he have?"

She takes a long, conscious breath. "Mind if we don't talk about it?" Grinding her jaw, she turns into the hospital parking lot.

"Not at all." His tone soft with regret or embarrassment, something that tells her he wishes he hadn't asked.

She turns off the engine, killing the air-conditioning, and the car immediately heats up. "There's a café in the lobby where you can wait for me, if you want," she suggests.

"Good idea."

He follows her into the revolving doors that land them in a high-ceilinged atrium, linoleum floors buffed to a hard shine. He makes his way to the café while she heads alone to the elevator.

Riding up to the fifth floor, she tries to ignore the turned-cheese smell that she associates with embalming fluids, formaldehyde, and methanol—*hospital smell*. Someone must have cleaned in here recently, leaving behind that unctuous chemical odor. Since her father's ordeal began, he's been in and out of the hospital twice in two weeks—first after the drama of his diagnosis, now for what one doctor called a "readjustment"; in expectations, apparently—and she's found that every visit here resonates with something new, a sensation that clings to her.

Oncology reception is unmanned; the hallway quiet.

She turns into her father's room and finds Roy sound asleep. The bathroom door gapes open, spilling shadows that evoke visceral recollections of last night: her fingernails scratching at the blazing scars, almost feeling relief until shame crept on top of it; her folded-together knife watching from the sink like a discarded old friend, waiting to be included; Elsa resisting and stopping and getting dressed and walking away, tossing the betrayed knife into her bag. She won't look at the bathroom now and instead fixes on Tara, sitting at their father's bedside, pecking away at her phone. Solitaire, probably, as she's practically a champion.

"Winning?"

"Shhh." Tara rests her phone on her lap and smiles at her sister. Then she looks past Elsa as if expecting someone else.

"Mel's at home. Don't worry, she's fine," Elsa whispers. "Has he been sleeping long?"

Tara seesaws her hand side to side: yes and no. A nonanswer that leaves Elsa without any sense of when he might wake up. The morphine button is loose in his hand, suggesting that he sent himself off into oblivion, and those journeys tend to last hours.

The sisters decamp to the hallway where they can talk. Elsa asks, "How is he?"

"Same, but he sleeps a lot now that he has that button."

"Can't blame him."

"That's another reason I want to get him back to Atria"—his assisted-living home—"and into hospice. Don't you think he should experience the end of his life?"

"Maybe, but I wouldn't mind some morphine right about now."

"Tough day?"

"Yup, and it isn't over." She says nothing about Mel showing up at the Haverstock house that morning, which would only upset Tara. "My partner's waiting downstairs. We're on our way back from Vermont."

"Vermont?"

"You don't want to know."

"You're right, I don't." It's long been understood that Tara can't bear any mention of the travails suffered by "your kids," as she once referred to the victims Elsa devotes herself to rescuing. Tara's aversion to speaking of it, as if that could bring disaster on her own family, has created a habitual silence between the sisters whenever the subject comes up.

"So," Tara says, "I guess you have to leave."

"Probably should. Tell Dad I was here. I'll come back tomorrow if I can."

"Okay."

They kiss good-bye as the rhythmic slap of footsteps comes down the hall, a gait that surprises Elsa with its familiarity. Hard leather on linoleum, not the more typical squish of a hospital worker's rubbery shoe.

Cowboy boots.

An uneasy feeling jitters through her and there is Lex, carrying a round glass vase sprouting a colorful arrangement of orange African daisies and magenta snapdragons—hopeful, summery *Get well soon* flowers, not *I'm so sorry* flowers in autumn hues of a defeated season.

"I hope this is okay," he says. "I have a soft spot for people in hospitals."

"They call that Munchausen by proxy," Elsa snaps when what she really wants is to remind him of the barrier she thought she'd erected between them earlier, establishing her need for privacy. She can't imagine what he's thinking, coming up here with a gift.

"That's when you *make* someone sick, not visit them," Tara corrects her. Then, turning to Lex with a smile, she says, "You must be the partner. I'm the sister. Thanks for the flowers. They're beautiful."

"It's not a bad gift shop down there," he says.

Elsa takes the vase from him. "Dad's out cold; we shouldn't have bothered coming. I'll bring this in and then we can go."

"You're welcome."

"Thank you."

She senses his gaze following her into her father's room as if he's disappointed that he wasn't invited to join her. It was a mistake, this detour. Roy's slow breaths in and slower breaths out suggest that his sleep has only deepened. She places the bouquet on a shelf within his view. When she kisses his warm forehead, his papery skin seems to hold the form of her lips a moment after she pulls away.

"I love you, Dad," she whispers.

As she's watching him, his breathing seems to grow even more lethargic, but she isn't sure; his eyelids quiver, or maybe they don't. He seems alive and he seems dead and the contradiction of it makes her dizzy with sadness.

Back in the hall, she tells Lex, "It's time to go."

Lex says, "Nice to meet you, Tara," and follows Elsa out. The elevator smell is more complicated now, someone's incontinence having added itself to the mix. They don't look at each other and don't speak until they're back in the parking lot.

"I guess I should thank you for the flowers," she says.

"You already did."

"I didn't mean it."

"Do you mean it now?"

"Not really."

"Elsa, I'm sorry, I wasn't thinking. I encroached on your privacy and I shouldn't have."

"Forget it." With the key fob, she unlocks the car doors with a pair of bleeps. "Let's just get back to work."

"Want me to drive?" he offers.

His compassion feels suffocating, but she *is* tired. "Sure. Thanks."

As soon as they're on the highway, Lex at the wheel, she leans back and nurses the sensation that she might just fall asleep if she doesn't talk to him or allow herself to think of the day's failures. Of how, for the half a day they've spent on Ishmael Locke, they aren't any closer to finding Ruby. Of how even her visit to the hospital amounted to nothing but wasted time. Of how if she does return to Whitclaw Street tonight, creeping in under cover of darkness like a burglar, it will probably end only with more disappointment.

The car whizzes south. She leans her head back and parses her strong reaction to Lex's interest in her life, how the slightest hint of curiosity stirred her defenses. How hypocritical it is of her to have cornered him yesterday about where he went to college when he clearly didn't want to tell her, and now, when he wants to know about her, she slaps him down.

But she doesn't know how to talk about the hovering loss of Roy. From the moment his terminal illness was announced, her thoughts have spun enough on their own without the interference of people's inquiries, which only add velocity to the sensation that she's about to exit her known orbit. Only lately has she begun to realize how the pact of silence she's shared with her father all these years has somehow kept her grounded. He's been someone to talk to about *everything,* she realizes now. *And when he's gone, you'll be sealed alone in your echo chamber, locked in your dark closet forever.*

She closes her eyes as the old loneliness for her father washes over her, but worse, and allows in the white noise of mindlessness until she's no longer aware of the roar of the highway. In her half-wakeful drifting state, an image of Ruby approaches her, reaching out her hand. The lock on Elsa's defenses gives way, unlatching like it always does in these cases—opening her wide to the girl in trouble.

12

Her hand on your back, in the milk-chocolate darkness, is a creamy swirl of heaven. It's as if her light touch has been perfectly calibrated to send tingles to your scalp. Shivers cascade through your nerves and you sigh without sighing and relax like falling into sleep again and again. You force your eyes to stay open, force yourself to stay awake because you don't want this to end. Her fingers brush down toward the bottom of your pajama top.

"Good night, Elsa," your mother whispers, respectful of your incremental drift toward sleep.

"Five more minutes."

"It's already been ten"—sounding gentle, the way she can when she wants to. No one is sweeter than your mother when she's in a good mood. Her voice luscious and just-right. And you love her.

"Please."

Her fingers climb back up the trellis of your ribs and fan over your shoulder blades. Your back so small under the wide span of her tender hand. And you believe she loves you too.

But then, the next day, you believe she can't love you.

Three skips of the jump rope, alone in your bedroom, three skips in your stocking feet on the thick carpet when you're sure she won't hear you. Downstairs, with the noisy vacuum running, it's impossible to hear anything. But then suddenly she's in your room, her face a distortion, eyes ablaze, screaming, "Stop!"

"But *Mommy*—" The rope now snaking at your feet.

Her hand is so fast and tight on your wrist that your bones hurt. She jerks you into the closet and slams the door and the key turns on the outside and she leaves, *her footsteps leaving,* and then the quiet is complete. You slump among your shoes and hit yourself for your stupidity. *Why did you do it?* Last night's bedtime ritual made you feel safe, but you ought to know better by now.

The light that filters into the closet through the cracks in the door gradually fades until the dark becomes a kind of liquid drowning. You can't see anything. There is nothing to hear, not even the vacuum, not a single footstep coming to you. The smell in here is peculiar, sour, and it fills your nose. Running your small hands up and down your arms and legs, you begin to wonder if you're even real.

Your insides start to shake, and you're unbearably thirsty, and you need to cry, but you're afraid of making any sound until your father gets home. You wait, and wait, but he doesn't come. Where is Tara? Doesn't anyone wonder where you went?

Finally, after a thousand years, you begin to evaporate. You *aren't* real. Your hands roam the floor, counting shoes—seven in all, one of a pair is missing—and then you feel the wire hanger just lying there. You pick it up and trace the funny shape, like bent elbows with a hook. When you reach the sharp end, you can't resist pressing it into the pad of your fingertip, just to see how it feels. The puncture of metal, the breaking of skin, comes with a rush of sensation that assures you that you *are* real after all.

You bend the hook and use the sharp tip to etch what you believe is an *E* in the top of your thigh. Your skin burns, not unpleasantly. You press harder. You think you feel blood rising out of your skin, but you're not sure, so you dab the wound with the tip of your finger. Taste it. Yes, you have made yourself bleed, and if that isn't proof of life, what is?

You miss dinner. Your stomach growls and the thirst grows and grows. The last thing you remember is a dry clawing inside your throat.

In the morning, you wake up in your bed, a whiff of your father's sweet vanilla scent in your nostrils replacing the closet smell of isolation. The thought that he kissed you good night when you were sleeping reprises a memory of safety, and the closet, you think, was a dream, just a dream. But then you feel the tug of a bandage on your thigh and you sit up in bed, fast, covers puddling at your knees. And there it is: evidence of your self-inflicted wound.

E for Elsa. Who is real. And alive. Even in the closet, alone.

Carefully, you pry loose the edge of the bandage and peel it back.

And it's true, you *were* locked in the closet. But you were wrong; it isn't an *E*. In the darkness, all you managed was a deep, ragged trench, an angry scribble.

13

The city's density gathers force as they near Manhattan, Lex at the wheel.

Elsa's mind drifts back to the crusty old problem of her mother's violence and the indigestibility of her father's failure to protect her. In some ways she's still waiting for him in that closet, has been waiting all her life, but now that he's dying, how will he save her? And why, why, why hasn't she ever asked him *why* he didn't rescue her back then, when he might have used his parental authority, his love for her, to yank her away from an unpredictable mother? Still, despite the slow-drip betrayal of those years—the way he essentially stood back and watched what was happening to his own child—she has learned to resist bitterness when it sizzles up. She just doesn't have the emotional energy to resent (too deeply) her admittedly imperfect father, and she knows he loves her, and after her mother's death he was all she had left. It's been a real comfort, all these years, just the idea that he's out there, that he knows her, knows she exists in the realest ways, knows everything about her, despite the tentative promise (the tempered scar-like relief) that the worst memories will die with him. The anguish that has yoked her for decades, which he wants her to *let go of*. It occurs to her for the first time that he probably understands she will never forget the past but hopes she'll learn to let it drift out of the forefront of her consciousness so that she can live more fully. Can she?

Elsa turns to look at Lex, his nice profile blocking the view of New Jersey across the river. Traffic on the FDR moves swiftly. To their right, the towers of New York stagger higher and higher. Skyscrapers reaching into the sky and seeming to touch it but really not even close.

He parks the car two blocks from her Brooklyn building and they walk together to Smith Street in a blooming twilight. It's late enough that boutiques have started closing and restaurants are filling up. Elsa's stomach lurches with hunger. She won't return to Whitelaw Street tonight, she decides in that moment; she'll stay in the here and now, no looking back. She'll go home and eat something, fried eggs and a beer, in front of her laptop while she checks for updates on the Amber Alert and the APB; waits for the lab results; digs deeper into Ishmael Locke's background; tries to find out what Ruby did with her father's fake gun and how or if it connects with her disappearance; wonders whether she's missing the lead she *should* be following while she chases Locke; waits for Mel to get home from her night class; and, not least important, calls to see if Roy is awake yet.

"The subway's that way," she tells Lex, pointing left. "Let's keep in touch tonight. I'll be ready at a moment's notice if anything comes up."

He nods, says, "Me too," and sighs. "You know what I could use right now? I could use a drink."

"I hear you." She thinks of the beer waiting for her at home, lonely, inviting.

"What's that place over there?" He looks across the street at the sleek façade of a vintage-inspired bar she has never been to despite having lived around the corner for four years. She rarely goes out for drinks with friends because she doesn't really have any, and her colleagues in CARD generally rush home with heavy hearts after another day hunting for missing children, unequipped for levity or banter or jokes.

"It's the Clover Club," she tells him.

"Looks nice."

"I wouldn't know."

He surprises her by taking her arm, gently but with enough confidence to be forceful, and guiding her into the street between the red blink of receding taillights and the glare of an oncoming car. They run to the curb.

Exhilaration mixed with annoyance, she asks, "Are you trying to get us killed?"

"Let me buy you a beer," he says, "to make up for before. An apology." He leads her toward the door, a flourish of gold lettering on finger-smudged glass.

"Lex, thanks, but—" She stops talking when she realizes that he isn't listening. He holds up a finger, begging her patience, his thumb dancing across the face of his phone. "My brother, David, works nearby. I told him I'd see him tonight if I was back in time and there was any chance."

"You mean there are two of you?"

"You'll join us."

"Thanks, but I'll pass. I should go home and see if I can get some work done before my niece gets back from her class."

"Yup," he tells her, reading his brother's reply, "just coming out of the courthouse now, says he can be here in fifteen."

"What, is he a lawyer?"

"Very good, Detective."

"Special Agent. Okay." Feeling guilty for the severity of her reaction to the flowers. Wanting to give him an inch. "Just one beer."

Low lighting douses the carved mahogany walls and ceiling with a sense of reminiscence for a time that probably wasn't as prettily lived when it was happening. Thing is, the faux atmosphere really is enticing—like a generous, frilly scoop of ice cream. There's no point wasting a place like this on just a beer. But because the drinks menu is long and complicated, and Elsa's tired, she keeps it simple and orders the bar's namesake concoction of gin, vermouth, lemon, and raspberry. Lex tells a few jokes and she manages to dredge up some thin laughter, but after a while thoughts of Ruby still being gone and Ishmael Locke out there with answers to her questions vine tightly around her. Her skin prickles. She has to go.

Standing, she says, "Thanks for the drink."

"You haven't finished."

She picks up her glass and downs it, the final quarter inch of gin racing into her brain.

Just then, his brother appears at their table, a man of medium height with thick disordered hair, the knot of his necktie pulled down to allow for the release of his top button. He strongly resembles Lex, but he's older and has about him the look of a hard day that Elsa instantly relates to. She sits back down.

"Sorry I'm late," he says to Lex, and turns to Elsa. His smile is wide and without his brother's gap. "Whatever he's told you about me, it isn't true."

"Elsa Myers."

"David Cole—good to meet you." His hand is warm and soft. She impulsively pulls hers away, because she knows herself; she has defective radar when it comes to men. So far, not a single one has failed to bolt after the darkness and booze have worn off, and, in daylight, the cryptography of her skin screams *trouble*.

"She's FBI," Lex explains. "We're working together on a case."

"Oh?" David borrows an unused chair from a neighbor's table and pulls it up to join them.

She says, "We just spent the day driving up and down the East Coast."

David offers an understanding nod, a shadow of concern moving through his eyes. He flags the waitress and orders an old-fashioned. Elsa already feels floaty from one drink. She begins to anticipate another.

"Nice place," David says, obviously looking for some way to direct the conversation away from work. She wonders what kind of lawyer he is. "Definitely a step up from where we usually meet."

"Which is?" she asks.

"Any old Blarney Stone."

The brothers have the same happy laugh.

"This place is toned," Lex says.

David corrects him. "Tony."

"Fancy place for a man with fancy brains. For David, only the best."

"Hey," David protests, "I like the place, but it wasn't exactly my suggestion."

"Fancy brains," Elsa can't help repeating, "as opposed to…?"

"Mine, brains of a gamer. Moldy-basement brains. And you?"

"Uh-oh." Elsa trades an amused glance with David, enjoying this.

Lex assesses her, his eyes booze-glossy. "Brains like a corn maze."

"How's that?" she asks.

"Complicated, can't see over the top, easy to get lost in, but will definitely find a way out. And corn—under the husk, it's very sweet. Hard to get to but worth the effort. See what I mean?"

Elsa cocks her head, sips from the melted ice cube at the bottom of her glass, not seeing it at all.

"It's a compliment," Lex explains.

Patting his brother's shoulder, David says, "I think we all know who's got the fancy brains here. Especially after a drink."

The brothers share another laugh. Despite a significant age difference, they are obviously close. Elsa thinks of Tara, and then of her father, and then of Ruby, and the coil of anxiety returns.

Their smiling young waitress approaches. "Another round?"

Without a glance at the current state of their drinks, David nods and opens a tab on his credit card.

Elsa reflexively digs into her bag to check her phone.

"Why don't you just put it on the table?" David suggests.

She doesn't like leaving her phone out when she's with people; it's rude, plus she worries she'll forget it. But he's right, and so she sets it down beside her drink, explaining, "You never know, and my father's in the hospital, so…"

"Hospital?" David asks.

"She doesn't like to discuss it." Lex, kindly, protecting her.

"Cancer," she blurts out. When she's intoxicated, her defenses peel away like dead skin.

David lets out a long breath. "I'm sorry. What kind?" Asking the next logical question, just as his brother had earlier in the car.

Lex intervenes. "David, enough."

"Lung," Elsa says, wearied of her own reticence. "They caught it too late. He never even smoked."

David says, gently, "Mind if I ask why you don't take personal leave? You have the right to, by law."

"That's a good question," she says in a tone more measured than she feels, because it is in fact an excellent question, another question his brother already asked, a question she's repeatedly failed to answer for herself, "but I've decided for now to keep working. I thought I should hold on to as much leave time as possible to use at the end."

"This isn't the end? You're sure?"

"There's no way to *tell*." Her voice squeaks regrettably

high on the last word. "The doctor gave him two or three months, but what does that really mean?"

"Good point."

If she were willing to admit the truth, she'd tell the Cole brothers that she thinks she'd go crazy if she had to sit there watching Roy die. Her sister is at the hospital. Isn't that enough?

"I remember when our mother was dying," David says. "It was fourteen years ago already. Not an easy time."

Lex's eyes seem to dull, rejecting the sharp edge of memory. He would have been a teenager then.

"How old was she?" Elsa asks.

"Only forty-nine." A note of wistfulness in David's voice. "Pancreatic cancer."

"It was like a freight train," Lex adds. "Wham. That fast."

"I'm so sorry." Elsa looks from brother to brother, their expressions hazed with recollection.

David says, "I don't think either of us really believed we'd lose her until she was gone. It was—"

"—surreal," Lex says. "Mama was the best. She loved us no matter what, even when we were little shits."

"Well, I wasn't a little shit." David looks at Lex and smiles wistfully. "You, on the other hand—"

"Ha! I was the worst. But Mama, she loved me best, you've got to admit it, David. Even if she wasn't my actual mom."

That catches Elsa's attention. "What?"

"Sure, Mama loved you," David says. "Who doesn't love a surprise gift?"

"Maybe she would have loved me even more if I was a box of candy."

"It's true—she loved chocolate. Every night, two squares for her, one each for us."

"*Even,* she called this calculation," Lex says. "Bad at math, that woman."

"She wasn't your actual mother?" Elsa asks.

"We have the same father," David clarifies, "but my biological mother raised us both after my dad's second wife left him high and dry in Moscow."

"Good old Dad," Lex says. "The door was barely closed, she was gone like half a minute, and he put me on a plane to the United States of America to live with a woman and a brother I'd never met. Nice guy."

Elsa asks, "What was your mother's name?"

David answers, "Yelena Chkalov. She immigrated here when I was a baby and changed it to Cole."

"Well"—she lifts her cocktail—"here's to Yelena. Brave woman."

They clink glasses over the table.

"She was a great lady," David says, tipping his head with affection. "She had a good sense of humor. Lex basically shows up on our doorstep when he's eight years old and all she says is, 'I have only three rules. You always do your homework; you set the table, which is your new job; and every night, I require a kiss on the cheek.'"

Lex recalls the moment: "She's wearing a muumuu with flowers, her feet are bare, she's got on lipstick, and to me she looks like a wrinkled old lady, even though she's only forty-three. 'Where you been?' she says to me. 'Set the table.' I swear, the second I saw that woman, I knew I was home."

"When we lost her," David says, "it was…unbelievable."

He looks at Elsa with such genuine caring, it startles her. "Would it be better if we don't talk about this now?"

"No." She lifts her third drink, nearly depleted but still with a tempting inch of numbness sitting at the bottom. "It's okay. I know what's coming. I'm ready."

The brothers look at her in silence, politely ignoring what is clearly either a delusion or a lie on her part. Her father is dying. It has to hurt. And here she is, adrift in her corn maze again.

"Why didn't you tell me?" she asks Lex.

He shrugs deeply, drunkenly, neck sinking between lifted shoulders, one eyebrow arching. "You didn't want to talk about it, and I understood that, I really did. Losing a parent is one of the hardest things you ever go through."

"I was twenty-nine when I lost Mama," David says, "but you know something? There's still this feeling of abandonment, and you're helpless against it."

"How old were you?" she asks Lex.

"Fourteen." He shakes his head at the memory of himself back then. "I reacted badly."

Elsa smiles. "Tell me."

"Let's just say"—David shares the smile—"that Lex sealed the deal on my specializing in criminal defense."

Not, she assumes, in the public sector, given his freewheeling spending on these overpriced drinks. "You must be good," she tells David, knowing that the NYPD would never have hired Lex if he had anything serious, or recent, on his record.

David deflects. "Well, in the end, he turned out okay."

"What about your father?" She looks back and forth between them.

"Bastard was dead one year after he put me on that plane," Lex says. "He was *zapoi*."

"Casualty of the vodka wars," David clarifies. "Drank himself to death."

"And your real mother?"

Lex answers quickly, "My real mother was Yelena. My biological mother was the woman I never heard from after the day she walked out."

"I'm sorry I asked."

"No, it's okay." Lex uncrosses his legs and recrosses them in the opposite direction. "As soon as Mama Yelena was gone, David, he was stuck raising me."

David laughs. "Fourteen going on ten."

"And now look!" Lex grins.

David slaps his brother's back and says, "Twenty-eight going on twenty-one. We're finally getting somewhere."

Lex flushes, as if it's just occurred to him that Elsa is the senior investigator on their team and the affectionate ridicule might not be good for his budding reputation. But she's pretty sure she won't recall much of what they've said other than its friendly substance and the fact that she's grateful to have joined the Cole brothers instead of going home by herself to wait and worry.

"What about your mother?" Lex asks. "You haven't mentioned her."

"She died when I was in high school. She was killed in a home invasion." A pulse of silence, shock drifting across both brothers' faces. And then Elsa bangs down her finished cocktail, what's left of the oversize ice cube dinking the inside of the empty glass. "But here's the thing: She wasn't exactly a saint—she used to beat the shit out of me. Why can't I just say it? It's the truth." She has never before come right out and said it so plainly, and she is instantly overcome with shame.

They stare at her, speechless.

"I'm sorry." She pushes back her chair and stands, wobbly. "I've had too much to drink. I've got to get home." Remembering, suddenly, that Mel will probably be back by now.

David stands with her. "Never apologize for telling the truth."

"The truth is a fucking bitch," Lex mutters.

When they emerge from the bar, Lex heads toward the subway, hands jammed in pockets, eyes down—presumably thinking thoughts she wishes she hadn't made him think. Alone with David on the quiet street, the chilly late-night air infiltrating her long sleeves, Elsa folds her arms in an attempt to warm herself up.

"Come on," he says matter-of-factly, "I'll walk you home."

Normally she'd refuse the offer, but the copious alcohol has relaxed her. And so, instead of responding with her usual line—*I'm a big girl, I can get home on my own*—she says nothing. They walk in silence to Butler Street and stop at the foot of her stoop.

He says, "Well."

"Well."

"I'm drunk."

"Me too."

"I really want to kiss you—is that crazy?"

"Actually, it—" *Is,* she's about to say. *It's very crazy, kissing isn't in my wheelhouse anymore, because, because* ... Their lips touch, tender, soft, before she flinches away.

"Sorry," he says.

"No, it's okay, it was just…habit."

Humor, acceptance, appears in the corners of his eyes. It feels easy to be with him, and she likes him, and she wants him, but she can't allow herself.

"I'll bet you're married," she says, as if that explains her reluctance.

"Divorced. You?"

"Just plain single."

He smiles.

"My niece is staying with me," she says, glomming onto the first excuse that comes to mind. She cannot let this man into her life just so he can see her ruined skin and leave her. She glances at the apartment window, lit up yellow. "Looks like she's home."

He presses the side of his nose into her neck, and she feels the warmth of his exhalation, and something inside her badly wants to melt. But she can't. "It's okay, but tonight was nice," he whispers, amazingly, given what she just dumped on him in the bar.

She has to agree, despite all that. "It was."

"Here." He reaches into his jacket pocket and pulls out a business card.

She holds the card, looks at him. "In the morning, you'll wake up and wish you hadn't given me this."

"No, I won't."

"I'm damaged."

"Who isn't?"

"You." She smiles. "Unless I'm missing something."

"See this face?" He presses a hand to his cheek, slackening

and puckering his skin in a way that ages him comically. "I've earned every one of these wrinkles."

"Wrinkles are nothing." She hesitates, and then: "You know how some people are covered in tattoos?"

A slanted smile. "My ex-wife has a little bird tattooed on her shoulder."

"Sounds tasteful. But mine? Let's just say they're doozies."

"Trust me"—his voice a soothing whisper—"nothing would surprise me."

He has no idea.

"Call me," he says.

"This case is taking up all my time."

"You'll find the kid. From what I understand, you always do."

In her mind, she searches through the thick fog of alcohol, trying and failing to recall any mention of that at the bar. She cringes at how much she drank, how vulnerable it made her, how stupid.

"Good night, David." She steals another whiff of him, sweet, milky. "It was really nice to meet you." She stumbles up her stoop, aware of him watching her until the door closes between them.

14

Loud music seeps out of Elsa's apartment into the common hallway. She cringes to think of her neighbor's young children being kept awake. Inside, it's vastly louder—something she doesn't recognize, a metallic genderless auto-tuned voice. Mel is sprawled on the couch, her long legs hoisted and ankle-crossed, hands drumming her stomach. Her jackknifed laptop sits open on the floor, pumping out a heavy beat.

Elsa crouches down and mutes it, issuing a quiet "*Shh*. Neighbors."

"Oh, shit!" Mel slaps a hand over her mouth. Whispering: "*Sorry*." She swings her feet to the floor and they *tap-tap-tap* in place.

"How was class?"

"Oh, class, *great*. The teacher, Mr. Bernard, gave us an assessment test to find out where we're at and we graded them together in class and, strangely, I totally aced it."

Elsa says, "Well, that's good."

"I mean, it's Algebra Two, it's not like I don't know any-thing, but the point is I just failed it in school and now I got like the best grade in class and the teacher was wondering why I was even there."

"I guess you know more than you think you know, if that makes sense. You ate something, I assume?"

"Actually, no. I wasn't hungry but now I kind of am. Hey—want to go out? What's good around here? Coming back from the subway I noticed tons of restaurants along Smith Street. I mean, it's never this hopping on the Upper East Side, which is *so* boring. I wish we lived here."

Elsa stands back and looks at Mel. "How much coffee did you drink today?" Mel seems, somehow, high—but Elsa her-self isn't exactly sober at the moment and the thought of asking her niece if she's impaired feels hypocritical.

"Not much. I mean, a lot." She laughs. "Is four cups too much?"

"Depends." On if you've slept or haven't slept. On what time of day it is. On if you've eaten anything. But four cups shouldn't be enough to produce this much hyperactivity.

"Exactly." Mel stands and quickly collects the things she's strewn around—laptop, socks, phone, magazine, used tissue—as if they're about to go somewhere.

"I can make us some eggs," Elsa offers. "How does that sound?"

"Oh—sure."

"Fried okay?"

"What can I do? I know—I'll make toast!"

Mel zips around the small kitchen while Elsa checks her phone. A few junk e-mails but no messages from the lab and nothing about the APB on Ishmael Locke. She sets about making the eggs, the blur of alcohol and the surprise of the unexpected kiss giving way to domestic routine. She will never call David, and he'll never call her, but she's grateful for tonight.

"So," Elsa says, "tell me about your day."

"I put up, like, a *million* signs again this afternoon. I mean, I've been looking for stuff about her on the Internet but it's all the same thing, nothing new, but *you* must know something."

"You went back?" Elsa, incredulous.

"Are you mad?"

"Are you *kidding?*"

"Sorry."

"I hate apologies that could have been avoided." Elsa's thoughts swirling as it sinks in that her beloved niece, whom she trusts, *trusted,* defied her. She pictures it—Mel leaving the apartment building after Elsa drives away; taking the subway back to Queens, to the Haverstocks'; that man, Teddy, handing her another stack of flyers, maybe adding a button; heading back into the woods—and feels a loss of…what? Control. What on earth was the kid thinking, going back after Elsa (thought she'd) made it clear that the Haverstock house was off-limits? "You knew I didn't want you there, and you went back anyway?"

Mel, slack-jawed, looks surprised at her aunt's reaction, disappointment having never before played out between them. "It's just that she's *missing*. And I thought I could *help*. And I had nothing to *do*."

"You could have read a book. Called a friend. Gone to the movies."

"I met some more of Ruby's friends," Mel tries, as if she could possibly think that by investigating in her own way, she was helping Elsa, not creating unnecessary distractions. "They're pretty cool."

Cool. Elsa does her best to ignore the ineptitude of that observation. *Cool. Nice. A regular person.* When in fact, no one, examined closely, is ever any of those things. She gathers herself, and asks, "How long were you there this afternoon, at the Haverstocks'?"

"Two hours, maybe, hanging more signs. And then Allie and me and Charlie—"

Allie and Charlie and I, Elsa thinks but doesn't say. "Please tell me you're not talking about Ruby's ex-boyfriend Charlie."

Mel's eyes lower; she's realizing (Elsa hopes) the error she's made in socializing with someone who is, at the very least, a person of interest in a missing-child investigation. Her voice softens. "We walked over to his house—well, Allie went home, I don't think she likes him very much, but I stayed for a while. I'm sorry, I really am. He was just…there."

They stare at each other a moment, two, three. Mel shrinking, ashamed; Elsa sobering quickly. And then Mel says, "Auntie Elsa? The eggs are going to burn."

Elsa's attention jumps to the stovetop, where the edges of their sunburst eggs have curled into blackened crisps. She pulls the pan off the burner, shuts off the gas, and switches on the exhaust fan. After catching her breath, she says, "They're still good to eat. Let's just calm down and have some dinner."

Mel nods, more submissive than Elsa likes to see her. She feels bad for yelling at the girl, but what was she supposed to say?

Mel barely eats and Elsa, ravenous, finishes off both their meals. She tries not to stare when Mel sets to biting what she can of her cuticles, as if they've suddenly grown long and bothersome.

"What else is going on with you, Mel?"

"Nothing." Her gaze lands on Elsa and just as quickly flits away.

"I realize," says Elsa, leaning forward, "that we haven't spent a lot of time together lately, and I'm sorry about that, because I love being with you. So maybe I missed out on something, but tell me what's going on and I promise I won't tell your mother."

"I feel like I want to rip my head off!"

"I can see that."

"You won't say anything?"

Elsa shakes her head. "No. I promise." And poses a question she's hoped never to be in a position to ask her own niece: "What are you on?"

Mel buries her face in her trembling hands with their raw half-moon cuticles.

Elsa breathes deeply, trying to keep calm. She knows what drugs can do to teenagers, to anyone, how they have the power to bring whole families down, but she never expected it to happen to Mel. To them. Tara hasn't mentioned anything, but it's possible that she doesn't know. That Mel has saved it for Elsa, her trusted aunt who's never judged her and has always said, all through her sixteen years of life, that she could tell her anything.

"Talk to me," Elsa says as neutrally as she can.

Mel squirms in her seat. Wipes a distracted finger across her empty plate. "I never did it before."

"Okay." Elsa, calm on the outside. "Never did what?"

"It was just one."

"One what?"

"Adderall. Charlie said he takes one every morning for his ADHD and it wears off after eight hours and he's done *so* much better in school since he started taking it but it's been like ten hours now and it hasn't worn off at all!"

"Charlie gave you one of his Adderalls?" Relieved to learn that it's a prescription drug, as if somehow that makes it safer.

Mel nods, staring down at her plate.

"Does he know who you are—that you're my niece?"

"I don't know. I didn't mention it."

"Did Allie? Mention it?"

"Not that I know of."

"Of course she didn't, otherwise he wouldn't have dared to do this."

Mel seems to shrink with embarrassment. Her eyes slam closed. "You're right. I never should have gone there."

Elsa asks, "What was the dosage?"

"Dosage? I don't know—one pill."

"But Mel, one pill can mean anything."

"It'll wear off. *Everyone* takes it. It was just one pill and it's really no big deal."

"Is that what Charlie told you?"

Mel nods.

"What about Allie—is she into it too?"

"*Into* it, Auntie Elsa? Seriously? One, she was gone by then? Two, it's medicine? To help you concentrate? Because school is too boring and too hard?"

"But Mel, you took someone else's medicine. You don't have ADHD that I know of."

"But sometimes I wonder if I do."

Elsa bites her tongue, on the verge of saying, *Yeah, you and everyone else—why don't you just put down your phone?*

"Don't worry"—Mel gets up and paces the room—"because I'm *never* taking it again. I *hate* it. I'd rather fail school than feel this way."

Mel sits back down, now facing her aunt, the two of them knee to knee. Elsa strokes the girl's soft cheek, unsure what to say.

"You won't tell Mom?"

"I probably should—"

"You *promised*."

"I know I did." Elsa hesitates. "Don't worry. It's between us."

"Thanks." Mel's smile is a little sweet and a little conspiratorial, reminding Elsa of how things have changed over the years, how friendship with a small child and friendship with a teenager are not the same thing. She's on shifting ground with Mel now.

"Listen," Elsa says, "I'm wondering—did Charlie offer you the Adderall? Or did you ask for it?"

"I didn't know he had any, so why would I ask for it?"

"Why did he offer it? He hardly knows you."

Mel shrugs. "Well, I guess maybe because he's kind of nerdy and that's one way he can get girls to like him? I told him I had to go to summer school and he just was kind of, like, *Here, this will help*. He said I could have it at no charge."

"He sells his meds?"

"I guess so. But he said he liked me and he wouldn't make the same mistake twice."

"What does that mean?"

Mel shrugs. "I'm not interested in him or his shit, so as far as I'm concerned, it doesn't matter. And anyway, I'm not going down that road. *I'm not.*"

Something about the change in Mel's tone triggers a new concern. "Is Adderall the only thing Charlie sells?"

Mel nods, then shrugs her shoulders—and then she shakes her head.

Elsa pitches forward. "Talk to me, Mellie."

Mel hesitates before stooping to the floor to unzip the front of her backpack. She pulls out a yellow globe-shaped lip balm and snaps it open. She removes a tiny plastic bag she's jammed in the globe and hands it to Elsa. The clear bag, smeared with the greasy lip balm, holds about a tablespoon of white power inside.

"What is it?" Elsa asks.

"I think it might be cocaine."

"You *think?*"

"He said it was better not to label experiences, to try something first and find out for yourself what it is. He told me that if I wanted to, I could snort it, so I figured it was coke."

Elsa holds the bag up to the light. It looks like cocaine, but then again, it could be white heroin.

"Auntie Elsa, I'm really sorry. I really am. I was never going to snort anything. I never should have taken the Adderall in the first place. It was stupid. I swear, he pushed that into my pocket when I was leaving and he whispered in my ear.

It happened so fast. I should have thrown it in the garbage can—I didn't know what to do."

Elsa lies there, wildly awake. Teenagers, drugs, a convincing replica of a gun. There is something here she needs to see. Finally, she gives up on sleep and gets out of bed. Puts on a clean pair of slacks and fishes out one of her lightweight long-sleeved summer shirts, tired of broiling under the strong June sun. Slips the bag of white powder into her purse. Creeps through the living room, where Mel sleeps soundly on the couch. Pulls shut the door, bracing at the heavy *thunk* of the turning lock, pausing for a reaction from Mel. Nothing.

She parks on lower Tenth Avenue. A middle-of-the-night visit to the DEA's Northeast Lab used to mean negotiating desolate streets on the edge of the Meatpacking District, ignoring gaggles of transvestite prostitutes who'd decry her boring sartorial choices—the pants and long sleeves in any season, never a bright color. Now, the massive government building sits entrenched in the trendy, well-heeled bar scene of Chelsea, a geek sitting on a billion-dollar property.

Elsa presents her credentials to the security guards in the lobby. Upstairs, a block of weak light falls from the glass window in the door of the lab, illuminating the sleepy hallway in which her footsteps echo. The moment she pushes open the door, a head of thick graying hair rises above a microscope.

"Clyde!" Elsa says. Glad to see the seasoned tech she's worked with often.

His coffee-stained smile and his eyes winked up at the corners greet her. "Elsa! Long time."

She hands him the bag of powder and asks for a quick

analysis, knowing from experience that sometimes, in the middle of the night, you can get a lab tech to nudge your job to the head of the line. But Clyde does even better, touching the white powder with the tip of his finger and tasting it.

His eyebrows shoot up. "Sure, but I'd bet you money it's heroin. Where'd you get it?"

Unwilling to implicate Mel, she answers, "A case I'm working—friend of a missing teenager."

He shakes his head. "Well, I'll be in touch later. Good luck."

Elsa makes her way downtown to Federal Plaza and her desk. Alone in the quiet, she leaves a message for Lex, then sits down to wait for him to call her back, feeling ashamed for drinking too much and talking too much—for telling the brothers about her mother. And for allowing herself to want something she knows she can't have; enjoying David's kiss was a mistake. She closes her eyes and tries to exile the memory. She has learned, or tried to learn, not to punish herself too harshly for her lapses. She thinks of Whitelaw Street and banishes *that* thought as well. Then her thoughts swing to Mel. Promising to keep the drug use a secret is one mistake she can correct before she lets it go too far. She picks up her phone and dials Tara.

On the other end of the line, she hears the workaday clanks and voices of a 24/7 hospital ward. Tara whispers "Hello" and then "It's so late."

"Sorry, it's been a hell of a day."

"That's all right, I wasn't really sleeping anyway. When are you coming back?"

"Not sure."

"Bring your partner—he's cute."

"Very funny. How's Dad doing?"

"The same." Tara yawns. "The transition lady came in before to talk about transferring him to hospice."

"So he can do hospice at Atria?" Relief at the prospect that he could return to his own apartment, his own whittled-down life, and fade there amid his personal comforts.

"Looks like it."

"Did you talk to Mel tonight?"

"No. How'd her class go?"

"Well," Elsa begins, "that's the thing." And then she tells her sister everything.

Tara takes the news with uncharacteristic silence, punctuated by a moan. "I can't believe it. I *never* thought Mellie would do something like that."

"Teenagers try stuff."

"But *heroin?*"

"I'm not a hundred percent sure that's what it is, and anyway, she didn't touch that—she was never going to."

"What am I supposed to do now?"

"Do?"

"I'm her mother, and Lars isn't good for . . . well, I can't just do *nothing*."

"Maybe you can. I thought you should know, but she seems pretty sincere about not doing it again. Adderall, I mean. And I believe her. Why not just let her feel the impact of the experience?"

"Elsa, that's not the point."

"I think it is. I think—"

"You're not a parent. You don't know. There have to be consequences or they don't learn."

"They?" Something hard drops inside Elsa. Mel isn't a *they*.

"I have to process this. Shit, *shit*. Why did she have to do this now? With Dad in the hospital. I'm calling her right this minute and telling her to get back up here."

"Let her sleep," Elsa begs. "You can talk to her in the morning."

"Thank you for your input," Tara snaps, "but I'm the mother here and I'll decide what to do."

After the call, Elsa rests her head on the back of her chair, feeling suddenly overwhelmed. Tara, who thinks she knows so much. Her father, lying there, sleeping, dying. Ruby. Mel. Locke. The day. Nothing sits well; everything fights.

15

As soon as the commercial comes on, you pick up your chart and add a name: Angie. You fish out your red marker and draw a line from Angie to Marian, complicating an already chaotic web. Babe is connected by blue to Greg and Jenny. Orange and green lines intersect to unite Tad and Liza. Every color connects in one way or another to Erica. You look over your work; it's coming together.

All My Children comes back on and you pay close attention. You don't know why they call them soaps—maybe because the story is slippery? In the two weeks that you've been unable to walk without throwing up, spending your days trapped on the island of your parents' bed, you haven't missed the program even once. The chart is for Tara, a visual aid to help you explain, so that she won't get so confused.

"Are you hungry, Elsa, honey?" Sitting at her fold-down desk, paying bills, your mother turns to look at you. She took the day off from her teaching job to stay home. For some reason, this embarrasses you. There is no doctor's appointment today, nothing special, just another day with you stuck here and no one knowing why. Then something occurs to you.

"Where's Sally?" The housekeeper whose bright teeth make the prettiest smile in her dark face. Her favorite show airs directly after yours, and you always watch it together on the bed.

"She called in sick. Do you want me to bring you a tuna sandwich?"

Tuna is stinky, but you don't want to complain. "Yes, please."

"Sally should be back tomorrow." Deb gets up and on her way out lays the palm of her hand gently on your forehead. You haven't had a fever at all, that's the funny thing. No one can figure out what's wrong. Not your regular doctor, who came to the house to visit you. And not the other doctor, the one to whom you were carried and driven, whose strange metallic smell lodged itself in the top of your nose for a whole day.

"Nothing seems to be wrong with her," the smelly doctor said, three whiskers flaring from a mole on his chin. He had chalky eyes that smiled when he talked. "Let's wait and see how she does. If there's no improvement, bring her back in a week."

Here's how it works: You feel fine until you stand up, and then your stomach heaves and if you don't get to the bathroom pronto it's a terrible mess for the adults to clean up. Every couple of days, Deb or Sally comes in with a bucket and a towel and stands you on your feet to see if the mysterious affliction has passed, but so far no luck. Because Roy has been away for a long time, he's never the one with the bucket. He's traveling with a string quartet that's performing some chamber music he wrote. You know what a string is and Deb told you that *chamber* means room and *quartet* means four, but you don't understand. You are only seven.

You have to pee but you don't want to miss even a moment of your show, so you hold it in. While Deb is out of the room, Erica slaps a policeman across the face, and then a grizzly bear comes after her. While the credits roll you note these new developments on your chart. By the time your mother is back with your lunch tray, your bladder feels like a water balloon on the brink of explosion.

"Mom?" you say. "Mommy?"

"Yes, Elsie?"

"I gotta go."

Deb settles the tray on her bedside table and bends to lift you, cradling you in her arms like a giant baby. When she carries you to the bathroom you bury your nose in her neck so you can smell her perfume. She lifts your nightgown and sets you on the toilet, and you wiggle your underpants down to your knees. You can't pee with her standing there, which she knows, so she leaves you alone. Obviously she listens outside the door because the second it's quiet, she's back. She carries you to the bed.

Another whole week goes by.

Your chart grows more complicated and colorful, but Tara can't follow the story no matter how hard you try to explain.

"You've missed a lot of school," your mother points out.

You nod. It's true. And no one seems to know when your confinement will end.

The best day is when Sally brings her baby, Roger, along and he takes his nap lying on top of you. He's the softest, springiest creature you have ever held, and the fact that his sleep is so heavy still feels like the greatest honor of your life. Because he trusts you. Somehow he knows that you would never, ever hurt him.

Then one day your father returns with stuffed monsters for his girls, matching except that yours is red and Tara's is blue, and you're so happy to see him that you jump off the bed and run into his arms and don't throw up, because he's home now, and for some mysterious unknown reason your inner topsy-turvy regains its careful balance.

TUESDAY

16

The quickest way to get to Forest Hills from lower Manhattan is to cross the Brooklyn Bridge and do some time on the expressway before turning onto Flushing Avenue. But Elsa can't resist. Off the bridge, she detours onto Atlantic Avenue instead. From there, it's a direct shot into Ozone Park.

Darkness, quiet, the day still so young that it masquerades as night. She flies along the normally congested avenue, making such good time that she doesn't pause to question what she's doing. Where she's going. Tricking herself, through speed, into believing that this is a good idea; a passable idea, at least. She turns on the radio and coasts from station to station, never finding one that pleases her. The music is too harsh or too boring, and at this hour talk radio only seems to care about extreme religion or the concerns of insomniacs. Finally, she reaches Whitelaw Street.

The house, her house, the lady-with-dyed-blond-hair's house sits quietly on its plot, windows darkened. Elsa notices that an upstairs pane is broken, a long jagged crack running diagonally from the top right corner all the way to the sill. It was her bedroom window, once. All those nights she used to lie in bed, unable to sleep, watching the moon shine silver through the glass while shadow patterns slid along her ceiling and bent onto the walls.

"Why am I here?" she mutters to herself, the note of bitterness sharp, unheard by anyone else. *"Fuck."* But she can't stop herself.

She eases the car door closed behind her.

Creeps up the driveway to the back door, which this time is unlocked.

Walks through the demolished kitchen and dining room and up the stairs to the second floor.

Nothing is left, just scratched floorboards covered in white dust. Footprints of round-toed work boots. She steps past heaps of broken drywall, inspecting the raw beams laced with ancient dust, little piles of mouse droppings. A rusty nail. The pleated metal cap of a beer bottle. As a girl she used to wonder if she'd find old love letters hidden in the walls if she ever had a chance to look, which she was sure she wouldn't. She scans every open wall. There are no letters; none.

Her father was right. There is almost literally nothing left.

Back in her car, she no longer needs headlights. Dawn opens the new day like the soft flesh of a perfect peach, sweet, promising. She drives into it, enjoying the moment, allowing herself the respite of having proved her father right by proving herself wrong. Could it be true? That what she feared no longer exists? That when Roy is gone, the worst of her past really will go with him? That she is safe, or as safe as she could hope to be?

Woodhaven Boulevard is sparsely trafficked; every bleary-eyed driver has one hand on the wheel and another on an over-size travel mug, a phone, a tube of lipstick. Windows down, music, voices, tender early sounds filtering into the simple quiet.

Elsa drives and drives, willing herself to believe that it *is* true, that the house really is devoid of everything that was once them.

Puts on the radio. Stops dialing at the luscious sound of Adele.

Turns onto Yellowstone Boulevard, into the heart of Forest Hills, her thoughts now realigning themselves to the official reason for her visit to Queens: Ruby. Allie. Charlie. Mel. Adderall. *Heroin,* Clyde confirmed, and Elsa was finished waiting for an appropriate hour. It's time to make demands, and she wants it all: everything the missing girl's so-called friends have not been ready, or willing, to tell.

The doorbell chimes into the lush quiet of a sleeping neighborhood. Ten to six, the sun streaking orange on a white-blue sky. Too early in the sane world for an unannounced visit, but tough luck. Elsa rings Allie's bell again and again, finally summoning footsteps.

A diaphanous curtain inches aside and a pair of eyes peers through the glass half of the door. At first she thinks it's a child but then realizes that it's a very short woman. The woman's curiosity gives way to alarm when Elsa produces her identification card. She stares at it, brow creased, and finally unlocks the door. Her robe hangs open over a too-large sleep shirt bearing a half-washed-away slogan about TEEN-RAGERS AND PSYCHOPATHS.

"Is something wrong?" The woman's morning voice is scratchy, belligerent, a little afraid.

"Sorry if I woke you," Elsa says. "Are you Mrs. Franconi, Allie's mom?"

"Yes."

"I was hoping to have a word with her."

"Good luck with that."

"Isn't she home?"

Mrs. Franconi shrugs. "You're welcome to take a look. First door on the left." She points to a hallway. In response to the startled expression Elsa fails to hide fast enough—how could you not know if your child is at home?—the mother explains, "Listen, she's eighteen years old and does whatever she wants. I learned when she was sixteen that I can't stop her, and now that she's legal, it's even worse. I keep my eyes and ears open, and I can tell you she wasn't here when I went to bed at one o'clock and she didn't answer any of my calls or texts. I try to keep up with her. I always try. But is she home? Honestly, I don't know."

The hall smells musty, as if the doors and windows are never left open to air the place out. An odor of mildew seems to waft up from the beige carpeting. Mrs. Franconi follows closely as Elsa knocks on the door with a stop sign nailed dead center, its red metal twisted and frayed where it was wrested off its post.

"Go the fuck away," a voice moans from within.

"Hallelujah," Mrs. Franconi says, "she's alive. Can I get you some coffee or tea? A glass of water?"

"Thanks, but I'm fine." Elsa knocks again.

"I said—"

"Allie, it's Elsa—Special Agent Myers. We met yesterday at Ruby's house."

Feet thump and the door swings open to reveal Allie, eyes alert despite her rat's-nest hair and smeared makeup. "Did you find her?"

"No. Can I come in?"

Allie slumps back to her bed and doesn't object when Elsa pushes clothes off the desk chair so she can pull it near and sit. The shades are open, sunlight trickling in. She must have come in pretty late and fallen into bed. Clothes and shoes and books and used dishes are strewn everywhere.

Elsa says, "Would you talk to me about Ruby and Charlie?"

Allie rolls her eyes, yesterday's restraint abandoning her. "Why don't you ask *him?*"

"Because I want to hear Ruby's side of things and I think you're the one who can tell me."

"Tell you *what?*"

Elsa pulls her chair closer, nearly touching the mattress. "How long has Charlie been selling?"

Allie stares, calculating her answer. "Selling…?"

"Stop jerking me around, Allie, and tell me what you know."

"I don't know anything."

"What, how much, to who, when, where?"

Allie turns over so that her back faces Elsa. Under the covers, the dips and curves of a womanly silhouette she hasn't yet earned.

The standoff soaks up a long, slow minute, until the bright smell of coffee wafts into the room. Mrs. Franconi follows closely, bearing a tray with two mugs and what looks like homemade scones. "In case you change your mind," she says to Elsa. "And this one can't think without caffeine." Using the corner of the tray, she edges open some space on Allie's crowded bedside table, knocking loose change and an EpiPen to the floor.

Allie sits up and reaches for a mug, her eyes rolling back at the first gulp. "Thanks, Mom."

Mrs. Franconi's weathered fingers stroke the hair off Allie's forehead in a loving gesture her daughter accepts grudgingly but accepts nonetheless. "Shout if you guys need anything."

"Thank you." Elsa adds milk to her coffee and gratefully sips. Then she looks at Allie. "I think your mother might actually love you."

"The woman who loved too much." That eye-roll again. But Elsa is sure she sees a trill of pleasure as Allie bites a chunk out of one of her mother's scones.

"Ruby's parents are having a hard time," Elsa tries. "Do you think they know Ruby's into drugs?"

"She isn't *into drugs*." Scowling, Allie stares at Elsa and then says, "I promised I wouldn't tell."

"But *Allie*—" Her friend has vanished. The rules need to change.

"I know, I know." She lays her remaining fragment of scone on her blanket. "The thing is…" She retreats into her stubborn silence.

"You're Ruby's best friend."

148

"Exactly."

"So act like one."

Her forehead scrunches and she exhales a long breath. "Just Adderall, to help her grades. None of the other shit he sells."

"Like?"

"Coke, smack, X, bath salts, TNT, whatever." The girl's gaze scuttles around the room. And then she looks squarely at Elsa. "But you didn't ask *why* Charlie sells his meds when he's got all that other stuff."

"Okay. Why?"

"It's how he hooks them. *Us*."

"You too, Allie?"

"No way. I mean *girls*."

Elsa nods, listening.

"His parents are rich but they keep him on a tight budget. So he deals. But he has a prescription for Adderall and he gives it to girls when he feels like it."

"Gives, or sells?"

Allie wiggles up in her bed, and her tone hardens. "He *gives* his prescription meds to girls he likes, like it's a 'special friendship thing.'" Hooking her forefingers around those last three words. "He reels them in, and then, when they realize he's a dick and they don't like him anymore, they still want the meds, so he makes them pay. And if he can, he'll sell them the harder stuff too. He starts out with this 'nice guy let me help you' thing and then he turns into a major asshole."

"What about Ruby? Did Charlie give her his meds?"

"Yup."

"And she took them."

"Duh."

"Why?"

"We just finished eleventh grade, and that's the year that matters for colleges."

"And she wanted better grades."

"Who doesn't? The thing is"—Allie shifts out from under her covers and swings her legs over the side of the bed, now facing Elsa—"she didn't want to take Charlie's friggin' pills at first, and he convinced her, and then when she wanted to keep taking them, he said she'd have to pay for them and so she dumped him, but really, I think it was him dumping her, don't you? By asking her to pay. That's why he's a scumbag. He plays these stupid games. I mean, if you want to break up, just break up, you know?"

"Sounds complicated," Elsa says. "But yeah, I know what you mean. So Ruby must have been feeling hurt."

"She was pissed."

"Of course."

"And then"—Allie's eyes widen—"the asshole actually wanted her back. He said he'd give her his meds like before, he'd give her anything she wanted, but she told him, she said, *No way*. She found someone else to get drugs from."

"Drugs?"

"Meds, okay? Ruby never went near that other stuff. She started copping Addies from someone she wasn't hooking up with. She really learned her lesson."

"Which was?" Elsa's stomach churning now from the strong coffee.

"Fuck if I know." Allie has a beautiful smile when she lets it show, as she does now, a smile infused with irony and humor, as if for a split second she sees herself from a future vantage point. "I *mean*," she says, "what she learned was to keep business and personal, you know, separate."

"Who is Ruby's new dealer?"

"*Dealer?* It isn't like *that,* not with Ruby. I mean, it's just Adderall."

Elsa listens with forced calm, but her patience for Allie's spiky little tantrums starts to wear thin. "The kid she got meds from after Charlie. Who is he?"

"It has to be a he?"

"Is it Paul?"

Allie shrugs and returns to her scone, breaking the last piece into two parts and releasing a cascade of crumbs that will undoubtedly be left for her mother to clean up. "Maybe. I think so. Okay, yes."

Elsa leans forward. "Why didn't you tell anyone this before, Allie? You think you were helping her by keeping all that to yourself? She's been missing for four days."

"Ma'am, Paul wasn't Ruby's problem. It was Charlie. He'd stop in at Queens Beans like every night looking to talk to her, because she blocked his texts."

"When did she tell you that?"

"Last week, I guess. And Friday night, right before I left? Ruby said he hadn't come by yet so she figured she'd see him soon."

Elsa sets her mug in a free spot on Allie's bedside table. "Thanks." She stands, itching to see Charlie, hoping to also catch him half asleep and vulnerable.

"That's it?"

"What did you expect?"

"I want to know where Ruby is."

"Allie, if I knew that, I wouldn't be here."

Mrs. Hendryk answers the door in her gym clothes and in full makeup. The Hendryk household, apparently, does not sleep in.

"Charlie is already gone," she chirps, as if it's absurd of Elsa to think she'd catch him at home at seven a.m.

"Mind telling me where?"

The mother's carefully plucked eyebrows arch, but she obviously decides against taking an attitude with the detective, given the circumstances. "He's on his way to the Haverstock house to help, and then he has a history Regents at eleven at school."

"Thank you."

Elsa starts down the bluestone walk toward her Beetle, hunched red at the curb. Behind her, the front door claps shut and the lock swiftly clicks into place.

She drives until she spots Charlie walking along Whitson Street, hairy-legged in baggy shorts and flip-flops, drinking a frothy iced Starbucks through a straw. Two sharpened pencils and a blue ballpoint protrude from his back pocket. She pulls into an open metered spot, sticks her permit in the windshield, and continues on foot. The morning is warm and summery but it isn't as hot out as his attitude suggests. He's moving in the direction of the Haverstocks', walking casually, in no particular hurry.

"Charlie!"

He turns around. A smile appears. He even waves.

"Okay if I walk with you?" she asks.

"I'm on my way to Ruby's to help out, but you probably already deduced as much."

Good thinking, Sherlock. But she doesn't say that. "Mind if we have a frank talk?"

"Not at all."

The morning is getting on, and a woman dressed for work in a skirt and heels rushes past in the direction of the subway. A man pushing a stroller comes up alongside them, his toddler belting a song happily and off-key. Elsa has to raise her voice to be heard.

"So how much do you charge for the dope?"

Alarmed, the father outpaces them, moving his child out of earshot.

Charlie stops abruptly. Sucking hard on his straw, his cheeks compress, draining away years of innocence. He turns and keeps walking.

"How long before Ruby started needing an Addy to get through the day?"

The slurping sound of Charlie's straw, vacuuming up bubbles at the bottom of his cup. "I have no idea what you're talking about."

"What were you thinking, giving that shit to my niece?"

He stares at her, caught by surprise. "Your niece?"

"Mel, your new friend."

"Fuck."

"When did you last see Ruby? No bullshit this time."

"*She* dumped *me,* you know. I never did anything to her. Why would I?"

"It doesn't matter who technically ended it, Charlie. You were supplying her with drugs and now she's missing."

153

He tosses his empty cup into a trash can on the corner and turns to her, acned cheeks inflamed. "Not drugs. *Meds*."

"Keep telling yourself that same story and see how far it gets you in court."

"I didn't push anything on her—she wanted it. It was only Adderall and it helped her. She wasn't exactly the best student."

"Allie tells me that you still want Ruby back."

"Allie."

"Do you?"

"Maybe."

They turn onto Ascan Avenue, two lanes of traffic under leafy trees. "Charlie, did you pay Ruby a visit at Queens Beans on Friday night?"

"What?" But his indignation sounds weak. "Look, I don't know what that pathological liar *Allie* told you, but I haven't seen Ruby—I mean, seen her alone—since we broke up."

"Ruby told her that you'd go by Queens Beans, hoping to get back together. Allie says that Ruby blocked your phone number. Not true?"

A man in a suit and tie Rollerblades by so quickly that he creates a stiff breeze. Charlie's bottom lip quivers. "Well," he says, "yes, she did block my number."

They stop walking, face each other now in front of a dry cleaner's store. MONDAY SHIRT 4 FOR $12, TUESDAY SUIT $8, WEDNESDAY SKIRT W/PLEATS $5, THURSDAY DRESS $8, FRIDAY SWEATER $4. The morning sun rises on the plate glass and, like a magic trick, transforms it into a mirror, obliterating the daily sales. Elsa watches as Charlie notices the reflection of his waning confidence, the way his eyes dart and how he looks like he might cry.

"I," he says. "I...I would go see her sometimes, it's true."

"But?"

His cheeks blaze. "She still wouldn't talk to me. It was humiliating."

"Did she buzz you in on Friday night? Did she turn off the video feed and buzz you in?"

He nods, cringing. "But only so she could tell me to leave her alone and not ruin her sweet-girl reputation. So I did."

"Did what?"

His voice flares: "I went away."

"What else, Charlie? Keep thinking. Because this is a very serious situation for Ruby and also for you. Selling Adderall is one thing. But heroin?"

He pushes past her, walking quickly.

"Charlie, come back." She trots after him, picking up speed as he breaks into a run. "Charlie!"

He stops so abruptly that she nearly crashes into him. Taller than her by nearly a foot, he looms, angry.

"You think I *hurt* her, don't you?" Crying. "But I *didn't*. She told me to *fuck off* and so I *fucked off*. She actually had a gun—I couldn't believe it. *A gun*. What was I supposed to do?" Shaking. "You should talk to the guy who drove up when I was leaving, find out what *he* knows about it. Why don't you talk to *him*?" He heaves forward, snot drooling out of his nose, fat drops splashing onto the sidewalk. A little boy in a big body. Elsa refuses to give in to the sympathy creeping up her spine.

"What guy?" She asks again, *"What guy?"*

"Forget it. I don't know anything. I wasn't even there—I *fucked off* so I don't exist."

"What did the guy look like, Charlie?"

"I don't know. It was dark out. I didn't really see him."

A woman with an armload of plastic-sheathed clothes struggles through the cleaner's door and heads down the sidewalk in their direction. Elsa steps aside and pulls Charlie with her, holding tight to his arm in case he tries to bolt again. "Try to remember."

"He was in his twenties or thirties, maybe. His hair was kind of long, kind of pushed back off his forehead." As details return to him, Charlie calms, face relaxing, eyes growing brighter. "When he got out of his van I noticed he was on the tall side. But it was dark out; it was hard to see."

"Van? What color?"

"White, kind of beat up."

Elsa's pulse quickens—Charlie has just described Ishmael Locke and his ride pulling up at Queens Beans on Friday night. "Why didn't you tell us that before?"

"I was ... scared."

"Ruby's life could be in real danger, if she's even still—"

Her phone rings. An upstate number flashes on her screen. She turns her back to Charlie, puts the phone to her ear, and answers, "Special Agent Myers," trying to temper the heat in her tone.

"This is Forensics up in Albany," the caller says. "We heard this was important so we bumped you forward. He left some juicy DNA on that cup."

"Talk to me."

"Guy's got a rap sheet a mile long."

The remark throws Elsa; she'd checked out Locke's record and it was clean. Something isn't right. "Are you sure?"

"Absolutely—this is one scary dude."

"Zap me the official report; I'll need to take a look at it. And thanks."

17

She feels them, her little tattoo people, crawling up the side of her neck. Their tiny feet tickle as they laugh and cry and wander up the steep climb to her ear.

Carrie, who leads the way, slaps the bulbous end of her earlobe so it swings and she catches the lowest rung on the ladder of earrings. And then—*wup-wup-wup-wup*—she catapults up to the ear canal, slides right in, and down she goes. Velma next, followed by Arnold, then Jesus.

Yes, she feels them, all her peeps now inside her head, her mind, minding her, helping mind her business. And what is her business now? Ranged around the conference table at the center of her mind, where she herself is chairman of the board, she doesn't know. They bang their tiny fists on the table, demanding her attention. Wake up! Wake up and smell the coffee!

Her swollen eyes crack open now; she wakes to the inside of a cave. Her body shudders from the cold. Both of her wrists are raw, her throat is sore, pain flares across her back, her hips *hurt,* and she can't tell which side she's lying on. Right or left? Her brain can't grasp the vocabulary of her body.

Addressing her board, she silently demands: *Come on, people! Little people! Tell me what's what. Tell me where I am. Tell me how I got here. Tell me how to get out.*

He sits cross-legged on a towel, sipping from a Styrofoam cup. Her stomach grumbles. And she's thirsty. She tries to lick her lips but there isn't as much saliva as she's used to. The smell is good, sweet and spicy, and she wants some. She wants some. But she can't get her body to move.

He looks at her. Bound, cold, everything hurting.

"So," he says, a lilt at the end of that small word, "you like jewelry, I see."

Confused, she blinks, whispers, "Yes." Did he notice before when she slid off two rings on their way through the woods, crumb-dropping a path to wherever he's brought her? She can't see the color of his eyes in this dimness. His head is tilted a little bit, like he's waiting for more of a conversation.

"One of my sisters was big on rings," he offers.

"What?"

"Rings—I said rings." He holds up both hands and wiggles his fingers.

Mustering more voice, realizing that talking could be the very thing to save her, she tries again. "What kind of rings?"

"Silver." He makes a fist with his right hand, knuckles glowing white, and startles her by punching at the air. "*Wham,* a ring on every finger, right in my shoulder blade, right here—" He twists to point out the spot on his back, knotty muscles and bone showing through the fabric of his shirt, where his sister apparently hit him. "That's got to be what brass knuckles feel like."

"I'm sorry she did that to you." Almost meaning it, but how could she actually care about him, and why would he want her to? "Is it okay if I shift position? My leg is starting to go numb."

"You want my help?" A creepy tease in his tone, she thinks, unless she's misreading. And no, *no,* she doesn't want his help, but without it the numbness will spread through her body and turn her to stone. She nods.

He stands up, kicks aside the towel, stoops over her, and she can smell him. Like manure, like he's been in a barn. There's a scratch down the side of his face. Did she do that?

How long has she been here?

She was on her way to school. She missed the bus. She was walking. And then. And then.

He slips his powerful hands under her arms and rearranges her, roughly, like she's a rag doll. Her back is now straighter against the wall, her leg moved off whatever jagged rock was digging into her. "That better?"

She nods.

"Okay," he says, and then, "There's something I've got to do, but I'll be back. Try not to miss me too much." He crosses to the other side, hops down somewhere lower than the cave's floor, and is gone.

All sounds of him evaporate and she's alone again with her board of directors. *Alone.* In the cracked sodden belly of this dark cave, rays of silvery light coming from somewhere she can't see.

She listens to air moving on the raceway of the walls,

coursing along its hidden paths, a trapped trajectory, a sound like moaning. Velma, Arnold, Carrie, Jesus, racing their cars around and around, their pitched cries to *notice, notice, notice*.

And then she does. She notices.

A rock formation across the cave moves faintly up and down in a breathing pattern.

Her own breath stops.

She is *not* alone.

The rocks aren't rocks; they're ribs and a spine, shoulders, a waist, hips, a sloped valley of twined legs. At first she thinks she's looking at herself, a girl tied up in a cave. But then she knows she isn't. There are no tattoos on that girl's neck. *Her* hair is dark. And their breathing, when hers starts again, isn't in sync.

"Hello," she says, but the girl doesn't answer. "I'm here too." Still, no response.

Across the cave, against a craggy wall, sits a bright red tool-box. On top of it is a paperback with a broken spine and faded title. On top of the book, his gun.

Keep your eyes open, Carrie instructs. *Whatever you do, don't fall back asleep. Without awareness there can be no action. Pay attention. Think. Study.*

The answer to your question, says Velma, *is lysosome.*

The fourth organelle. Aha! Nucleus, mitochondrion, endoplasmic reticulum, lysosome, Golgi body.

18

A familiar face stares at Elsa from Lex's monitor. Around them, the detectives' unit sizzles with the heady waft of takeout bacon and coffee and commingled voices as the early shift gets its footing on the day. Raw sunlight arcs up the dirty windows, projecting silvery rectangles onto the scuffed walls. She moves her chair to the right, creating a shadow, blocking the glare on the screen, so she can see the face better.

The face that belongs to a man named Sammy Nelson, whose DNA was found on the cardboard cup that Ishmael Locke tossed into the trash at Greenberg's lumberyard.

Without the aviator sunglasses, the face is easy to recognize. Sammy Nelson. She wonders how many aliases he has; usually, where there's one, there are many.

She leans close to the screen, examines the bend in his nose, the backward sweep of brown hair, and remembers him. The much-read book, lavender bows in his daughter's hair.

"He was helping at the Haverstocks' house yesterday," she

tells Lex, her voice quavering. "I talked to him. His name tag said Teddy."

Panic branches across her skin.

How did she fail to recognize him when they were face to face?

But how could she have known it was him?

"Teddy's short for Edward." Lex grinds his teeth, muscles lumping along his jaw. "Ishmael Edward Locke."

Sammy Nelson's screen face is hard, the way he looks right into the camera, and suddenly she's back to yesterday, standing at the volunteer table, the messy scratch of his handwriting when he wrote down her name and how he knew her title meant FBI. The close attention he seemed to pay to her and Mel as they walked across the lawn. The pleasure he must have taken in their encounter, knowing that in looking for Ruby, they were also looking for him. The clarity of hindsight; yesterday suddenly in focus.

Elsa reaches under the desk for her striped bag, her hand searches the bottom, where all the small things fall and gather. And finds it. Round, smooth, a little prick where the pin nestles in its hook. She drops the bag back onto the floor, her stuff clunking around inside, and hopes the laptop didn't suffer.

She hands Lex the button. "He gave me this. He pinned it right onto my shirt without even asking. The guy was really weird."

He examines the button, front and back, running a finger around the smooth round edge of the laminated metal.

"He said it was his daughter."

Lex exhales. "No shit."

"I thought he was one of those nuts who—"

"Yeah, I know what you mean. I saw him too—one of those helpers who come equipped and never stop talking. Kept my distance." He looks at Elsa. "But you didn't."

"I should have." Knowing, as she says it, that it's just the opposite: she should have stayed longer, drawn him out more, grown suspicious, done something other than walk away.

Lex closes his fingers around the button; the girl's face vanishes under his fingers. "What else did he tell you?"

"He has sisters." She closes her eyes, thinks back. "He knew I was FBI. I could tell something was wrong, but I..." She reaches under a sleeve and digs in her fingernails, hard.

A look so warm it could be misread as pity radiates from Lex's face. He shifts toward her and says, softly, "Been there, Elsa. Done that. Everyone has. This one time, in Vice, I spent a whole night with a kid I thought was a runner for the local dealer before I realized he was the head of the operation. Well, not a kid—he was twenty-five."

"I could have had him," Elsa says. "Right there. I should have known."

"You know why kids think Santa Claus is real, until they don't? Because it's what they want to think. It's how our minds work."

"Not mine."

"Last time I checked, you were human too."

"Thanks, I guess."

"It's just a fact. Elsa, no one's as good at this job as you are. That's your reputation and now I see why. It's *because* you let it get to you. *Because* you're willing to admit mistakes. *Because* you suffer."

"So now I'm a martyr too?" Using her grin to break through his compassion, to stop this misguided attempt at... what? Understanding her? Forgiving her? Giving her permission to forgive herself? He has no idea how deep her guilt goes, or exactly why.

"I wouldn't go that far." He puts the button down on his desk, a clack of metal on wood.

Gathering herself, pulling her hand out of her sleeve, scooting closer to Lex's screen, she stares at the face. Teddy. Ishmael Locke. Sammy Nelson.

"I wonder if she's really his daughter," Elsa says.

"Good question."

"So, who is this guy?" she asks. "Who is he really?"

"Nelson was a suspect in a missing-kid case seven years ago in Indiana. Sixteen-year-old girl. They couldn't prove anything so they let him go. Look at this fucking guy's rap sheet." The monitor shows the long, detailed list of crimes Nelson has been accused of over the years.

"He was at Queens Beans," she tells him.

"What?"

"I was just with Charlie Hendryk. He went to see Ruby on Friday night, right before she disappeared. He'd been feeding her his Adderalls until she moved on, starting buying them from Paul. Charlie deals his meds, but also drugs. And he wants Ruby back, but she's blocked his number, so he shows up at her work and tries to talk to her, and she scares him off with the fake gun. But before he leaves, he watches a white van drive up, park, a tall guy with brown hair get out."

"He saw this freak and he didn't say anything?"

"Nelson has Ruby's credit card, Lex. He was with her." She

feels an acid burn in her chest. Forces in a deep breath, allows it out slowly, eyes landing on the button, that little smiling girl. She picks it up and returns it to her bag, not wanting to lose it.

"What the fuck was he doing at the Haverstocks' yesterday?" Lex asked.

"They do that sometimes, turn up to witness the havoc they've caused. Gives them some kind of twisted, voyeuristic enjoyment. He might have even used her credit card for attention—to taunt us. They do that sometimes too."

The look on Lex's face as he absorbs what she's just said, the implication of *them,* that Sammy Nelson, aka Ishmael 'Teddy' Locke, is operating off a different set of instructions. That bending their minds around his intentions will be difficult, and it will hurt.

"I can't understand it." Lex leans forward, presses his thumbs to his temples. "I talked to Charlie *twice*. He seemed credible. I didn't get a single vibe that he was lying or holding anything back, and I'm usually good at reading signals—how did I miss this?"

"Santa Claus," she reminds him. "You're human too."

"I never believed in Santa Claus, that's the thing."

"Neither did I." A tremor slips into her voice. "Lex, what if he's still there? It's unlikely. But."

He makes the call, phone pressed to his ear, asks the question, his eyes locked with hers as together they wait for an answer.

"Thank you," he says, and ends the call. He tells Elsa, "No one's seen him at the Haverstocks' since yesterday afternoon."

"Where did he go?" And then her thoughts veer upstate,

to Locke's cabin. Nelson's cabin. Teddy's breadbox full of snacks. A prickling along her skin. "Call Sang McCracken. Tell him everything we know and ask him to go back to the cabin. Then ask your sergeant to pull together a task force—we need help."

"Good idea." Lex reaches for his phone.

"I'm calling Greenberg—there's something I've got to find out. Remember how that cabin floor creaked, especially in one spot?"

She dials, and as she waits for Greenberg to pick up, the ringing phone is swallowed by the recollection of walking across Locke's floor. *Nelson's* floor. It's all Elsa can hear now above the workaday din of Lex's colleagues, the *creak, creak, creak* of those rough-hewn boards, echoes from a hollow space they'd been unable to find. While the phone rings in her ear, she notices a greasy film on the surface of her untouched coffee, a purple reflection from the overhead fluorescents that someone has turned on unnecessarily. The room fills with too much light, skewing everything.

"Yello!" Greenberg answers.

She explains what she wants, and he puts her on hold. Minutes later he returns to the line and rattles off items and their costs in a blur of Ishmael Locke's prosaic home-improvement projects going back six years. One jumps out.

"Stop," Elsa tells him. "Repeat that last one."

"August seventh, 2009." Greenberg's tone deep and quick, eager to help. "Six planks of two-by-ten raw pine. Fuckin' A, I remember that sale. Pardon my French."

"What do you remember?"

"He brought in an old plank, actually pried up an existing

one from his cabin floor. Had to have an exact match. I mean, two-by-ten pine is some of the cheapest wood you can buy— no one brings in a sample."

"You ask him why he did?"

"I figured he was one of those prissy summer people, wanting every nail in their precious houses just so. Vintage. Know what I mean? A couple of local guys have made a killing selling yesterday's junk to the second-home people."

"Did he strike you as someone with a second home?"

"If you'd seen the people coming in here dressed like bums and driving away in Maseratis, you'd know why I don't judge anymore."

But if he'd ever visited Nelson's bare-bones cabin, he'd know what she knows: This is not a man who cares about his home, let alone home decor. If he wanted to match floorboards, it was for a very practical reason.

"Do me a favor," she tells him, "and send me a copy of that purchase record."

Next, she calls Detective McCracken, who answers with "Elsa. We're here. What do you have?"

"Take up the floor."

"All of it?"

"All of it. And careful not to damage anything—we might need to trace wood lots."

"On it."

She ends the call, looks up, and discovers that Lex disappeared while she was speaking with Greenberg. On his desk, a note: *Task force assembling in conference room 2.*

19

The narrow room with two utility tables pushed together between half a dozen mismatched folding chairs is not the nicest task-force home Elsa has ever seen, but it's a private space to work in and it'll do. Along one wall, a large old-fashioned chalkboard is covered with a haze left behind by the erasure of someone else's notes, the ghost of another case.

A steel-haired man and a pregnant woman sit facing each other.

Lex does the introductions. "Special Agent Elsa Myers, FBI Child Abduction Rapid Deployment division. Detective Owen Tate, State Bureau of Criminal Investigations. Detective Rosie Santiago, Queens Special Victims Bureau."

Tate half rises to offer his hand, and when Elsa shakes it, he looks right into her eyes. His are surrounded by thick folds of skin networked with deep lines. She knows from experience that the BCI has some good people on its team, and she hopes he's one of them.

Elsa says, "Thanks for being here, Detective Tate."

"Owen." The raspy voice of a smoker.

She walks around the table to greet Santiago, saying, "Don't get up," her pregnancy ballooning under a denim skirt and a tight-fitting floral T-shirt. A gold band pinches the detective's swollen ring finger, and Elsa fleetingly wonders why she doesn't just take it off for the duration. But people get attached to their things, tokens of deeper meaning, like Elsa with her Swiss Army knife. Without it close at hand, she panics. Just the passing thought of it now sends a call across her skin, an appetite for the touch of cold steel.

Santiago pushes herself up to standing, maybe to prove that she can despite her girth. Elsa gets it, and they share a quick smile. "Lex filled us in. It's a doozy."

"If you're lucky"—Elsa shakes the detective's hand—"maybe you'll have the baby soon and get a pass out of this one."

"Not due for another coupla months. Anyway, this shit doesn't get to me anymore. I mean, sometimes it does, but not really."

"Glad you could join us, Detective Santiago."

"Rosie."

"Elsa." She drops her bag on the table and takes a seat. "So here's where we are right now. I've got Detective McCracken upstate taking up Nelson's floor, and Dr. Bailey, the BAU analyst, is on her way here to work with us on-site. Meanwhile, I'm hoping we can shed some light on *this*." She fishes the girl-button out of her bag and slides it across the table like a hockey puck.

Rosie stops the button with a slap of her hand. Looks at it. "Cute kid. Who is it?" She passes it to Owen Tate.

Elsa says, "He said it's his daughter, that he wants to keep her safe."

Rosie's lips gather into something that isn't a kiss.

Lex adds, "We're also waiting on Charlie Hendryk. We're going to show him an array, but he's underage, so we've got to call in one of his parents too."

"We shouldn't waste any more time on that kid today," Elsa says. Angry that his delay in speaking up lost them time on Ruby. If he'd told Lex about the van when he was first questioned three days ago, they might have found her already—they'd have known, at least, to look for the van.

Lex argues, "I know, but we have to get it done," and he's right even though she hates it. A positive eyewitness account of Sammy Nelson showing up at Queens Beans moments before Ruby's disappearance will give them greater resources to work with in the hours ahead. Later, in a court of law, it could be the detail that shifts a jury against him.

They get to work on Nelson, who he is, where he's been, what he's done, charting what came before so they can map, with as much accuracy as possible, what might come next.

Sometime during the blur of a quickly passing hour, Tara's ringtone rattles for Elsa's attention: a happy marimba beat that tends to lift her spirits. But not today. She ignores the call and then, as it slides to voice mail, thinks better of it. Maybe something is happening with their father. Turning away from the group, she holds the phone to her ear and listens.

Tara's message-voice is controlled at first and then spirals into agitation: "Sorry about before, on the phone. Dad's hanging in there for now; he woke up and he actually ate something. And Mellie, well, I ignored your advice and called her in the middle of the night. She got on the first bus up so she's here now—but I really screwed up and I have to talk to you. I lost control and *I hit her* and now I feel like shit. Call me."

The silence after the click is followed closely by a wave of dark blue misery, a powerful revulsion. Elsa stares at the wall, a fissure racing across her skin, blood memory, opening her. Tara has struck her child and *she* feels like shit? The hot sting of Tara's hand on Mel crawls all over Elsa. She scratches, once, hard, sits on her hand, and faces the group.

Dr. Joan Gottesman Bailey hurries in. "Got here as fast as I could from DC."

The behavioral psychologist appears to be about Elsa's age, pretty, with a bodacious Afro. She wears brown slacks and a short-sleeved yellow blouse that shows off her sculpted arms, igniting a prick of jealousy that Elsa swallows. She hasn't worn short sleeves in public since she was a kid.

"Thanks for coming, Dr. Bailey," Elsa says.

"Joan, please." She sits down, unbuckles her leather bag, pulls out a laptop. She unfolds a tiny pair of reading glasses and puts them on. "I worked on the flight so I'm ready to go. You guys want to kick off, set me up with some more context?"

Lex stands, goes to the board, and takes up the first piece of white chalk he finds. He jots notes as he speaks.

"Sammy Nelson, aka Ishmael 'Teddy' Locke, is thirty-six years old, born in Utah, youngest of four children. His three older sisters bullied him—so badly it shows up in school records all the way through middle school."

My sisters told me always to bring a book, you know, in case things got boring, Teddy had told Elsa, friendly under the tent. *Boring.* Not a chance, not if they were punching away at his existence. How did *he* hide from the assaults? She thinks of the book he had with him that day, *The Invisible Man,* how worn it was, and wonders now if it's some kind of emblem for him. A way to talk back to his sisters, to decipher them and make a statement that they didn't succeed in erasing him.

She thinks of her own sister, the cruelties that lie between them, but also the love.

"All of his sisters bullied him?" Joan asks. "That's unusual."

Lex raises an eyebrow, nods. "Yup. When he was five, the family moved to Washington State. They belonged to the Christian Identity church—white supremacists, basically. Later, he dropped out. When he was twelve, his grandfather gave him a gun as a birthday present, and apparently he really took to hunting."

"Nice gift," Elsa mumbles. She feels reassured by the weight of her Glock, a necessary evil, heavy on her ankle, but in fact she hates guns for what they can do and have done to the wrong people at the wrong times.

"As soon as he could," Lex says, "he joined the army, spent time at Fort Lewis, Fort Hood, and a few months stationed in Egypt. After the army he landed in Alaska, worked as a handyman, carpenter, contractor. As we know, he's on record in Indiana as a suspect in the disappearance seven years ago of a sixteen-year-old girl, Gerri Wagoner, but nothing came of that. Eventually he found himself in Oregon, which is his current address. Visits the Northeast once or twice a year.

When he's here, he goes by Ishmael Locke—uses a New York State driver's license and credit card under that alias."

Elsa adds, "It looks like he never flies. He drives, and somewhere between Ohio and Pennsylvania, he slips into the Ishmael Locke identity."

"His mom passed away about a year ago," Rosie says, "and his dad died eight years ago. I spoke with one of his older sisters, Beth. She's married with a couple of kids, lives in Seattle, seemed a little irritated when I first called but then she calmed down. My impression was that this is not a very nice family. Anyway, once I got her talking, she admitted she feels bad about pushing him around as a kid, tried to apologize to him a few years back but he didn't want to hear it."

"Has she spoken to him lately?" Joan asks.

"Beth says she hasn't seen or heard from him in a long time," Rosie says, "and that he isn't close with either of the other sisters. Sammy is a loner, always has been."

Joan reaches toward the middle of the table, where the button has settled, and lifts it up. Sits back, studies it. "This the daughter? I'm kind of surprised no one's mentioned her yet."

"He told me it's his daughter," Elsa answers, "but we haven't found anything about a kid or a wife or a girlfriend, nothing like that. Have you?"

"Took a little digging, but yeah. Zoe, she's five now. The girl's mother, Maryanne, says they weren't together very long. They weren't married; that's probably why she doesn't show up in most of his records. He was violent with her and she kicked him out when Zoe was an infant. Sent him a picture of the kid a couple of times but otherwise keeps her distance."

Lex asks, "You talked to her?"

"I did."

Owen clears his throat. "If it was me, the minute the Amber Alert went public, I'd worry my time was limited, I'd want to go see my kid."

Joan nods. "Of course, that's what most people would do. But the ties there sound weak; Nelson hasn't shown any interest at all in Zoe since he left Alaska."

"He wears a button with her face on it," Elsa argues.

"Yeah, maybe that means something, or maybe it's just for show. Obviously, I recommend we put a pair of eyes on Maryanne's house, keep a lookout."

"Agreed," Lex says.

Rosie's stomach grumbles so loudly, everyone laughs. Tate gathers lunch orders and twenty minutes later they're picking at sandwiches, salads, coffee, water, a mess of refuse gathering in the center of the table as they continue to work.

Elsa's phone rings, screen flashing a number she now recognizes as McCracken's cell. She drops her turkey-on-rye onto the mayo-smeared sheet of wax paper it came in.

"Sang—hello."

"Good call, Elsa, about the floor."

"What did you find?"

"He dug out a space and buried two toolboxes. Same size, same make, holding pretty much the same stuff. But, strangest thing, one's a lot older-looking than the other one. Rusted. The tools inside that one look real dirty and caked. To my eye it looks like it's been down there longer. My tech sprayed them with luminol, and, Elsa—there is definitely the presence of blood in both toolboxes."

Her stomach turns; she pushes away what remains of her sandwich. "Get it all to the Bureau's Albany lab right away."

"On it."

"Take photos?"

"I'll zap 'em right over."

"Perfect. Thanks."

"Wait." He stops her from hanging up. "One more thing. Two, actually. Locke's van was found this morning at Manchester Commons, abandoned, in the parking lot outside the Yankee Candle. And a blue Ford Escort was reported stolen a little while later from in front of Crabtree and Evelyn."

"Manchester Commons is a mall, I take it."

"Big one, parking lots sprawling every which way. Cars get stolen from there every week, but because of the van, this one seemed worth mentioning."

"Put an APB on it."

"Already done. And we've impounded the van—going over it with a you-know-what."

Immediately after the call, McCracken texts half a dozen photos to her phone, and she scrolls through them. Two red toolboxes containing a matched set of items. A screwdriver, a wrench, pliers and a hammer, masonry nails, along with things that wouldn't make sense in a typical handyman's kit: a variety of carabiner hooks, cuticle trimmers, a shrimp fork, loose cigarettes, a partially burned stick of incense, a plastic lighter, a knot of filthy rope. Two identical sets of illogically gathered tools, everything crusted and bloody and used.

Elsa thinks of Sammy Nelson and hates this, hates *him*. Suddenly she hears her mother's voice from thirty years ago:

Hate *is a strong word. Try* dislike. Emotion fountains and Elsa pushes it back.

She thinks of Ruby.

If you wait long enough, someone comes to get you.

But they don't always. Sometimes, you wait and wait.

She feels the hard smack of hand on flesh, terror rippling through icy surprise. You recoil, as if that will protect you, but it won't, not when the person holding all the rage is stronger than you are.

She reaches to the center of the table, pulls a tissue from a half-empty box, and wipes dry her forehead. Sits there, hiding her growing panic in the intentness of listening as the task force continues to analyze the true nature of the man they'll need to understand if they have any hope of finding Ruby in time. The thing is, Elsa feels she already understands him, more or less, but she doesn't know how to begin to explain.

A quote she'd used in her Ralph Ellison essay jumps out of a deeply buried memory bank and into her thoughts: *I remember that I'm invisible and walk softly so as not to awake the sleeping ones. Sometimes it is best not to awaken them; there are few things in the world as dangerous as sleepwalkers.*

Yes, she understands that, not as a black man unseen in plain sight in racist America—"the novel's major theme," as teenage Elsa had dutifully informed her eleventh-grade English teacher—but more generally, as a person who learns how to hide her true self, how not to leave footprints. She hadn't made the association when she was a teenager but now it resonates in the most awful way.

But her *Invisible Man* isn't Nelson's; she doesn't know *his* book. She goes online and calls up a sample from the Wells novel, her eyes landing at random on a passage: *A feeling of extraordinary elation took the place of my anger as I sat outside the window and watched these four people…trying to understand the riddle of my behavior…I was invisible, and I was only just beginning to realize the extraordinary advantage my invisibility gave me. My head was already teeming with plans of all the wild and wonderful things I had now impunity to do.*

And then another: *To do such a thing would be to transcend magic. And I beheld, unclouded by doubt, a magnificent vision of all that invisibility might mean to a man—the mystery, the power, the freedom. Drawbacks I saw none. You have only to think!*

But what does it mean? What does this idea, or vision, or whatever it is, of the temptations of invisibility and impunity—what does it mean to Sammy Nelson? She doesn't even know whether the invisibility is supposed to be literal or figurative, if he's reacting to some powerful metaphor by carrying that old book around or if he's just out of his mind.

Or maybe it means nothing. Maybe at home, wherever home is for him, maybe he has a whole shelfful of spine-broken books he's studied for clues to his place in the universe. Books his sisters pressed on him to better himself.

His trio of cruel sisters.

Lex's voice interrupts her thoughts: "Elsa? You okay?"

She blinks. "I think the sandwich made me a little queasy."

"Deli mayo," Rosie says. "Gotta watch out for it."

"Charlie and his mother are here," Lex says. "Come on, Elsa, let's get this over with."

20

Mrs. Hendryk's heels jitter a staccato rhythm on the linoleum floor. Charlie, seated beside her in the interrogation room, stares at his folded hands on the table. The mother refuses to let them begin without their lawyer, which wastes another fifteen minutes. Finally he appears.

"Apologies for holding you up," the lawyer, Norman Osprey, says without a hint of remorse. He yanks out a chair and sits beside Charlie, but Charlie, Elsa notices, doesn't even glance at the older man, whose horseshoe of black hair, she also notices, looks as if it's been painted on.

Lex pushes the stack of mug shots across the table. "Let's get started."

As Charlie studies the array, his mother coaches him, saying, "Listen to your instincts, Charlie," as if helping him prepare for a tricky exam. "Don't overthink."

Elsa says, "Please, just let him look."

"Can't I talk to my own son?" Mrs. Hendryk turns to her lawyer for guidance.

"Of course you can," Osprey answers firmly.

Satisfied, she resumes her rigid posture, spine straight, hands joined, knees pressed tight. She instructs Charlie, "Go ahead."

He slumps, reviewing every face. Elsa sits across the table, leaning back as if they've got all the time in the world, which they emphatically don't. Charlie's omission about Friday night has already cost them valuable days they couldn't afford to lose.

Ignoring Mrs. Hendryk and the mind-warp she emits is almost impossible, and Elsa's thoughts loop to her own mother, then to Mel, then to Tara. She's glad she isn't a mother because she wouldn't have a clue how to correctly raise a teenager.

Suddenly, Charlie's face brightens with recognition. His finger stabs hard on Sammy Nelson's mug shot from the Indiana case in '08. "This is him."

Lex responds by striding briskly to the table from across the room, where he'd propped himself against the wall. Elsa leans forward, galvanized by the sight of Charlie's fingertip on Nelson's image. She asks, "You're sure?"

"That's enough," Norman Osprey says. "We're done here."

Charlie continues as if the lawyer hasn't spoken. "Absolutely, yeah."

Lex asks, "You'd testify to it?"

"Norman said stop." Mrs. Hendryk stands abruptly. "Charlie, I mean it, don't say anything else."

"Come on, son." Osprey lifts his briefcase from the floor and stands beside Mrs. Hendryk. "We'll talk about this outside."

Charlie defies them both. "Yes, I'm sure this is who I saw that night, and I'll definitely testify if you need me to."

"Charlie!"

"*Mom*. I already fucked up enough. I have to tell them what I know."

You could practically see Charlie's future draining out of his mother's eyes. Elsa holds back the vitriol percolating in her mind—what's the point? Once the DEA gets their rope around her son, Mrs. Hendryk will face a *real* reckoning. Norman Osprey opens the door for his clients. Elsa and Lex follow them out.

"*Svolosh,*" Lex mutters, just the two of them in the windowless hallway. Somewhere in the near distance, a door slaps shut. Another opens, releasing a pair of investigators who move in silence in the direction of the elevators. "So now we know for sure."

Whether Nelson still has Ruby is another question, four days and nights having been squandered since she vanished. She says, "I feel like such an idiot."

"Elsa." Lex's hand on her back zippers warmth across her skin. "You couldn't have known." She wants to lay her head on his shoulder, but doesn't. Wants to fall in love with his brother and be part of their family, but can't. Whenever Lex Cole comes too close, warning bells go off, familiar, confusing.

"I thought she probably ran away. You came to me—your instinct was right. I was wrong."

"We're all wrong sometimes."

"I can't afford to be wrong, not in this kind of work."

His palm rubs a circular motion on her shirt and her skin ignites. "Come on, let's get back to work."

"Meet you there." She gestures toward the women's room down the hall. "Nature calls."

In the quiet of the bathroom stall, Elsa lets her mind rip free. It's been years since she cut herself but today the urge is calling so loudly, pulling so hard. Thoughts racing and crashing with things she'd like to say to Charlie, narcissistic Charlie, who might have cost his former girlfriend her life; with thoughts of Ruby, and Sammy Nelson, and Roy, and Tara, and Mel.

Mel, whom Tara hit. Beloved Mel.

Elsa always believed that the violence would end with her if she didn't have kids; another thing she was wrong about.

Clearly, telling Tara about the Adderall was a mistake. But when Elsa thinks of that greasy little packet of heroin, she also knows that she had little choice.

She wonders how long it will be before Roy dies.

And she wonders about Ruby: What will her death be like?

She can't bring herself to return Tara's call. Instead, she leaves a message for Mel: "Hey, sweetie, how are you? Can we talk? I need to hear your voice, okay?"

And then the separateness of the stall, it's cold isolation, engulfs her. No one will come for her here. Even if someone enters the bathroom, they won't notice her, not if she's quiet.

She unhooks her bag from the door and finds her Swiss Army knife. The neat, reliable package of it, its parts tucked together like sleep, lends a perfect weight to the palm of her hand. She runs a finger along the smooth steel edges, flat on the sides, rounded at both ends. And then her fingernail finds just the right notch and pulls out the reamer. Calmness overtakes her. She rolls up her pants leg, sits on the toilet, props her leg up against the wall, and gets to work.

21

"Why is it always me?"

A fist forms in your gut. Your parents' words volley above you as you stand there between them, trapped, small. Monkey in the middle.

"It isn't always you, Deb."

"You *never* discipline her."

"I still don't know what she did."

"She threw a hairbrush across the room. It nearly hit me."

"No, Mom," you protest, "*you* threw the hairbrush and it hit *me*." A tender spot still echoing on the back of your leg. You'd been trying to get away.

The veil of reasonableness snaps off, her tone blistering with heat. *"Roy."*

"I don't know."

It's her silence that does the trick. No one is as scary as she is when not-speaking. A decade of volatile marriage roils her features. You think that when your father looks into your mother's face, he sees both his daughters, one lodged in each fierce eye, around which the storm of troubled mother-hood swirls. You think he thinks that if he obeys the face, the eyes won't blink. He must keep his daughters safe how-ever he can.

He addresses you while looking at her: "Elsa, come with me."

You are eight years old. You follow him up the stairs. She stands below, watching.

Your bedroom door slaps shut and for a second you think your cat's been caught in the door and you feel horrible be-cause it's your fault (again) but then you remember that Pea-body ran away two months ago. *Good for Peabody,* you think while your father looms beside your narrow bed and says, "Pull down your pants."

You do it. You pull them down.

He unbuckles his belt and snakes the leather out of the loops.

"Daddy," you whisper. The fist in your stomach reaching into your throat. He has never hit you before. If you lose him too, you'll have no one. You feel yourself slip out of your body and flee to the ceiling, where you look down and commit the moment to memory. *"Daddy, please."*

His lips purse in a silent *shush*. He winks.

He sits on the edge of your bed, nods at his lap, and speaks like an actor trying a new line that comes out too loudly: "Bend over!"

You do it. You bend over. Ashamed of your naked butt.

"When I slap my hands"—his whisper so low, you can barely hear it—"scream."

He claps the air above you as hard as he can, making a loud

flesh-on-flesh noise. One. Two. Three. Four. Five. Pause. A second set of five. He knows the drill.

For every clap, you scream your heart out.

He isn't touching you but still you feel the fear, knowing that she's downstairs, standing where you left her. Listening.

22

Elsa walks through the detectives' unit, the fresh wound on her shin chafing under the crisscross of too-small bandages she fished out of the bottom of her bag, and then stops at Lex's desk. She puts down the rain-soggy cardboard tray of ordered-in specialty coffees that she just retrieved from reception and is taking back to the conference room. The weak department coffee isn't cutting it anymore, and she needed an excuse to step out of the room, where the task-force members have circled everything they collectively know, again and again, in a mind-numbing roundelay—*the presence of blood in both toolboxes*—while they await results from the lab. Whatever the tech comes back with, presumably it won't be good news about Nelson's intentions—this man who presumably abducted Ruby Haverstock right out of Queens Beans and also presumably means her harm.

Everything a presumption now. No, not everything. He carries that book around. Wears the photo pin. Collects identical sets of tools in matching toolboxes that he might, presumably, revisit in order to…what?

What does he think he's doing? What does he want?

The task force has gone round and round the questions, trying to make some kind of sense of it, but the presumptuous nature of every answer makes it impossible to latch onto anyone without a hard set of facts to anchor them.

And anyway, what does it matter why he's doing it or what he wants? All they need is Ruby back. And to stop Sammy Nelson from ever doing it again.

Elsa sits at the desk, then bends underneath it. She uses her phone's flashlight app to illuminate the dusty shadows where apparently neither sunshine nor broom has visited for some time and sees it: the spare ammo clip missing from her bag. She already checked the bathroom, thinking it might have fallen out when she rescued her knife from its oblivion or succumbed to it in desperation, so blinded by a desire to cut herself that she might not have noticed anything else. Tracing further back in time, she recalled the clunky sound of something shifting inside her bag—maybe, she guessed, not shifting but falling out—when she tossed it onto the floor under Lex's desk after retrieving the Zoe button to show him. Little Zoe Nelson, cherub-faced on a souvenir that the man who happens to be her father but doesn't know her wears on his shirt.

What does it mean?

She grabs the clip and, sitting back up, drops it into her bag as her gaze counts all the investigators in the room who failed to notice loose ammo lying around the unit. Eight, and not everyone appears busy.

The things we don't see that we don't want to see.

The things we do see that aren't there.

The things we miss simply because we aren't looking.

She stands and picks up the tray. If she takes too long getting it to the conference room, her colleagues will wonder where she is, and she isn't keen on letting anyone know she mislaid her spare clip.

She crosses back through the room, afternoon sucking at the windows.

And it hits her: *Memories.* Nelson is collecting memories. Souvenirs, mementos, proof that he has allies in the world when it appears he's utterly alone. Maybe the book reminds him of his sisters, who were cruel to him when he didn't deserve it. Maybe the button reminds him of a child he abandoned for her own good. And the bloody tools—proof that he connected with other people? Is he building a story that works better for him than the one everyone else sees? Adding emotional inflections to inexplicable actions so he doesn't have to identify himself as a monster?

She picks up her pace, eager to share her theory with the others.

The door to the detectives' unit slaps shut behind her and she almost doesn't hear her phone but catches it on the fourth ring before it goes to voice mail. An Albany area code— another presumption, but she'd bet anything it's the lab.

"Myers here, what do you have for me?"

"You Myers?" An older man's voice, a little too loud.

"I just said I am. Who is this?"

"Upstate Forensics. This is the lab calling to tell you we've got some information for you, if this is Agent Myers."

Elsa stops walking and takes a breath. She makes it a policy not to show her impatience with older folks who are hard of hearing, and she won't do it now. "Yes, this is Special Agent Elsa Myers. I've been waiting to hear from you about some blood samples—what do you have for me?"

"Blood and hair, both. You want me to read it to you, or should I e-mail it?"

"E-mail, please. Right away."

Elsa bursts into the conference room. Conversation stops abruptly; eyes turn to her. She announces, "It's in—the lab's e-mailing me right now."

She puts the tray on the table and hurries around to her laptop. E-mails stream in but not the one she wants. "*Fuck*. Where is it?"

"I can't just sit here." Joan pushes up from the table, goes around to the tray, and removes the various-size paper cups with methodical patience. Lex sits there, thinking or maybe not thinking at all, while Elsa stares blankly at her screen. Rosie bites the inside of her cheek. Owen leans back and yawns enormously, willing equanimity. Everyone finding his or her own way to wait without waiting for the information they've been waiting hours for.

Joan hands Lex a tall cardboard cup and sets down an identical one beside Elsa. Takes a tiny paper vessel of espresso and slides it across the table to Owen. Walks around the table to give Rosie her chamomile tea.

"Okay," Elsa announces, seeing the e-mail, "here we go. I'm forwarding it to everyone so we can read it together."

All at once they lean into their screens, tap open their mail, read through the report as quickly as they can take in the information. Elsa forces her mind to slow down so she won't miss a single detail.

A variety of different hairs were combed out of the van.

And the blood of six people was found on the tools, three in each box.

Elsa tries to take that in, *six people,* but the words, the concept, the reality of it slips off her brain, just won't go in. Six. *Six.*

"All right, here's what we'll do." Elsa's hands lift off her keyboard; she faces the group, somber eyes looking up from their screens. "We'll run every sample through CODIS and NDIS. Then we'll call NMPDD and see what they can give us by way of matches."

If the hair from the van or blood from the tools sparks a match in the National Missing Person DNA Database, they'll have something to work with. Until then, all they can do is ask Sammy Nelson about it—if and when they catch up with him. So far, like the Amber Alert for Ruby, the APB for Nelson has yielded nothing but hot air from enthusiastic callers—the kind of rubberneckers Elsa mistook Teddy for at the Haverstocks' yesterday. The force of her voice pushes against a rising feeling: her failure to recognize him *and now this* curdling in her stomach and oozing into her heart, into her brain, where it stews with reminders of her innate ineptitude. How can someone so damaged expect to think clearly, ever?

Lex asks, "How long does that usually take?" pulling Elsa out of her inner detour, wanting facts.

"Five minutes to three weeks." She clears her throat, rights her mind. "In my experience."

"We don't have three weeks."

"Lex, no one whose blood is on those tools is still alive."

"What if one of them is Ruby?"

"Every indication is that both toolboxes were buried a long time ago," Rosie says. "According to the report, all the blood is old."

"She's right." Elsa pops open her latte long enough for a puff of steam to escape, realizes she doesn't want it, and re-caps it for later.

The calls are made and then the minutes tick forward. A quarter hour. Twenty minutes. Twenty-five.

At last, a flash of red on the screen announces a message from the NMPDD.

Elsa clicks it open and announces, "We've got a hit on one of the samples: Tiffany Shamouz, Nevada, eighteen-year-old college student, went missing in April 2008. Never found."

The air seems to drain from the room; in its place, a heavy silence.

Elsa recognizes the numb anguish of where this is going. Knows how much she doesn't want to go there. Knows they have no choice.

Soon, her screen flashes red, red, red; more samples spark-ing results.

"Kelli Jefferson, sixteen, vanished in July 2012 in eastern Pennsylvania. Gerri Wagoner, sixteen, went missing in April 2008."

Owen says, "That's the Indiana case they almost had him on."

"Yup." Elsa's voice catches when she reads the next one. "Maisie Campbell, seventeen, Oregon, also April 2008."

"Fuck." Rosie leans back and folds her hands protectively over the planet of her unborn child.

Elsa steels herself and reads the next two. "Angela Diaz, Pennsylvania, July 2012. Fannie Mann—"

Lex cuts her off. "Also taken from Pennsylvania? July 2012?"

"Maryland," Elsa corrects him.

"Right next to Pennsylvania."

"That's correct." Elsa checks the victims found in the nearby states against the samples found in both toolboxes. "The 2008 girls' blood are on the set of tools from the older toolbox. The 2012 one, the newer box. None of them were ever seen again."

"I have to pee." Rosie's voice small, vaporous, as she pushes herself up out of her chair, knocks the door open hard. Her quick footsteps resonate unsteadily down the hall.

Joan's concerned gaze rests on the door until it clicks shut. She gets up. "Think I'll go too."

Watching the flight of women from the room, Elsa realizes that she also needs to relieve herself, but she can't return to the bathroom, not yet. She hopes she buried the bloody paper towels deep enough in the trash can. At the sound of someone coming, she'd jammed the knife into her pants pocket, where it now presses against her leg, a tempting and chastening reminder.

"You okay, Elsa?" Lex's voice brings her back to the moment.

"Hunky-dory. You?"

"Fan-tastic." But he's frowning, and she can hardly breathe.

Owen stands at the chalkboard with printouts of Sammy Nelson's and Ishmael Locke's credit card and cell phone records and cash withdrawals going back years. Elsa watches as he gathers facts in two columns, one for Nelson, another for Locke. Plucking details off the lists, he makes notations beneath their names. Under Nelson, calls and charges in Oregon, Nevada, and Indiana during the month of April 2008. For Locke, activity in Pennsylvania and Maryland in July 2012.

Rosie and Joan slip back into the room, a serene quiet between them. Elsa guesses that the good doctor administered some flash therapy in the ladies'. A glance at the soft slope of Joan's face, her calm eyes, makes Elsa wish she'd joined them after all.

"So that's it." Owen stands back to look at the board. "Nelson's movements connect to all six of the cold cases, 2008 acting as himself in the Midwest, in 2012 as Ishmael Locke in the Northeast. He'd drop into town. The girls would vanish. Within a week or so, he'd be gone. Interesting note: He has the same issue credit card from the same bank as Ruby's, Chase, which probably accounts for his smooth move charging that lumber to her card. There are *no* credit or debit card records from 2012 or 2008 or before of his purchasing the first two toolboxes or any of the tools inside. Best guess, if he was smart about it, he bought them in cash, in different places, over time—with one exception. Five weeks ago he places an order from eBay for a twenty-inch flattop toolbox made by Homak, red. The particular model was discontinued a few years back for a defect in the way the shelf fit into the top. They reissued it as a new model, but apparently

Nelson wanted the old one. Had to have it. Shipped to his address in Oregon."

Rosie scoots heavily forward on her chair. "Anyone from the local PD out at his Oregon place yet?"

"Yup." Lex. "They'll ping us if they find anything, otherwise we'll see a report later."

"So," Joan says, "he keeps the toolboxes as souvenirs and buries them so he can visit them whenever he wants. And it was important to him to build an identical murder kit for both clusters of killings. Why?"

"That last part's an assumption," Owen argues. "Yes, he built matching kits. But the cases are open; we don't know what happened to those girls."

"Shit, Owen." As soon as she says it, Elsa regrets the edge in her tone, but only because it's unproductive. To her, the idea that any of the six girls are still alive seems ludicrous. Nelson was a stranger; he didn't know them and didn't love them. Why would he have spared their lives? She places her elbows on the table, leans in. "The souvenirs—I think it might be more than keeping reminders of the crimes. It's hard to describe, but I think he might be trying to define himself, to himself, as better than he really is. He doesn't hold on to blood just as a memento of something he did. It shows him something about himself that he needs to remember— or believe."

Joan nods. "And he wears that button of his kid."

"Right. And the book," Elsa adds, "*The Invisible Man,* it reminds him of something his sisters urged him to do to improve himself."

"So what?" Owen's tone a little sharp.

"Yeah," she says, "you're right, I get it. It doesn't really matter—I mean, who gives a crap how this guy feels? But then again, maybe it does matter. Have any of you ever worked a repeater before?"

"Unfortunately, yes," Joan answers. "In some ways they're all the same, and in other ways each is unique. The key is to focus in on how."

Rosie says, "Me, never."

Elsa looks at Lex, who shakes his head, then at Owen, who answers, "Once. Guy hated immigrants. Killed four people over two days, but he was stupid and we caught him pretty fast."

Those are the good cases, Elsa thinks, when the surprise of what's happening merges with an adrenaline rush like no other, and you forge ahead with blinders on, eyes fixed on the empowering righteousness of your goal. And you save the kid, and you nail the fucker, fast. Those are the best ones, the best of the worst, because all of them are bad by nature. But in cases like this—the ones that limp forward, tripping over minutes and hours and days, allowing in variations of light that trick the eye elsewhere—doubt infects purpose and you can't be sure that anything you think or say or do is leading you where you need to go.

"I've worked a few of these before," Elsa says, "and they're always ugly. Believe it or not, on some level you'll get used to it, though it will never not hurt. You know that thick skin they probably told you about at cop school—"

Lex rips a page out of his notebook, balls it up, and aims it at the nearest trash can. Scores. "I'm up to this, Elsa. I don't want you to think I'm not."

"Yeah"—Rosie, vanquishing any trace of hesitation from her voice—"me too."

Owen lowers his chin in a formal, stoic nod of agreement.

Elsa says, "I know you are." But she knows they aren't, because no one ever is. "And we're going to find Ruby. We will. He takes them in clusters of three. If he's following the same pattern now, he'll want two more girls. We'll start by looking at all the teenage girls who vanished on the East Coast during the past week."

The immediate list is long, over a hundred girls reported missing since the previous Tuesday. The four investigators divvy up all the East Coast states, with Joan consulting as they pare down the lists.

The list shrinks and shrinks by the dozen until finally they pare it down to just under thirty girls spread across a triangle reaching from Ohio to Maine to Delaware. Girls who failed to come home after school, work, church, the park, a friend's house. By eliminating every girl with a plausible reason for her no-show—an inappropriate boyfriend, history of drug use, mental illness, repeat disappearances ending in return—they cut the list to twenty.

Minutes tick through an hour, two.

The list shrinks to ten. Any one of these missing children could be somewhere with Ruby right now, but to join each of those investigations to theirs would be to squander their resources. They have to look harder, to be sure.

Elsa reaches for her cold coffee, foamed milk crusted on the top, and drinks. Everyone else has his or her head buried in a laptop or notes. She takes another long sip, feeling her own concentration evaporate like hot mist in cold air. Evaporate like girls everywhere. Like she did as a girl in her closet.

Exhaustion sinks through her, heavy as a stone. She finishes her coffee, but it doesn't help.

Her thoughts drift to her father, the creeping shadow of his inevitable death. And then she thinks of her mother, how suddenly she was gone and how helpless Elsa felt after. Horrified, afraid, and now she'd never find out if Deb actually *had* loved her, if she'd just plain hated her, or something in between.

To this day, Elsa can still feel the smack of her mother's hand all over her body, yet she can also feel the gentle caress of the same hand during the last minutes before sleep. She can smell the fresh tang of blood inside her closet, and she can smell the sweet cocoa brewed for a pair of frozen-fingered sisters on winter afternoons. She can hear her mother's thundering approach, and she can hear the same woman's soft footsteps recede after a tender good night.

How can you make sense of a person who confuses suffering and love, with such devastating results?

No one can.

And yet, somehow, Elsa does.

She sees it. Feels it. Remembers it.

Power is bartered for survival. Survival traded for love. And despite the costs, after each beating, the conversation between you goes forward as if you might still find your way to a truce. But regardless of what is said—before, during, or after—the real currency of the negotiation between violence and its cessation is dread, the knowledge that it will inevitably happen again. That's the trap. You can't talk your way out of it, or wish your way out of it, or forgive your way out of it, though you can try and try and try. And through it all, you crazily hope that there is still a sun up there capable of casting warmth, even on you, if you could just get to a clearing where it could find you. Which it never does. Or hasn't yet. And you are always, always cold. And the scars don't go away. And despite your best intentions, you will apparently never stop replicating the unfathomable punishments of your childhood.

Elsa knew without knowing as a child that her mother's love for her fed on a cycle of violence and guilt. Her whole life, torn and bruised as she fled past the husks of memory, she pecked at any sweet kernel that tumbled out. (*That* is her corn maze. How did Lex read her so well?)

With each blow comes the abnegation of another chunk of your self.

Your weakness is her strength.

His strength.

His *power*.

A spark ignites and Elsa sees it: Sammy Nelson's drive to vanquish girls in groups of three sets off fireworks in her mind, a flaring symmetry that reveals the contours of his childhood. Why, she wonders, didn't he learn to resist it? To hurt himself instead of others?

23

The kitchen wallpaper is decorated with vertical rows of yellow teapots tilting right and left, alternating like leaves up a vine. Deb stands at the stove in her apron, stirring something in a big pot. Soup, or stew; she is an excellent cook. You sit at the table, doing homework, on the verge of solving a vexing math problem. Tara sits cross-legged under the table with her Barbies, which have decided to throw a party and use your feet as furniture.

"Get *off*." You kick the dolls away.

Tara wails, "*Mom*. Elsa *kicked* me."

"No, I kicked your stupid Barbie."

"Mommy…" Tara whines.

"I'm trying to do homework," you protest. "She should take her dolls somewhere else."

Deb looks over her shoulder, annoyance glowering. "Can't you just move your work over?"

"Why should I? I was here first."

"Because you're the oldest, and you're supposed to be the mature one."

You continue your work, pretending not to hear. Your heart races but you stay put, stubborn to the core. Because it isn't fair. It isn't fair. It isn't fair.

Deb repeats, "Move down."

"Mommy says *move,*" Tara echoes from below.

If you press the pencil harder into the page, the gray darkens and the numbers grow bold. Mrs. Fisher will appreciate that.

Even before it starts, you know what's coming. The metal cooking spoon whacks hard against the back of your neck and then, when you turn to face your mother so she can see your eyes at the moment of her cruelty, it slams your shoulder. There will be bruises, maybe blood, depending on how long she keeps it up this time.

Pain carries the report of a new attack quickly through your nerves, lighting you up with an impulse to bolt, but your brain is ready. You rarely run anymore because Deb always catches up with you, and sometimes it's easier just to get it over with. At eleven, you've *grown up* and *accepted your punishment,* though punishment for what, you're still unsure, except that it has something to do with your innate badness or wrongness or nastiness or all of the above.

The reddish-brownish sauce splatters across the kitchen with every strike before Deb runs out of gas. This time, eight in all, two short of the usual ten.

You learn another lesson: with endurance comes progress.

By the end of it, Tara has snuck away with her Barbies. Your homework has been ruined with sauce from the stew. And Deb, who has exhausted herself, has retreated to her room with a glass of wine. You clean up the kitchen, change your clothes, and redo your math on a fresh sheet of paper.

When your father gets home from work, he kisses you on the cheek and asks how your day has gone. "Fine," you tell him. But you know that he knows, because he has to, doesn't he? The kitchen is too clean for this hour of the day, the house too quiet, everyone in a different room.

24

I t has something to do with his sisters," Elsa says.

The faces of her fellow investigators come into focus, turning to her with surprise as if she'd left the room and barged back in with an interruption. She *had* left the room, in a way; she'd zoned out deeply enough to miss a whole section of their conversation.

Lex asks, "What?"

"His sisters bullied him—three sisters. He could be reenacting something."

"Or reinventing it," Joan says, in energized agreement, "for a better outcome in which he's less hurt. He's scratching an unsatisfiable itch, for the third time."

An unsatisfiable itch. Yes, that's it. Elsa's skin electrifies with understanding, telling her they're on the right track. This is how it always happens. This is the feeling she gets when the pieces of a case start to fit. Lex was right—it's why she's so good at this work, and why it's so painful. Her skin tells her when a child is within her reach, her unstoppable, unfixable skin.

Elsa turns back to the list of girls. She pulls up all their Facebook pages and arranges them across her screen: rows of moody teenagers. Thinking aloud, she says, "Wouldn't it make sense that he'd play this out close to home? *Home* being the operable concept for a guy whose sisters tormented him. This one girl, Hope Martin-Creech, disappeared the very morning that Ishmael Locke went shopping in her town— Bennington, Vermont, just across the border from Sammy Nelson's upstate cabin."

A click and there is a happy selfie Hope recently posted on Facebook. Her wide smile defies a tapered chin. Lank dirty-blond hair, angled at her jaw, a flyaway wisp off her forehead. Pale brown eyes. Freckles sprinkled across her cheeks and nose. Tattoos of impish figures climbing one side of her neck. "Sixteen. Tenth grade. Lives with her parents and two younger brothers. Good student, no boyfriend, no drugs, no problems. Hasn't been seen since Monday morning when she left for school."

"It makes sense to me," Joan agrees.

Lex says, "Me too."

"We've got DNA profiles from some of the hair samples in the van," Owen says. "Let's see if we can get a sample from this Hope girl. See if there's a match."

Lex says, "If she's not on file, then maybe her parents have her hairbrush. I'll make some calls."

"No," Elsa says, "I'll do it."

Reaching for her phone, she uncrosses her legs abruptly and feels a warm, wet trickle along her shin. It's happened before: the wound weeping too generously for the bandage to hold. Most women fear getting their period on white pants in front of other people. Elsa? Her blood has been known to flow embarrassingly from anywhere.

"You okay?" The way Lex is looking at her, like a concerned brother. He reads her too well.

"Fine." The phone is already ringing. There's no time to get to the bathroom so she reaches down to adjust the bandage, if only temporarily. Her call is answered halfway through the first ring.

A woman's voice, thin with distress: *"Hello?"*

"Is this Mrs. Martin-Creech, Hope's mother?"

"Yes."

"I don't want to alarm you, Mrs. Martin-Creech, but this is Elsa Myers, I'm with the FBI and I'm calling because—"

The woman says to someone near her, "Ernie—it's the FBI."

A man comes on the line: "This is Detective Sergeant Ernie Bennett."

Elsa introduces herself. "We're looking for a seventeen-year-old girl missing from New York City since Friday, and we've connected her to someone who traveled from here to Bennington in the last twenty-four hours. This man, he's a known repeater, and we're concerned that—"

"You're calling about Hope."

Elsa's bandage breaks loose again; blood moves down her ankle. "Yes."

"She's been missing since yesterday," Bennett tells her, "and this morning we found two items of her jewelry in the woods near her house, so we figure she was in there at one point. Now, with what you're telling me, Special Agent..."

"Myers. If he does have Hope," she says, "then he's

probably got our girl too. In the past he took them in groups of three."

Bennett falls silent so abruptly, she suspects he's swallowing a curse he won't let loose in front of the frightened mother.

Holding the phone away from her mouth, Elsa asks Lex, "How fast can you get us a copter?"

Lex answers, "Right away."

"Do it."

To Detective Sergeant Bennett, she says, "Hold tight, we'll be there as soon as we can."

25

#getmethefuckoutofhere, Mel types after uploading the selfie of her blazing-red cheek, deleting the addendum #hatemymom because *that* just feels too harsh. But still. *Post.* And now the cold fact that her mother just slapped her, hard, is out into the vast cyber-cloudy nether-space of whereverness that is Facebook. Part of the conversation. Feels good and right for one split second and then embarrassment sets in.

Delete.

High noon in the hospital parking lot, bright and unfiltered. Mel holds a hand over her eyes and contemplates her next move. She'd stomped down the hall with her mother chasing her saying "You can't leave when Gramp is about to die!" actually saying *die* in her mad voice right there on the cancer ward where everyone really *is* dying and no one needs that kind of tell-it-like-it-is reminder practically shouted in the hallways because it is what it is and they already *know* that. Mel knows Gramp is dying but he isn't dying *today*.

"Well, Mom, you fucking *hit me*."

"Shhhh."

"You don't want anyone to hear about it but you didn't mind *doing it*."

Ding and the elevator door opened and Mel stepped in and pressed the close-doors button over and over until they finally closed. Her mother just standing there looking shocked that her sweet little daughter would actually leave.

Her mother has never hit her before.

Her aunt has never betrayed her trust before.

Adults are such hypocrites.

She'll go back to the city. Live her *own* life in a way that feels honest.

She swipes her phone for an Uber and, presto, up drives a blue car. Great app. You don't have to wait.

She doesn't see an Uber sign anywhere but the window rolls down and the driver looks at her through his sunglasses and nods so she knows it's her ride. She leans into the air-conditioning, says, "Train station," and gets into the backseat. Some button he's got pinned to his shirt glints for just a second; it's a face, but she can't see whose.

The car curves out of the parking lot and she feels good, really good, making a break for it. The look on her mother's face when the elevator doors closed. She'll head to a friend's place, not home—scare her mother, just overnight.

After about ten minutes she notices fields, not buildings. "Excuse me, sir? Isn't the train station the other way, in town?"

His face looks sweaty, and now she notices a nasty scratch down one side. His left hand stays on the wheel while his right elbow crooks over the seat and he half turns for a quick look at her. When he smiles, a bend in his nose flattens out, but it isn't really a smile. He says, "There's a better train station in the next town."

She doesn't know how one train station can be better than another unless it's closer. But she doesn't ask. This guy gives her the creeps. Just so long as he gets her there.

She thumbs a text to Charlie: Can you meet me Met steps one hour? She should be back in the city by then.

Her mother called him a drug dealer, *but* she doesn't want his drugs and she only sort of likes him, but *still,* if she can get a selfie with him and throw it onto Facebook and *not* delete it, *well,* guess who wins round one? Her mother didn't listen when Mel told her it was a stupid mistake and wouldn't happen again. She just wouldn't listen.

yup will be there

cool

So that's set.

She feels the car swerve to a stop and looks up, expecting they'll be at the train station. But they're not. They are nowhere—not even a house in the distance. The bright blue sky from before has gone all gray, like rain is coming, like they've entered a different world.

He turns around fast, his arm reaching all the way back to snatch her phone right out of her hand. "I like you," he says, and he hurls it out the window.

"What the fuck!"

The back of his hand slams against her cheek so hard, she feels each knobby bone of his knuckles. Pain spitfires through her face, into her brain, silencing her.

"Met your aunt yesterday"—lifting his sunglasses, showing

her his eyes—"she was looking for you. Gotta say, you made this pretty easy; usually I have to work harder to get my girl. Only one hospital in Sleepy Hollow. And you—you got right into my car."

She recognizes him now: that weird guy from Ruby's house who watched them, Auntie Elsa whispering, "Shhh."

A worm uncoils in her stomach.

With a click, he locks the doors from up front. She rattles the handle but it won't budge. He jerks the steering wheel and speeds back onto the road.

26

Faded white clapboard, chipped black shutters, a saggy porch. The Martin-Creech house would look neglected if not for the well-tended flower beds seaming the front walk with vibrant color. Deb was also that kind of gardener, Elsa remembers, keen on decorating the outlines. A FOR SALE sign is staked on a front lawn glistening wet from a quick rain amid the familiar chaos of neighbors and visitors who have gathered to help search for Hope.

Every time Elsa thinks that—*search for Hope, look for Hope, hunt for Hope, find Hope*—the banal phrases confront an awful reality. Hope, in this case, is an actual girl, the second girl in a week to go missing at Nelson's hand, her hair now positively identified in his van along with Ruby's and the hair of two of the girls missing since 2012.

Elsa glances around at the hive of state troopers, local detectives, FBI agents, neighbors, and strangers who have come to join the search, and she flashes back to yesterday at the Haverstocks. *Scar tissue,* she thinks; families and communities surging together to heal an unexpected injury. Lex and Joan stand beside her, taking it in.

Just arrived, she group-texts Owen Tate and Rosie Santiago, who stayed behind in New York. How's it going there? Elsa doesn't envy them their task of contacting the families of those long-lost missing girls, ripping off the old scabs, poking a finger into the wounds. Asking questions and offering nothing but hopeless answers.

Rosie responds: Painful. You?

Circus, zoo, are the first words that spring to mind, but Elsa plugs the defensive sarcasm. Instead, she types, Still getting the lay of the land.

Startled by a weight across her shoulders, she looks up from her phone and there is Joan Bailey administering a sideward hug. Elsa doesn't know what to say; she doesn't know if she likes the unexpected affection or if it crosses a boundary. Both, maybe. Fresh off a helicopter flight during which they chatted about irrelevant things, the two women numbing themselves with words while Lex shifted his focus between his phone and the obscurity of passing clouds, Elsa realizes now that that was not idle conversation. Joan had been sussing her out, therapizing her.

Joan says, "I see an agent I know over there. He might have some insight." The behavioral psychologist looks at Elsa with the kind of contemplative pause, ever so slight, that expresses an unspoken request for consent to step away.

"Go ahead." Elsa keeps her tone level, professional, despite a spark of emotion.

Joan crosses the lawn toward a pair of men, one in uniform.

Lex asks, "What was that?"

Ignoring his question, because she doesn't know what it was, not really, she says, "Let's get started."

They go in search of Detective Sergeant Ernie Bennett but cross paths with a tall woman who stops when she sees them. An inch of gray roots borders the center part of her blond hair; her eyes droop, wet, heavy.

"I'm Becky," the woman says. "Hope's mother. You must be Special Agent Myers from New York."

"Elsa, please. This is Detective Lex Cole, NYPD." As she reaches to shake the mother's hand, a wind gust lopes out of nowhere and she has to push hair out of her eyes and tug down a sleeve to fix herself.

"Thank you for coming," Becky says, "thank you so much, this has been such a nightmare."

"We understand," Elsa says. "We're going to do everything we can to help find your daughter. Becky, I know this is awful for you, but do you mind if we jump right in?"

"Please."

"You've been shown the mug shots?"

Becky nods. "I didn't recognize him."

Just then a school bus pulls up and discharges a pair of blond boys, one slightly taller than the other. They wear matching blue backpacks. One has neon-orange sneakers, the other's are green. They shout hellos to their mother, drop their backpacks at her feet, and, ignoring the clumps of people on their lawn, run to the driveway, where a basketball hoop is attached to the front of the garage. A ball is quickly produced and a game started.

Elsa says, "We should speak with Detective Bennett."

"He was in the kitchen a little while ago," Becky offers, "unless he's back out in the field."

In the field. Already she's adopted the lingo of a search.

Becky sighs. Picks up her sons' backpacks. "Check the house first?"

"Sure," Elsa answers. Restless to find the detective, who probably *is* back in the field by now, but also feeling pulled by the family, the sense that there is always something important to learn on the inside. Knowing that houses, and mothers, are rarely as they appear on the surface.

They follow Becky into a comfortable, lived-in kitchen with pushed-aside piles of paper competing with gadgets and condiments for counter space. Ernie Bennett is not there.

Becky catches Elsa glancing at the fridge where the family's last holiday card is prominently displayed: red plaid border, holly boughs, and bells; a tall, handsome father smiling beside his well-groomed wife, their poised teenage daughter, and the two grinning boys. "Tim's a pilot for United," she says. "He was based out of Boston until last year, when they switched him to Chicago."

"That why you're selling the house?" Lex asks.

"He's hardly ever home. We thought it would give us more time together if we moved there."

Elsa asks, "Where is he now?"

"En route here from Anchorage. He's worried sick." In an instant, she seems to melt. "I don't know how much longer I can take this. That other girl... what did that man do to her?"

"We don't know." As for what Elsa guesses he did, she won't say.

"Do you really think there's a chance Hope is…okay?"

"Definitely." An exaggeration, but it's in everyone's interest to bolster Becky's optimism.

"Maybe Ernie's upstairs," Becky says.

They follow her up a carpeted, bending staircase. No Bennett, but Elsa can't help pausing in Hope's room. It's small and full, the walls painted a faded lilac and covered with whimsical pencil drawings. The intricate illustrations are everywhere that's not blocked by bed, dresser, desk, or bookshelf. A copious assortment of stuffed animals crowd her headboard. On her nightstand, a ceramic bowl is filled with a tangle of rings and bracelets, and a jewelry tree is strung with a webbing of necklaces. By the position of a bookmark, she is halfway through *A Confederacy of Dunces,* presumably for school, unless she's an independent reader.

"I tried to stop her from drawing on the walls when she was little," Becky says, noticing their interest, "but it was useless, so I just let her go at it. I've grown to really like them. I wish there was some way we could take the walls with us when we move."

"She's got talent, that's for sure." Lex steps up for a close look at a group of little figures on a boat, mobilizing to fight a giant wave.

Elsa follows his gaze and before she knows it is pulled into Hope's imaginings, they're drawn with such conviction—the way a tiny hand raises to the monster wave as if to halt it, the bend of a little arm over eyes to block the terrifying sight, a face buried in a cage of spiny fingers, and the one rushing gleefully into the arc of water with a surfboard. That subversive act of resistance speaks to Elsa's heart; she doesn't know this girl, this young artist, and probably never will, but suddenly her desire to reach her before it's too late colludes dangerously with her anxieties over Ruby and her father and Mel, who still hasn't returned her call. Elsa can't save Roy from the disease that's consuming him, unsell the house, or force Mel to forgive her and pick up the phone—she can't pull back time and with it Tara's hand—and she can't uncut her skin this morning, but if she can save these lost, presumably injured girls...if she *can*...if Ruby and Hope at least can have a future, then maybe...maybe what? The impulse lingers in the back of Elsa's mind like an unfinished sentence and all she can think to say to Hope's mother is, "She could be a graphic novelist when she grows up."

"If she wants to. Why not?"

Elsa says, "She has a strong imagination," thinking that that's a good thing. Maybe she fought Nelson. Maybe she's struggling, internally, to keep hold.

Becky settles her hand on a biology textbook open on the desk. "She had a test on Monday. She was up late studying the night before."

A boy's voice sails in from outside—"Mo-ommm!"—and Becky's whole body reacts. She throws open Hope's window. "What is it, Sam?"

"We didn't know where you were."

"I'm right here. Down in a minute, okay?" She leaves the window open onto a lush view of blue hydrangeas. "The boys go back and forth between trying to pretend nothing's happening and worrying they'll lose me next. Look around all you want. I've got to get back outside. If I see Ernie I'll tell him you're here."

As soon as Becky's gone, Elsa says to Lex, "Let's go find him."

He nods but continues to study the wall illustrations. "These pictures are so—" he begins but is interrupted by Elsa's ringing phone.

She glances at the incoming number, tells Lex, "I'll catch up with you outside."

He leaves and she sits on the edge of Hope's bed, her weight sinking into the soft mattress. Feeling that she shouldn't be here, but that she can't pull herself away.

"Agent Myers?" A young man's voice, familiar, deep yet uncertain.

"Charlie?"

"You said to call if I thought of anything else."

"I'm listening."

"It's not about Ruby, though, and maybe I shouldn't have bothered you, but I thought—"

"Just say it."

"Mel was supposed to meet me and she never showed up. I've been calling her but she doesn't answer."

"I don't understand—you made plans with Mel since I saw you?"

"*She* texted *me!*"

"When?"

"Right after I left the police station. She asked me to meet her on the steps of the Met. I don't know why, but I said I'd go; I mean, I *like* her. Anyway, maybe she just blew me off. I wouldn't blame her. But to be honest, I'm kind of paranoid now about not telling you everything, know what I mean?"

"Thanks, Charlie."

"Should I call you if I hear from her?"

"Yes. Yes, please do."

Trembling, Elsa dials Mel and leaves another message: "Mellie, will you *please* call me?"

Next, she tries Tara, who answers with "Did you get my message?"

"Yes, I got it. How's Dad doing?"

"The same. Elsa, I can't believe this, all of it, happening all at once, and I—"

Elsa blurts out, "You *hit* her? You actually fucking *hit* her!"

"I reacted. I was upset. I'm her mother and—"

"I can't talk to you about this right now" is the best Elsa can come up with in lieu of the venom simmering on her tongue. No child deserves to be hit when it isn't in self-defense. But this isn't the time to explain that to her self-righteous, martyred, pampered sister. "I just wanted to make sure she's with you."

"She's at the hotel."

"You saw her there?"

"I've been here all day, with Dad. She stormed out of here like a, like a…well, I just assume she's at the hotel. Where else would she be?"

"Call her. If she doesn't answer, call the hotel. If she doesn't answer the room phone, call the front desk and ask them to go into the room."

"Why?"

Elsa doesn't want to invoke Charlie's name; there's no time for Tara's drama. "Just do it."

"Fine. I'll do it. But—"

"Call me after." Elsa hangs up.

Flames of worry lick the edges of her determination not to worry, to keep things in perspective, on the principle that 95 percent of the time, people worry over nothing. Tara will call back and report that Mel has been stewing in the hotel room all day, maybe racking up a big bill on room service in revenge. Elsa feels satisfaction in believing that Mel won't have taken being hit lightly. Mel will have reacted, rejected. Unlike Elsa, who quietly absorbed every assault.

She goes outside to look for Lex and is immediately drawn by the unmistakable sound of Greenberg's voice booming across the lawn. Lex is with him.

"Yello!" Greenberg greets her. "I hear our Mr. Ishmael Locke has himself a different real name."

"Unfortunately," she answers, "that's how it's turning out."

Lex asks Greenberg, "That him?" in continuation of a conversation Elsa missed. Greenberg nods his large bushy head.

"Yup, that's Ernie. Known each other since we were kids. That's how I know Sang McCracken, since you mentioned it." Another reference to something Elsa must have missed. "Met Sang at one of Ernie's annual Fourth of July barbecues."

Striding across the lawn in their direction, the local detective looks like any friendly dad in baggy jeans, sneakers, and a fleece zipper-vest over a T-shirt. But when he speaks, the sharp clip of his words betrays an efficiency you learn only on the job.

"You the folks from New York City?"

Elsa introduces herself. Their hands meet, both gripping harder and a moment longer than necessary. She asks, "Anything new since we spoke?"

"Unfortunately, no. We've got a task force put together in town. Why don't you folks come in with what you have; we'll put everything on the table and see what we can make of it."

To Lex, Elsa says, "Let's find Joan. She'll want to be there."

The three investigators pile into Elsa's rental car and head toward town along verdurous country roads. On the way, Elsa's cell marimbas a call from Tara. Driving, she says to Lex, "Answer that and put it on speaker. It's my sister."

"Okay." He fishes in her bag and finds her phone.

Tara wails, *"Mel's gone."*

"You're sure?"

"She isn't in our room. She never even went to the hotel. She isn't with any of her friends and she won't answer my calls. I don't know what to do now." Tara groans. "How do I find her? How did you know she wouldn't be there, Elsa?"

"I didn't know. I was hoping she'd be with you."

"She isn't. What do I do now? And don't tell me that teenagers take off sometimes. Some do, some don't—and Mel doesn't."

"I'm going to trace her cell phone," Elsa promises. "I'll call you as soon as I find out where she is."

"You didn't answer me. How did you know to ask me?"

"Talk to you later." Elsa hangs up and catches a glimpse of her phone's wallpaper photo before Lex drops the cell back into her bag: Mel at four, dressed all in princess pink, waving a sparkly plastic star-topped scepter that Elsa bought as a gift. Everyone starts innocent and sweet. Everyone.

"Your niece?" Joan asks from the backseat.

"Yes."

"How old?"

"Sixteen."

Lex asks, "When did this happen?"

"That's why Charlie called me before. Mel asked him to meet her at the Metropolitan Museum at about one. She never showed."

"And he actually went out of his way to let you know?" Lex says.

"Scared him before, I guess."

Elsa and Lex and Joan lapse into silence as they near the Bennington station house. Little explosions of heat pop along Elsa's skin as she struggles to convince herself that her niece's absence and the girls' abductions are completely uncon-nected. She steadies her breath and refuses to allow fear to overtake her, reminding herself that Mel's silence is probably intended as punishment for betraying her trust about the drugs. The kid's pissed; who wouldn't be? That's all it is. Nothing bad has happened to Mellie.

But each time one of those girls fell off the radar, wasn't there a plausible explanation at first? She's busy. Her phone's battery ran out. You hurt her, offended her, ignored her, and now it's your turn to see how it feels. And then, suddenly, she isn't ignoring you—she's gone.

27

Mel knows that she was in a forest before and that now she's in a cave: musty damp in her nose and on her face and seeping through her clothes.

At first, when he takes off the blindfold, she can't see anything. The complete darkness is blacker than anything she's ever experienced, a not-seeing that confuses her. Then, gradually, her eyes adjust, which must mean light is filtering in from somewhere.

He pushes her down so she's sitting and she feels sharp rocks through the ass of her jeans. Her bound wrists pull tighter in this position.

"Why are you doing this to me?"

"Say hello to your sisters."

"I don't have any sisters. I'm an only child. I'm—"

"Shut up."

The way he says it, she does.

She starts to make out shapes in the granular light. He's crossed the room and is hunched over something—a toolbox, she thinks, its red color shining through the dull lightlessness of the cave. Something yellow and crumpled near the red box: a nest of rough fabric. A towel, she thinks. Half off the towel, a book.

"Damn it." He slams shut his toolbox. Lifts the towel, looking for something. The book flips over: *The Invisible Man*. A curl of panic as she remembers she's supposed to read the other one, the Ralph Ellison one, this summer for next year's English and she was actually looking forward to it, but now...

"What's that about?" Thinking that maybe she can get his mind off whatever tool he's found missing, if that's what just upset him. She doesn't like that he's looking for tools at all, considering. "The book you're reading. I mean, it's so dark in here, how do you read? Unless you have a flashlight."

"I do have a flashlight, since you asked."

"What's the book about?"

Hunched on bent legs, he flattens a hand on the ground to steady himself. Looks at her, his button catching stray light again so this time she can see the face of a little girl. "A scientist uses optics to alter his refractive index so that no one else can see him. That's what he tries to do, but it doesn't work out. This is the third time I've read it. Great book."

"I like to read too. I mean, sometimes not even for school. I like to read in this one chair we have in the living room right next to the window."

"Not me. I like privacy, quiet."

"I like the light from the window."

"My room was the best spot. I put a sign on my door that said *Quiet Zone* but they just ripped it down."

"Who did?"

"Excuse me." An electric undercurrent in his tone now. He stands abruptly, crouching under the cave ceiling. "I left the nails in the car."

She makes out the whites of his eyes shifting in her direction, stopping when they land on her. He thinks a moment and then he reaches for something, a coil of rope, which he pulls out of a shadow. He ties her ankles together and says, "No funny business while I'm gone."

"I don't have any sisters," she says.

He hunches across the cave quickly. She hears something rip. He returns with a piece of duct tape and presses it hard on her mouth, his large hand covering her nose, and she can't breathe.

She can't breathe.

Then he lets go and dank air surges into her nose.

He crosses the cave again and clicks open his toolbox and suddenly a flashlight beam emanates from his hand. He waves it around the cave, saying, "Take a look. Those are your sisters."

The light lands on the back of a girl lying on her side, brown hair pooled at her neck, the long gentle slope from her shoulder to her waist, her legs ranged long across the rocky dirt floor, cinched at the ankles by filthy rope. Mel watches the back of the girl's ribs, waiting to see them move, looking for even the tiniest evidence of breathing.

The beam jerks to a part of the cave she didn't notice before. In the near-total darkness, the flashlight illuminates another girl. Frazzled blond hair, tattoos up one side of her neck. Bound and connected to some kind of noose that forces her to pitch forward. The rope around her wrists is entwined with several bracelets: the rubber kind they give out at school events, this one yellow, a charm bracelet, and some metal ones, the kind that jangle. Her wide eyes stare fiercely at Mel. When she realizes that Mel sees her, she blinks. Mel blinks in response.

"Chill, girls." He moves toward the mouth of the tunnel until it swallows him and he's all but gone except for his voice, trailing. "When I get back, we are gonna have some fun."

Near the tunnel's entry sits a stack of wood planks—is that what he needs the nails for? *Is he planning to seal them in?* Only when she can't hear him anymore does her brain stop spinning, and then a different, more frantic kind of panic twitches through her. She breathes as loudly as she can through her nose, in and out and in and out, trying to communicate with the other girl. The one who's still alive. When the girl reciprocates in kind, Mel's eyes flood and she drops her head forward and forces herself to stop crying. If her nose gets stuffed she won't be able to breathe, and she won't make it through the next ten minutes.

28

The pillared limestone building in the center of town temporarily housing the local task force reminds Elsa of an old country bank: ornate ceilings and tall windows opening onto a pastoral view. And the windows are clean, sparkling with sunlight. It's nice here, really nice, and yet the realization that she's more at home in the cramped-space, grimy-windowed fogginess of the city makes her feel urban, ruined, and separate. She can't stop thinking about what she did to herself this morning, cutting her leg. A scab is starting to form—she feels the tight pull across her skin—but nonetheless, beneath the film of healing, the voracious jaws are already opening.

Bennett is talking, catching them up, and Elsa forces herself to pay attention. But she thinks and thinks and thinks about Mel. Who hasn't called anyone back. Whose cell signal has still not been triangulated with enough precision to pin down a location. All they've been able to ascertain so far is that the phone is still somewhere on the East Coast.

No, Elsa assures herself, *nothing has happened to Mel;* she's just headstrong, flipping her mother the bird. She doesn't realize how worried they are about her; if she knew, she'd get in touch.

"We know that right after Hope dropped the chalk," Bennett says, standing at an easel, peeling to a blank page, starting a new list, "she turned toward the woods. Seems we can all agree that that edge of the woods is too densely traversed to pick out individual footprints, but given that the first ring, the copper one, was dropped five hundred yards in, when two sets of tracks are consistent, we know that he led her from the road into the woods. Deeper in, we find the second ring, the glass one." Purple, which according to Becky is often worn on Hope's right forefinger. "So we're guessing he's got her cuffed, and she's dropping rings because she can."

Holding the scrap of blue chalk in the palm of her hand, Elsa wonders how the girl managed to reach into her pocket to get it. But of course, that's assuming she had it in her pocket to begin with, or that she even had a pocket; maybe she was holding it in her hand when he took her. Elsa can see it: The animated Hope who has come alive in her mind—part herself, part Ruby, part Mel, a girl built of impressions—moving languidly toward school, in no hurry, having missed the bus anyway. An idea enters her thoughts. About to draw, she digs into her pocket for the chalk and then …what? Sammy Nelson, aka Ishmael Locke, appears in front of her. How does he do it? Does he ask for directions? Or does he come from behind and surprise her? If he surprises her, she drops the chalk before she manages to slip off the first ring. She's smart and intuitive enough to already be thinking about dropping clues. She's right about him. But why doesn't she run? Or does she try?

Without thinking, Elsa reaches down to scratch her leg, and then she corrects the impulse by folding her hands together on the table. She looks at her phone, faceup beside her. It doesn't ring.

"There are caves in these woods," Bennett finishes, "and we think there's a good chance he's got her—or them—in one of them. So that's where we are." He turns to the New York contingent, seated together across the table.

Elsa takes the lead, fast-forwarding through Ruby's disappearance and its connection to Sammy Nelson, who he is, what he's done in the past, and her theory as to his modus operandi. Bennett's people pay close attention, taking in the seriousness of how the two cases appear to be converging. And then the ruminative silence is interrupted by an old-fashioned ringtone that spills from Bennett's cell phone.

He listens, nods, hangs up. Announces: "Someone's turned up at the house with another piece of Hope's jewelry."

A rush to the door as they all hurry back to their cars.

Elsa's nearly at her Beetle, its top bright in the blazing sun, when her cell rings—a caller with an upstate area code. She answers immediately, "Special Agent Myers," hoping it's Mel, or about Mel, or at least about the whereabouts of her phone.

Lex and Joan both wait with Elsa. Around them, investigators slam doors; engines rev, cars race out of the lot. Standing in the sun, blinded by its intensity, Elsa doesn't turn her eyes away. She'll take whatever pain is coming, absorb it, devour it, let it consume her. Joan puts on her sunglasses and Lex lifts a hand to shade his face, both standing protectively close as she listens.

A deep male voice says, "This is Trooper Sullivan. Got something for you on that girl's cell—the signal pings on Route Thirty-Two, just above New Paltz."

"Heading north?"

"Heading nowhere, actually. We watched it a solid five minutes and it's holding still. Thought it might be a rest stop but it isn't. It's a field."

"You found it?" She closes her eyes, trying to divine a sliver of metal in a field of green—a phone. Nestled in the hand of a girl, Mel. Just sitting there, the way kids do, absently texting her friends. Detached from time.

"Not yet, but we're still looking. Just wanted to keep you posted."

Elsa doesn't realize she's trembling until she's in the driver's seat, starting the engine, and feels the weight of Lex's hand on her arm. She shakes him off and drives, wondering how and when Nelson got to Mel. Flashing back to yesterday, walking past the tent, sensing that he was listening. What had they talked about? *Ruby, the gun, Allie—returning to the hospital in Sleepy Hollow.*

Tara's slap resonates on Elsa's own face; she knows exactly how Mel felt, why she bolted, and she wonders for the umpteenth time why she herself never ran when she could have. The poison of rage spreads and spreads until the road in front of her subsumes the past, and she's helpless, because what they did to each other then can't be undone, the seeds cannot be unplanted. The only way for Tara not to have slapped Mel would be if Mel had never been born. And the thought of that is worse than almost anything.

29

Hope opens her eyes—shivering, ravenous, thinking of Jackson.

Jackson is a boy from school. A boy Hope likes, and he knows it.

She'd been with him in her dream just now and shuts her eyes hard and tight, hoping to re-conjure him, but the mildew smell of here and now is too strong and he evaporates.

On the craggy wall behind where the freak was sitting on his towel before he went away, a scant trickle of water drips, drips, drips. Her dry-as-Hades mouth opens and, thirst beckoning, she wills a drop her way. Just one. But she isn't magic and it doesn't come and her animal thirst growls.

And then out of nowhere the other girl comes toward her, the new one, like a rickety tripod, on bound wrists and legs that have somehow come free. Her muddled voice fighting the tape over her mouth, struggling to say something. She looks so bad, so scared, so energized; how Hope felt when she arrived a million hours ago. When the first girl was still breathing. Before she knew that she, too, would die here in this cave. She feels her eyes pool and blinks them clear.

The new girl's face is damp and dirty and she's shaking her head like a dog out of a lake, drops flying. Telling Hope not to cry. That's nice of her, Hope thinks; maybe if they'd met some other time and place, they could have been friends.

The girl hunches over Hope's hands and with bloody stumps of cracked fingernails picks at the ropes. Hope understands; it's how the new girl got her own ankles free. Hope lifts her hands as much as she can, a quarter inch, before the lariat tightens around her neck.

It will never work; it will never work.

She thinks of Jackson, tries to will herself back to the dream. Focuses on what she can remember of his face: roundish cheeks, coppery skin (they say his mother is half American Indian), a natural flare to his nostrils that says *I don't care* but means *I'll be passionate about love when I find out what it is*. He's younger than her by a year. Taller than her by six inches, and she isn't short. She took a bite of his pizza last week and he laughed.

Snap.

Hope widens her eyes and nods and nods. The rope has suddenly gone slack, and she unfurls like a chick out of its shell.

The girl lifts her own hands—her bound, shaking hands. Angles her head, pleading.

Hope shakes out her arms and rotates her neck and kicks her feet and gets to work unknotting the girl's wrists.

30

Becky's hand is trembling, holding a yellow rubber bracelet stamped LIVE STRONG with the ST scratched out and a w etched above it. Broken, roughly, as if bitten apart. Streaked with blood. "She was wearing this yesterday when she left for school."

The young man who delivered it, thick blond hair and a trimmed beard, explains, "I found it at SVC, on campus."

Elsa has heard of Southern Vermont College but knows little about it other than that it occupies the former estate of a nineteenth-century industrialist somewhere in or near Bennington.

"I work part-time at Everett Mansion and sometimes, before I get into my car after work, I go into the woods. Take a walk. Clear my mind. Today something yellow caught my eye. It was bunched up with some pine needles. I've been hearing about that girl on the news and when I saw this, I had a feeling it was hers, or could be hers. And then I noticed something—it isn't wet, but it rained earlier today."

Realizing the possible significance of the find—that Hope might have dropped it recently, after the rain; that she could be on the move again, either with or without her captor—Elsa turns to Becky and asks, "How well does Hope know the woods?"

"We used to take long walks there," the mother answers, "so she knows it more or less."

The grid of Elsa's forehead tightens. Pulse races. Skin burns. This clever girl thinks for herself; she's a survivor. She dropped clues on purpose—and recently. And Mel, shrewd Mel, would bring ideas of her own. Strength in numbers, Elsa thinks; it's always best to have an ally.

People scatter into the woods, vast and green, and Elsa is moving to join them when she hears her name. She turns and finds Lex facing her, his arms crossed over his chest. His smile isn't encouraging; he's tilting his head. Next to him, Joan stands in perfectly poised professional neutrality. Elsa knows what they're going to say before they say it—she can read it in their eyes—and she's ready for them.

"Elsa," Lex says, "we think you should sit this out."

"No."

"This is personal for you now," Joan says softly, "your niece—"

"No way."

"You can't be clearheaded," Joan argues. "Your judgment will be impaired. Sweetie, no one can operate on all cylinders when a loved one's at risk."

It's the *sweetie* that gets her. One thing Elsa has never been is sweet. She says, "There is no fucking way I'm going to sit this out," and turns toward the woods.

31

The staircase bends at the middle, the two parts joined by a small landing with a window looking out onto the backyard where your old swing set has grown rusty. Only Tara uses it now, occasionally. You have other concerns.

School has gotten harder. There's a boy you like who might possibly like you back. One friend got her period for the first time. Another girl's parents are splitting up. There is a lot for your friends to deal with without adding your own problems into the mix, and besides, what would you say?

Sitting on the lower half of the stairs, fresh from a bout with your mother, you try out excuses for the bruise that might appear on your cheekbone where she hit you with the back of her hand.

"I didn't mean to hit your face," she said. "You moved."

To which you replied, idiotically, "I'm sorry."

You still don't know why *you* apologized to *her,* but in some odd way it feels right. This is a kind of problem you wouldn't know how to begin to discuss with your friends. And so you don't.

The front door opens and Roy walks in. His smile fades when he sees your face. Normally the first thing he asks is "Where's your mother?" but not tonight. He puts down his bag, hangs his coat on the bottom curl of the banister, and sits beside you on your step midway up the first section of staircase.

He says, "Do you want to tell me what happened, Elsie?"

"Why does it matter?" Without acrimony. The truth at the core of your rhetorical question is apparent to both of you. It doesn't matter why it happens. Anything can trigger it. That it happens, and happens, and happens is a fact of your life.

You shrug your shoulders.

Your father sighs.

You've grown too old for him to avoid the question of his culpability, and he says, "If we got a divorce, would you come with me?"

Your heart dances. "Are you? Getting a divorce?"

"It's really just a hypothetical question."

You look at him; you don't quite understand that word.

"I'm just thinking aloud," he clarifies, "wondering what would happen *if*."

Oh. That means that nothing is changing here. Still, you want him to know: "Yes, I would."

"The only reason I stay is to protect you and Tara."

"But she doesn't hit Tara."

"And between you and me," he says, "we're going to make sure she never does. Right?"

"Right, Daddy." You allow him to take your hand. His,

so warm. Something doesn't feel right, but you can't put your finger on it. Finally, you ask, "How does it protect me, though?"

"As long as I'm here, you know you've always got an ally, a friend, nearby. You aren't alone. My eyes are open. I know— we all know—that she takes her anger out on you, honey."

You feel cold, even with his hand still holding yours. He squeezes, as if he senses you drifting and wants to stop you from floating away.

You ask, "Why me?"

"I think it's because you're special." A small, loving smile that you drink in. "You're feisty, you speak your mind, you argue back. And you know what?"

You look at him. It feels like watching a commercial on TV, half of you wanting to believe, the other half holding back.

"You're strong. She can't break you, no matter what."

"My face hurts so much, though."

His eyes squint, inspecting your cheek. "It's not too bad. Listen, do you want to go out to dinner with me tonight? Just the two of us? We can talk about whatever you want to."

You jump at the chance. But over dinner at the local diner, conversation falters; you end up finishing your grilled cheese sandwich mostly in silence, and both of you forgo dessert.

32

Bright daylight weakened by the density of trees, their summer-lush branches arcing high in a forest ceiling. Day becomes artificial evening, and, the farther in Elsa walks, evening becomes premature night punctuated by dreamlike flashes of sunshine. Outside sounds are absorbed by bird chatter, insect chirps, breeze-fluttered leaves, the searchers' footsteps soft on a thick carpet of moss and pine needles. Elsa and her group walk, armed, intent, as if connected by an invisible rope of their breathing. As if language has been reduced to only three words, voices repeat, "Ruby!" "Hope!" "Mel!" in an echoing cacophony. Every now and then a voice from somewhere else in the woods intrudes sharply, an unseen searcher, and each time they stop to listen for a note of urgency. Greenberg's voice, in particular, a howl.

A siren crescendos into the now-distant parking lot. An ambulance, at the ready. Dread burrows into Elsa. She takes a deep breath and forges ahead, leading her small group with the map, as if she can read it when her mind is spinning circles around the professionalism she struggles to yoke into place. Maybe Lex and Joan were right, maybe she should recuse herself, since Nelson's crimes have gotten personal. Maybe. But she can't stop. She just can't, now more than ever.

When the beaten path feels limiting, she veers off the trail, and the members of her group scatter into the brush. She ignores the thorny branches slapping at her, tearing her sleeves, and scans every inch of the forest for the girls. Trying not to think about the possibility that Sammy Nelson could be out there too.

Not realizing at first that she's separated from her search party, she reemerges onto the trail and finds herself with a different group, this one including Lex. The side of his neck has a bloody gash. They lock eyes a moment and continue on together.

Half a mile west of their starting point, Elsa's and Lex's phones vibrate simultaneously. Elsa pulls hers out of her pocket and sees that it's a text from Ernie Bennett.

Found it, Everett's Cave, northwest of the mansion.

Elsa responds: Anyone there?

Ruby.

Not Ruby alive, or Ruby dead. Just Ruby.

They have to clamber over jutting stones and then stoop into a narrow opening in order to enter the cave. Then a climb down takes them into darkness, weakly illuminated by Bennett's flashlight. The dark void pulls around Elsa. The mossy damp. The resonant *drip-drip-drip* that grows louder as they proceed.

Bennett shifts his beam upward. "The CSI techs just got here." The dripping is so close now, it gives off echoes.

On the second level, a nest of flowstones and dripping stalactites. Only a shred of natural light finds its way in. Bennett waves his beam back and forth over the cave to show them, but it's hard to see much of anything until one of the two techs setting up their work area switches on a floodlight. Elsa's stomach bucks when she sees it:

The stack of lumber Nelson loaded into the van at Greenberg's

A filthy towel

A roll of duct tape with a jagged ripped end

A cigarette lighter, orange

An empty Styrofoam cup lying on its side near the towel

A pair of rusty scissors

An unopened bag of carabiner hooks

A coil of steel rope

A flashy new toolbox

A small black handgun that looks identical to the one Elsa saw in Peter Haverstock's workshop.

The Invisible Man

A sticky-looking thread of something half dried, reddish, leads Elsa's eye across the cave.

To Ruby.

A wax girl.

Elsa's brain twists and twists; her heart plummets.

They are too late.

Days and hours and minutes *too late*.

Her mind pulls away from her body, like it used to when she was a girl, allowing her to observe the horror from a safe distance. Or a distance, at least. The last time this happened, her mother was dead in front of her. She squeezes her eyes shut and forces her parts back together.

Bennett crouches beside Ruby and says, quietly, as if he doesn't want the lifeless girl to hear, "We think she's been gone between four and twenty-four hours. She's still in rigor mortis."

Lex silently directs his flashlight to a haphazard pile of rope. A glint of something white brings a soiled feather earring into focus. "Didn't Hope's mother say she was wearing an earring like that when she left for school?"

Yes, Elsa thinks, *yes, yes.* Her eyes hunt for signs of Mel, anything to prove she's also been here, hoping that she wasn't, and in the darkness and panic she sees nothing. She says, "Maybe he doesn't actually have Mel. Maybe—"

Lex's hand on her shoulder is oppressive. She jerks away and heads toward the mouth of the cave. Recalling, suddenly, the thirst that clawed her throat after long hours in her closet. "If it were me in here since yesterday, I'd want water, first thing."

Bennett's voice trails her: "There are a couple of streams and a waterfall nearby. I used to bring my kids here when they were young."

Shaking, Elsa climbs out of the cave, into the tunnel.

Lex and Bennett are right behind her, the flashlight's beam opening the path forward.

33

"Come on, people, let's move it!"

Carrie leads the way, swinging her elbows like she's the captain of a marching band. She's tiny enough to get lost in the profusion of leaves but too bright to miss. Carrie is neon pink, and now, Hope sees for the first time, she carries an emerald-green baton. Behind her, sapphire Velma and Arnold wearing a big gold crown hold hands. This is new. Jesus comes last but he's grown a quarter inch and filled his outlines with rainbow stripes. Hope blinks her eyes. They disappear. Blinks again, and they're back, bigger and brighter than before.

Jesus turns to look directly at her, walking backward. "Don't give up, Hope!"

"I won't." Hope gasps. "I won't." Breathing is harder now. Her lungs feel deflated. Her throat is so swollen it's hard not to choke when she tries to swallow, which she can't anyway because she's out of saliva.

"Where are we going?" she asks the entire board of directors. She pays them to have answers, after all. It's their job.

"Who are you talking to?" the new girl asks. She's smaller than Hope, but stronger.

"Onward," Velma and Arnold say together.

And so they do—move onward. She follows, hoping for the best.

Carrie turns and raises her baton. "The cupcake. Drop the cupcake now. It's time."

Hope rips the cupcake charm off one of her bracelets and drops it. Carrie nods in approval. So does the new girl, who adds, "That's a good idea."

They tramp through the woods.

Everything dims. Hope feels scarily faint.

Jackson.

Her mother.

Her father.

Her brothers.

She forces open her eyes and thrusts her feet forward as daylight seems to drain away. In the dusky forest the entire army of her hundred and twelve little people appear, glowing, perched on leaves like candles on Christmas branches. *Tous ensemble* (Ms. Laroux, ninth-grade French), they raise their batons and lead her forward with a chorus of petty inquisition:

What is a quark?

The smallest unit of matter, makes up protons.

What are molecules?

Two or more atoms held together by *something*.

What is an organelle?

Part of a *something* that has a specific function.

What are the five types of organelles?

Nucleus, mitochondrion, *something something, something, something* body.

Order from smallest to largest.

"I hear water," Hope mumbles, tripping forward.

"No," the new girl says, "not now. We have to keep going."

"I'm so thirsty."

And then, laced into the gurgle of water, the leaf crunch of a footstep. Two.

Someone else's footsteps. *His.*

"Help me," she says to her little people. "Please."

They ignore her and repeat: *Order from smallest to largest.*

A third footstep, closer now.

And a fourth.

But it's an irresistible craving, not fear, that propels her. Water; thirst; molecular compound and human tongue. And then he can have her, if he wants her that badly. She can't fight him anymore, not even in her mind.

"Come with me," she begs the new girl, but she yanks her hand away and runs in the opposite direction.

The gurgling draws Hope forward and there it is: a sparkling, bubbling stream. She falls to her knees, laps at the shallow edge—sweet bliss!

Why couldn't the new girl at least wait for her?

She drinks again but it's not enough.

A plank across the stream promises passage to a clearing on the other side where it's deeper and she could dip in her face and gorge. The thought of it. She moves forward onto the plank, old wood warping underfoot.

The footsteps, faster, harder, louder.

His quick weight heaving onto the plank behind her.

When she's nearly there, it snaps and gravity releases her and as she's flying, her board of directors, *whom she pays to prevent just this kind of mishap,* swarm ahead, repeating the demand:

Order from smallest to largest.

34

Deb is a master gardener; she could be a professional if she wanted to. You learned early that she's happier around plants and have often wondered why she chose to make her living as an elementary school teacher. "*Always* around kids," she's been known to complain, "*never* get a break."

One springtime afternoon, on your way home from school, you and your mother and your sister stop at a landscaping center. Following your mother's instructions, you and Tara carry twenty-pound bags of rocks to the trunk of the car. The rocks are for Deb's garden—she's always creating something new—and you're proud that you're strong enough to assist in the effort. Then, with a heavy bag cradled in your arms, you recognize something vital: You have grown capable; you could resist her next time her rage flies.

Which it does, of course, not long after your realization.

It's just before dinner. You're alone with your mother in the kitchen. Roy isn't home yet, and Tara is at a friend's.

You dig in your heels about something and *that look* overtakes Deb's face, the mask of forced patience falling away, replaced by a contortion that makes your pulse spike.

You can't help yourself; you take off running.

She follows.

At thirteen you're quick but she's a grown woman and catches up with you in the second-floor hallway. She grabs your hair on both sides and smashes your head against the wall. And again. And again. She, enraged. You, in shock.

And then you remember your strength. You can hit back. Maybe you could get through to her if she got a taste of her own medicine.

You draw your hand back and slap your mother's face, hard. Just once. Shouting, *"How do you like it?"*

You've never seen her so surprised. You freeze, terrified of what might come next. You didn't anticipate that this warrior woman who has won every battle in your life would burst into tears and run away to her room and weep. But that is exactly what she does.

The guilt is overpowering. You've hurt your own mother. Proven your point by assaulting *your own mother*.

Her pain haunts you.

After that, the violence stops.

Gradually, over time, a new worry grows: What if someday you should become a mother; won't the cycle inevitably repeat? Because even though the hitting has stopped, the fear of it is still inside you. You are not to be trusted, because she made you in the likeness of her rage.

35

The group of searchers breaks past the dense trees and into the clearing where the nearest stream meanders, but Elsa senses they won't find the girls here. It appears thoroughly undisturbed except for the sounds of cheeping birds and the leafy crunch of the searchers' footsteps. In the near distance you can see the elaborate roofscape of the old mansion that houses the college. From their left tromps a group of half a dozen searchers.

"Water!" Elsa shouts to them. "We're looking for water!"

Bennett points. "This way—there's a reservoir."

They all veer to follow Bennett.

Elsa asks, "How far?"

"Not very—a thousand feet maybe."

As they move deeper into the woods, sunlight fades with an encroaching cloud, and with the loss of visibility, Elsa's heart begins to sink. They'll be too late, she feels it; feels, suddenly, that wrapped in the loss of Ruby is Hope, and wrapped in the loss of Hope is Mel, and wrapped in the loss of Mel is the renewed loss of Deb, and wrapped in the echo of the long-ago loss of Deb, as always, is the loss of herself…girls and women ribbed together by a single spine. In one's collapse, they all go down together.

Elsa shakes off the haunted thoughts and tries, tries to push past the inner headwinds of doubt and fear and shame and recrimination.

Lex moves ahead of her, along with two of the faster searchers. As Elsa watches him leave her, emotions conflict: resentment that he's abandoning her, and relief to be alone. Every now and then he glances back at her but he doesn't wait.

After a minute, Greenberg shouts, "I found something!"

In the craggy center of his broad palm he holds a thimble-size enameled pink-and-yellow cupcake frosted with rhinestones. A tiny metal loop shows where it would attach to a chain. Hope must have ripped it off a necklace or bracelet and dropped it as she ran or walked or crawled along. And if Hope was here, Mel could be nearby. Elsa rejects the images flashing through her mind of the girls blanketed under leaves, fallen or buried. No. She won't succumb to that yet.

The terrible thirst chafes at the back of your throat, closet-dark and insistent.

Another stream appears, this one longer. A pair of searchers follow Bennett in that direction, edging northward, while the remaining two stay with Elsa. Elsa, skin map tightening, slowed by a pull of dreamlike exhaustion. Soon, everyone has moved ahead of her. As the distance grows, she makes out the edge of what must be the reservoir Bennett mentioned. She can see searchers, like ants, fanning out around the bank.

She stops walking, so far behind now that there's no point trying to catch up. Alone and out of breath, she doubles over and gives in to the weight of helpless frustration.

They'll never find Hope.

They'll never find Mel.

Roy is going to die while Elsa is away, her past going with him but never really gone.

She will be forever unmoored. Lost. She has failed at everything.

She sinks to her knees. Pebbles and sticks dig into her flesh, rip through her pants. Her brain is sloggy, heavy; her skin alight. It's foolish to keep working when her father is dying. She *should* take a leave of absence, face the gathering storm head-on, race straight into it.

She should go back to Sleepy Hollow immediately. Sit with her father. Just be there, for whatever it's worth. Talk to him. Listen. It's suddenly clear.

They don't need her help finding the girls; it's presumptuous of her to think that her presence is of any real importance. Between Lex, Joan, Ernie Bennett, Greenberg, and the army of searchers, if the girls are still alive, they'll find them. And if they aren't alive, they'll find them. Everywhere, people swarm, looking. And Elsa does not want to be the one to find Mel if finding her will be anything like finding Ruby.

The pathetic wailing sound leaking through Elsa's tears embarrasses her, and she forces herself quiet, sucking back the flood of self-indulgent remorse. Standing, she brushes leaves off her knees and the palms of her hands.

And then, as the last searcher vanishes into the distance behind the tower of Greenberg, in the growing quiet she becomes aware of a low thrum, gulpy and emotional, as if she hasn't stopped crying, although she is sure that she's no longer making any sound.

A stream babbles somewhere near.

And then the hard crack of wood breaking.

She moves toward the sound, and there it is: water lapping onto a bank of pebbled earth. Just to the left, beyond a thicket of overhanging branches, the broken halves of a long board, someone's intention for a footbridge. It appears to have fallen in and obstructed the flow of water, creating the glurping sound. Her heart sinks lower. She'd thought, for just a moment, that the sound she heard could be someone else crying. That she isn't alone here. That she actually did hear another voice.

She steps into the stream and, pushing aside branches and prickly brush, moves closer for a better look.

And sees them.

Hope, obscured by the brush, wouldn't have been visible to the searchers. You have to veer in sideways, into the stream, or come in from the other direction to see her at all. She must have come across the plank while it was still in place. His sudden weight must have broken it—that crack. And now, here they are: she, curled into the muddy bank; he, kneeling over her.

Through the slick skin of his stream-wet clothes you can see the undulations of strain as his back and shoulders engage in some kind of effort. The cervical knobs of his neck appear grossly pronounced. Beneath him, her body subtly twists, legs barely kicking.

Alive.

Eyes glued to him, Elsa reaches into the water and feels for the Glock holstered to her ankle. She slides off the safety strap, grips the handle, tugs out the gun. Frozen in place, hand underwater, she studies him.

She focuses on the burl of neck and skull where his hair is skewed in all directions, a tender spot a mother might have kissed. She will aim exactly there. If she misses, Hope could die, but if she doesn't try, Hope will die.

She lifts the gun out of the water. And then, in a moment, the wet grip slicks out of her hand. Her weapon lands in the stream with a heavy plop, ripples orbiting. Nelson turns. Sees her.

His eyes blink like shorted neon. Mouth drops. The voice that sails out of him doesn't resemble the one that spoke to her on the Haverstocks' lawn, the voice of nerdy Teddy with his book and his button and his "analog message." This voice is massive, dense, guttural. Untamed. The sound of it spreads across her skin in high-voltage tendrils.

He shouts: *"You!"* And, like a bird of prey, launches himself in her direction.

She staggers backward, trying not to fall, and then pivots in an effort to skirt around him to get to Hope. Takes two steps, three, and then he lands on her, huge and powerful. Forces her down into the water until she's submerged. Eyes open, sinking in the up-bubbles of underwater breath, hands flailing on the streambed, drowning and drowning and drowning with shame for all her failures before this monster, who is herself, who is her mother, who is her past and present and future, when all she had to do was pull the trigger before he noticed her.

His fingers web around your neck with the tight, in-evitable feel of a Chinese finger trap; the more you struggle, the harder the grip, the worse your chances. Pushing down, he holds you underwater, his thumbs pressing into the hollow of your throat.

Oxygen drains away like the end of a brilliant afternoon, leaving you in a lavender twilight, and for a split second you're convinced that it's the most beautiful place you've ever been. You are unlatched; an inconsequential feather set afloat. The end of time is the beginning of time. You become a slippery birth out of yourself, at the hands of another, pre-pared for a simple release. Ready for it.

So this is how it feels when he kills them.

What surprises you most is how willing you are to give yourself to the prospect of your death.

But then you remember Mel, somewhere out there. And Hope, so close, at the edge of the stream.

Rallying, Elsa raises a knee into Nelson's groin, hard, and again, harder. He flinches briefly, enough for her to squirm partially out from under him. He recovers himself, fingers curling around her neck, but not before her right hand lands on a rock settled into the streambed.

She twists to the side, gets a grip on the rock.

His fingers bear down on her throat.

She sweeps her arm upward until she feels a shock of cold air on her hand. Calculates. Slams the rock into the side of his head. And again. And again.

His fingers flower open, releasing her, as if she's pushed a button and turned him off.

Water races into her mouth, fills her lungs. She surges

upward, desperate for air, expecting him to come at her again.

But he doesn't. He's stupefied, balanced on his knees like one of those inflatable punching bags that can't stand but doesn't fall. Moaning like an injured animal. Blinking, struggling to regain his equilibrium. His little daughter's face smiling, still smiling, from the dripping-wet button.

Now, she tells herself, *right now.*

She forces her hand into her wet pocket and pulls out the knife, *her knife,* with its array of implements she knows by heart. Plucks out the longest blade. Crashes through the water toward him.

His arm lifts, but slowly. She grabs his hair and jerks his head toward his left shoulder, revealing the long right side of his neck, his jugular vulnerable, all hers.

One cut. Precise. Swift. With force.

His flesh parts like the opening of a mouth. A lipstick-red smile. A yawn. A scream. Ribbons of blood pouring from the lips of his wound. His eyes seem to fix on her, staring, but empty. And then his body keels backward as if hinged at the knee. She thinks fleetingly of his mother, how he was once someone's beloved child. Even him. And then the reality of what just happened vibrates through her hand and arm and brain and awakens her.

She struggles forward, thrashing her way through the stream to Hope.

She can't see the girl's face, but the chain of her spine is still and her rib cage doesn't move at all. She doesn't seem to be breathing. There is no sign of life other than a trickle of blood that appears to be leaking from her wrist.

Shaking, Elsa crouches down. Hope's hipbone juts high above a sunken waist, a girl's narrow waist from which ribs flare to broad shoulders. Tattoos of impish figures, like those from her bedroom wall, march single file up the side of her neck, holding hands. Four of them: two laughing, one crying, one staring right at you with a look of curiosity. The side of Hope's rib cage rises, and falls, and rises again.

"Good girl," Elsa whispers, "just keep breathing."

"Auntie Elsa!" The voice calls from the opposite side of the stream. And there, there is Mel. Blood caked on her wrists. An angry bruise on her cheek. Shoeless. Sodden and filthy and *alive*.

THURSDAY

36

Lex Cole opens the chapel door for Elsa, continuing his trend of kindness, having covered for her over the past couple of days as she helped move her father into hospice, and she thanks him.

The cheerfulness of the airy chapel, with its blond wood and cream walls and the splashes of sunshine on the pale green carpet, feels disorienting, a counterpoint to the end-of-world hopelessness of the cave where Ruby drew her last breath. Elsa has hated funerals ever since her mother's, watching her father serve as a pallbearer, the blank misery of his expression, the deep sag of his shoulders under the unbearable weight, heavier than the casket or the body inside it.

Peter and Ginnie Haverstock wanted their daughter buried here, at Flushing Cemetery, because although neither parent came from Queens and they have no extended family here, it's the only home Ruby has ever known and they want to keep her close.

Lex, in a pressed black suit, slides into a pew. Elsa follows, too warm in a linen pantsuit, pale gray, with a black blouse and a triple-strand pearl choker. Real pearls, passed down from her mother, something she almost never wears. Tara got the diamond engagement ring and plans to pass it on to Mel someday.

Peter and Ginnie occupy the front-most pew, closest to the gleaming casket that encases their only child, bookended by white-haired couples, a pair on either side. No flowers anywhere, Elsa notices, but nothing surprises her anymore. The eyes of all three women are swollen and red, and one cries openly, presumably Ruby's maternal grandmother, as she sits pressed closely into Ginnie's side—Ginnie pale, bloodless, her shaking hand clutching a ragged tissue. Peter's utter stillness touches something deep inside Elsa, deeper than the sadness and regret that have rooted inside her since Tuesday—the burning seed of their failure to save Ruby's life.

That maniac, she thinks, wishing to reduce Sammy Nelson's culpability to something already made, inborn, inexorable; to strip him of his vengeful rage, the whole dangerous knotted tangle of a person who chooses—actually *chooses*—to prey on other people. But even now, today, sitting here in the solemn aftermath of a girl who came so close to reaching eighteen but had the bad luck of crossing paths with him first, even after everything Elsa has seen in her life and in her work, she can't bring herself to believe that anyone is born preprogrammed to kill. Even so, one way or another, we become who we are, and she will never forgive him for what he did to all those girls.

She doesn't realize that she's digging her fingertips into the tops of her thighs until she feels Lex's arm settle on the back of the pew behind her shoulders. She takes a deep breath and stops the grinding mechanism of her mind. They didn't get there in time for Ruby. They were too late for her. But Hope and Mel, they managed to save. Mel barely scathed, not physically, at least; Hope's recovery will take more time.

Elsa doesn't like working missing-kid cases, she decides for the hundredth time. She doesn't like it at all. She doesn't know how she's tolerated it all these years and then realizes she hasn't.

Two rows behind the Haverstocks, Ruby's friends cluster tightly together, talking, crying, glancing at their phones as if some vital piece of information might appear at any moment. Ruby, maybe, texting, jk lol i'm not really dead. Elsa knows not to underestimate magical thinking in the face of death, but these kids, they're just learning. Allie and Charlie sit at a distance from each other, and if they interact at all, she doesn't see it. People are scattered in the pews, waiting for someone to get up and speak.

No one can, not even Ruby's stricken parents, especially not them.

Finally, a bald man with a trimmed goatee ascends the platform, tripping on his long black robes, revealing Converse sneakers. He rights himself, stands behind the podium, and introduces himself in a soft voice as a "nondenominational pastor." He speaks long enough to put a few words to the overwhelming grief that has silenced everyone else. Both parents weeping now. Allie, among the gaggle of teenagers, heaves forward. Elsa takes another deep breath and doesn't cry.

Later, they follow the procession through a maze of

headstones, up a grassy slope to a plot of freshly dug soil. Beside it, a mound of dirt with a shovel poking out. The family sits in folding chairs lined up near the gaping mouth of the grave. Everyone else scatters, watching, as Ruby in her casket is lowered slowly into the earth. There is no marker for her, not yet; it all happened too fast. Elsa and Lex stand side by side, in silence, and watch from a distance.

The pastor pulls out the shovel, digs it into the mound, and holds out the first offering of soil to the family. After a moment of hesitation, Ginnie comes forward and takes it from him. She averts her eyes when he smiles at her, and Elsa wants to slap him for trying to cheer her up. Shaking, she carries the shovel in front of her, dirt raining in her wake. When she reaches the grave, she stands there, looking down. Her face seems to gather inward, like someone's pulled a string at the top of a sack, closing her off. A woman, a mother, finished. She tilts the shovel and the dirt falls in, thumps against the top of the casket. Quickly, she turns and hands the shovel to her husband, who has come up behind her. She makes her way across the lawn, back to her seat, where she hunches, cocooned in a private grief.

Peter stabs the mound, hard, provoking an avalanche of dirt.

Beside her, Elsa feels Lex's warmth. She steps away so she won't cry.

Reading her, he whispers, "Let's go."

They don't speak until they're sealed into the quiet of her car. Only then does she breathe. "That was awful."

"Yup."

"Poor Ruby." She starts the engine, steers onto the road

that winds through the cemetery. Lex, beside her, checks his phone.

"Wow—Elsa, we just got an e-mail from Oregon."

"We?" Thinking: *Oregon. Where Sammy Nelson officially lived.*

"The task force, all of us. The local PD went back to his place. There's a video attached."

She pulls the car up to the curb and parks, still inside the cemetery. "Open it."

He props his phone horizontally, and they wait while a two-minute file loads. A hearse with its headlights on enters from the street, moving slowly, leading a procession that snakes slowly past. Elsa stares at the small screen. Lex clicks the arrow and the video begins.

A man, young enough to still have a telltale crack in his voice, speaks over shaky footage that sweeps slowly left to right. "This is Officer Lloyd Bass, Winston, Oregon. I'm at the home of your perp. I was told to show you what I see, as you're on the other coast, so here goes. The outside of the building where he lived."

A low-rise apartment complex clad in beige siding, fringed with parking spots, half of them unoccupied. The lens rests on a windowless van, forest green, with a jagged scratch across the rear bumper, an Oregon license plate.

"This is Sammy Nelson's vehicle. Neighbors told us he has two vans, this green one and also a white one with New York plates. He takes up two spots, and some people don't like it, but occupancy here is low so management let it slide."

The camera jerks away from the van, back to the apartment building. Eight concrete paths connect the parking lot to a series of identical front doors, each leading to a down-stairs and an upstairs. Two buzzers per door, two apartments per unit.

"He lived in unit three, apartment B."

The officer's hand reaches into the shot to open the door. Hairless, not a wrinkle, a wedding ring.

"Up the stairs."

The image rocking with the officer's steps, the slaps of his shoes on cracked linoleum. His hand appears again to push open an interior door with 3B stenciled in black. "I unlocked it before, figured it would make a better shot, so you wouldn't have to watch the whole rigmarole with the landlord. Here we go."

Foot by foot, yard by yard, a living room takes shape. A room with off-white walls, brown carpeting, a low ceiling, two perfectly symmetrical windows with closed venetian blinds. On the wall above a long blue couch hangs, in pride of place, a poster-size enlargement of little Zoe—same as the button, but in this larger version a likeness to her father is evident around the eyes. Between the couch and the windows, a pair of tall bookcases lean into each other. Books, lots of books, and almost as many DVD cases, most with library stickers on their spines. *Ordinary People, Kramer vs. Kramer, Rain Man, Beginners*. The camera pans quickly past the windows: a large-screen television mounted on an otherwise blank wall, the inside of the front door on which a fringed macramé hanging is attached by a pushpin.

The lens makes a sudden dip to the floor, where, at the seam of living room and hall, an empty eBay box sits with its flaps open, a box just larger than the twenty-inch toolbox Nelson favored. With a shiver Elsa wonders if he'd been all ready to go, waiting for the package to arrive, if he'd opened it immediately and extracted the shiny red toolbox and filled it with his goodies and hit the road.

"Okay. Now the kitchen."

A small square room, windowless, with plain wood cabinets and the cheapest appliances you can buy. A round table fills up most of the space; it holds a red floral place mat, a saltshaker with an *S* and pepper shaker with a *P,* a plastic takeout cup with a lid and a straw and an inch of murky water at the bottom. A single chair. Inside the small sink sits a clear glass vase with a bouquet of dead coneflowers, bulbous black middles haloed with desiccated petals that might once have been purple. The camera lingers a moment on the front of the refrigerator, crowded with photos: people in pairs, trios, groups of picnickers, on boats and rooftops and swimming in lakes, smiling and laughing, a beaming couple with their arms around each other, a family raising their glasses at a holiday table laden with food. Every single photograph cut out of a magazine.

Loneliness punches Elsa in the gut. She blinks, and the lens turns away.

Bass announces, "Bedroom now. That's the last room. Well, and the bathroom."

The double bed is clumsily made with an Indian spread; two pillows hold the indentation of a person's weight—an empty space left by Sammy Nelson's body in repose. On a bedside table sits a short stack of books, titles turned to the wall, and one of those small clip-on reading lights—as if when he read, alone in his room, he wanted to make the smallest possible impact on the darkness.

"Enough," Elsa says, "I can't—I don't want to see any more." She turns to look out the car window, where just then a woman on a white bicycle whizzes toward the graves, a potted yellow begonia in the wire basket above her front tire.

FRIDAY

37

The FOR SALE sign on the lawn in front of the Martin-Creech house is gone. A pair of small boy's bikes is tangled together, tossed down by the front steps. Half a dozen camera-slung reporters stand at the edge of the property, talking casually, waiting out the family's reticence. As far as Elsa understands, Hope's parents have managed to keep the press at bay, practically a miracle, given the raging hunger of the news cycle.

The reporters come alive when Elsa and Lex take the path to the front door. Elsa rings the bell, sees a curtain part on a downstairs window, hears a voice say something and then footsteps. The father, Gary—gray-faced, dark swaths beneath his eyes—cracks open the door just enough to let Elsa and Lex inside. Behind them, cameras click and flash. He slams the door and locks it.

"They've been here since we got her home," Gary says. Three days.

He leads them to the living room, where all the curtains

are drawn against prying eyes, blotting out daylight. Hope and Becky sit close together in the bend of a sectional couch. On a low round coffee table, a pitcher of iced tea and five glasses have been set out, along with a plate heaped with clusters of green grapes.

"Sorry we're late," Elsa says.

Lex adds, "Traffic."

"No worries," Becky assures them. "We're happy as clams just sitting here."

They look it too. Even Hope, with her spectrum of bruises and bandages and sprained arm hoisted in a sling…even Hope looks relaxed.

Becky rises to greet them, kisses Elsa on the cheek. When a case ends well, the gratitude you receive is almost enough to remind you why you do the job. The real satisfaction, though, is in Hope's eyes. She doesn't get up or even smile. She doesn't really know them, after all; they were told that her memory of her rescue is dim. But the clarity of her eyes, the aliveness of them, is enough for Elsa. Despite popular belief, she feels that there's something elementally optimistic about teenagers, the way their bodies can operate as adults' while their minds still have a direct line into the good kind of wishful thinking, when you don't question the gumption of racing forward into life. Mel has that too. Elsa isn't sure if she herself has ever really been that confident. Sitting down across from the couch, looking at Hope, she wonders if the girls will take fewer risks now, and a renegade impulse rises up with optimism that the trauma may not necessarily distort their ability to trust people…but what's the likelihood of that?

"Are you guys, like, real FBI agents?" Hope asks.

Elsa smiles at the sound of Hope's voice, which she has never heard before: light and scratchy, as if she's recovering from a sore throat. "I am. My friend here is a police detective."

"Cool."

"So," Elsa gently probes, "how are you doing?" and elicits a sly grin from Hope.

"Seriously?"

"You don't have to talk about anything you don't want to."

Hope nods, her eyes darting to her mother.

"We've explained that to her," Becky says. "She understands."

"Okay, then." Elsa takes a breath. "What can you tell us about what happened to you?"

"He's dead, though, right?" Shifting in her seat, Hope winces.

Elsa answers, "One thousand percent."

"Are you the one who killed him?" Hope asks tentatively, like a child peering into forbidden dark corners, even though the time has passed to protect her from those.

Elsa nods.

"He was such a *freak*."

"You can say that again."

"I wish I could have helped Ruby."

"I know you do—but there's nothing you could have done to change the way things turned out. You had no control over him. None of this is your fault, honey."

Hope's eyes flash at the endearment coming from a stranger. Elsa regrets it. This isn't Mel, and it isn't a younger version of herself. She has no power to comfort the girl outside the reason for this visit: an exit interview, as it were, so that they can officially close the case file.

"He, like, came out of nowhere," Hope says quietly. "I missed the bus, so I was walking to school instead, and I was thinking about my biology test, and all of a sudden there's this guy in front of me." She sips her iced tea. Eats two grapes, slowly. "He kept wanting to talk, like we were friends or something. It was so weird. But then he also hit me. I didn't understand what was happening. And he had all these tools. And then he brought in this other girl, and I was so scared because the first girl, she was—" She slams shut her eyes.

"It's enough, angel," Becky says softly. "You don't have to say anything else." She lays a reassuring hand on her daughter's arm and glances sharply at their visitors.

Elsa and Lex stand and say their good-byes. Gary walks them to the door. At the last minute, Becky jumps up to join them.

"I didn't want to start crying in front of Hope," Becky says, "there's been too much of that around here lately—but I just have to tell you how grateful we are." She opens her arms to Elsa, envelops her in a maternal hug that feels familiar and foreign, comforting and off-putting, somehow right and somehow wrong.

"You have an amazing daughter," Elsa says. "I've never seen such a will to survive."

"If you hadn't—" Becky's words choke to a stop.

Elsa shakes her head emphatically—"Don't go there"—refusing to revisit the many ways in which they might not have found Hope and Mel alive.

"If you need us for anything," Lex says, "even to talk things through, give us a call. But if you never want to hear from us again, believe me, we'll understand."

Elsa could have loved the guy for having the heart to say that. She thinks of David. She wonders how much of the brothers' compassion comes from their late mother—the wise and affectionate Yelena—and how much comes from each other.

"The main thing is that Hope's safe now," Elsa agrees. "That's all that really counts."

Elsa holds a constant speed, just at the limit, as they drive through the bucolic village of Bennington in silence, past Greenberg's lumberyard, past the Blue Benn diner filled with patrons eating lunch as if nothing happened.

Lex says, "This town's got a big problem with heroin—dealers, addicts, the whole bit. Couple of colleges here—maybe a good fit for Charlie."

Elsa laughs, stifling the remarks that flit through her mind about the surfaces of things, about how meanness can lurk in the prettiest places. "Well," she says, "we're not college counselors and we're not DEA, so what do you say we get the hell out of Dodge?"

"*Dodge?*"

She explains but doesn't think it makes much sense to him, as he presumably missed out on *Gunsmoke* reruns during his Russian childhood and immigrant adolescence. She stops trying when they turn in the direction of the highway.

After a while, he surprises her with a question—or a challenge. "So, you told David you have tattoos."

She glances at him, speechless. Accelerating through the green-blue countryside, she grinds her teeth, wishes he weren't here, that he didn't know her, that he'd landed someone else for this case. But then she remembers that it wasn't random; he chose her.

He says, "You don't have tattoos."

"Excuse me?"

"A few days ago, in the wind."

She remembers. Standing outside the Martin-Creech house, a gust hit her hard. She was blinded for a moment by the swish of her hair over her eyes. She recalls the fabric lifting off her skin, how she needed to pull her sleeve back down.

And then he says, "Yelena was a cutter—our mother."

A cutter. No one has ever spoken that phrase aloud to her before. The few who know about her problem—her parents and sister—always held the secret as if it were their own. Each and every lover had fled in the sobriety of daylight. Avoidance, pretending normalcy, has been her creed for a lifetime. Competence has been her shield. She has found a way, barely, to live with herself, and she does not, not, not want to talk about it with Lex Cole or anyone else.

"Best woman I ever knew," he says. "She had some problems in her past. But she didn't let it stop her from loving us, or us from loving her."

Elsa stares at the road ahead, lap after lap of asphalt vanishing beneath the car. Her insides wither at the thought that Lex glimpsed her skin and might have discussed it with his brother. Well—the case is over; she never has to see either of them again if she doesn't want to. Her grip tightens on the wheel.

"I understand your predicament," he continues, "growing up with a tough mother. And then what happened to her. Terrible. But I'd also like to say this: Parents, they give what they can, even if it's shit. And you, Special Agent Elsa Myers, you didn't turn out so bad."

"Lex"—her voice gluey, the words difficult to force out— "I really can't discuss this." But the words do get out, just a few and nothing significant, and they have the desired effect of pushing him away. He's essentially right about her. But she doesn't need a friend; doesn't *want* a friend like him who will try to open her up, to know her, maybe even to fix her.

He nods. They sit in silence for a few minutes, and then she asks, "Would you mind if I dropped you at a train station? I'd like to go see my dad."

"Of course I don't mind." Warmly, gently, like a real friend. But he isn't. She wishes she could, but she can't.

38

Elsa walks through the white-pillared entrance of the assisted-living home where last year Roy parked himself prematurely, she'd thought at the time. But now she's thankful that he's here at Atria, with its genteel practical comforts. A nurse from the hospice program visits every day, like a philosopher-spa on wheels, tending his soul and rubbing out his kinks while no one pretends he isn't dying.

Everyone is dying, though, Elsa thinks, waving at the front-desk attendant with the pale blue coif she'd thought went out of style two generations ago. Everyone is dying, all the time. It's just a matter of when it becomes official. For Deb, it happened twenty-four years ago, right before dinner. For Roy, it will happen soon. For Elsa, the forecast is wide open.

"You're here!" Mel rushes over with a hug.

Elsa drinks in the love, holding her niece long enough to make the girl squirm away. "Where's Gramp?"

"With Mom, in the kitchen. She's slaying him at Scrabble—she's got no mercy."

Elsa finds her father and sister bent over the table in the small, sunny kitchen he uses only for morning tea. Roy has delighted in taking all his meals in the dining hall, socializing with the other residents, enjoying his freedom from even the smallest responsibility. Feeling a surge of gladness that he's had this one easy half-year, she pats his shoulder hello.

He turns his face to see her. "Hi, honey. I think I just lost this game." Behind him on the windowsill, Lex's hospital flowers, still mostly fresh in their vase.

"You know you did." Tara grins. "I'll run those errands now, Dad, since Elsa's here. Mellie, you want to come with me?"

"Sure. Auntie Elsa, will you be here when we get back?"

"Probably."

"Cool. Catch ya later, Rambo." Mel laughs at the new nickname she's apparently given her aunt.

Tara shakes her head, chuckling.

Roy forces a grin.

But Elsa's insides freeze. "Is that what you call me now?"

"Yep."

"You're a legend around here," Tara says. "Enjoy it."

They gather their purses. Elsa sits quietly with her father until the chatter is subsumed by the closing front door. "Wow, I don't know if I can live with that."

"We're lucky they have a sense of humor. So do you, Elsa. Don't forget that."

"Dad, I have to ask you something about Mom and—you know." The question that's long bubbled under the surface.

"Okay."

"Why didn't you stop her?"

The muscles of his face shift incrementally, creating the appearance of a deep shadow. "I didn't know how."

"Why didn't you take us away from her?"

He looks at his daughter and struggles to explain. "She was my wife, and she wasn't easy, and the thing was that I"— *Loved her,* Elsa is sure he's about to say. But instead—"was afraid of what would happen. I was afraid that if I left her and took you with me, it would make things worse."

"Worse how?" When obviously her life would have been so much better.

"I don't know," he says with a familiar hollow sigh. "I've thought about it and I can't really understand it myself. I was weak, confused. We were a family. I didn't know what to do."

You drop everything and save the kid, she wants to shout, but doesn't. What's the point? In this case, the kid has grown up and the consequences of all that violence are etched into her skin.

"Elsa." His hand creeps forward to take hers, dry, cool, and he holds tight as if she's a balloon and he's afraid she'll float away, as if no matter what he does or says, he's fated to lose her trust. "Something came to me just this morning; I realized that I was wrong; we did leave something behind at the house. So much time's gone by, years, and I'd put it out of my mind. And then suddenly I remembered. I'm sorry, Elsa, I'm sorry."

"The King of Denial" is what she and Tara used to call him behind his back, before Deb was killed. They'd laugh about it. They even invented a little Egyptian-esque dance featuring (in their imaginations) their father in imperial robes on the banks of the river Nile, pretending to ignore a bloody sacrificial ritual being enacted in the open.

Elsa asks, "What? Just tell me."

She watches his Adam's apple toggle up the reed of his throat and slide down. "Remember I had a concrete platform built before the shed was installed in the backyard? I buried something very, very deep at the far left corner, near the fence."

She instantly knows what he means.

Her mind flashes to the backyard, five days ago, on Sunday, and she realizes that the shed wasn't there. The new owners must have had it removed in preparation for their pool. All she recalls is that the yard looked overgrown in some places, empty in others.

A wave of queasiness overtakes her. "The shed's gone."

"It can't be."

"But it is." She pulls her hand out of his and stands. As usual, what he's offering is too little, too late. But she can't hate him for it, not now. He has never been quite enough, but for years he's been her only parent, her wobbly island in an incessant storm, and he won't be here for long. She leans over to press her lips against his soft, withered cheek. "I love you, Dad."

"I'm sorry," he repeats.

"Don't worry. I'll take care of it." Not adding the obvious: *If it isn't too late.*

"Elsa?"

She turns at the door. He looks gaunt, almost translucent, in the bright kitchen sun. "Yes?"

"I love you too."

39

A summertime chorus of air conditioners hums along with cricket song, masking Elsa's steps in the deep night quiet as she moves up the driveway and into the backyard. She kicks aside the long dry grasses that have fallen over the footprint of the missing shed, where the concrete slab has been removed. Uncovered, the earth is dark and moist, recently overturned. She removes a paper lunch sack from her canvas bag and sets it on the ground. Lays a brand-new spade on top of the sack. Puts her bag off to the side, where it won't get dirty from the mess she's about to make. She gets on her knees and begins to dig.

Roy meant what he'd said about burying it very, very deep. The soil remains loose and easy three feet down, releasing a loamy sweetness rife with memories of Deb digging in this very yard, preparing it for planting. Elsa digs all the way to the property line marked by the fence, and a foot to either side. She digs forward to where the middle of the shed had been. She digs and digs, stirring already loosened earth.

She plunges in her spade, hoping to find it and hoping *not* to find it; anticipating the contours of her mother's favorite chef's knife: the wood handle now baked soft by time, its sharp edge coarsened. *Nothing, there's nothing here,* she thinks, and then she feels something hard that isn't a stick or a stone—something man-made that doesn't belong buried in a yard.

And suddenly, after all these years, it's back in her hand: the rounded butt, the dip of the handle guard, the scales and tang and return. Not long after it happened, she'd spent hours studying the anatomy of a knife just like her mother's, hoping that if she could reconstruct every element of every moment of that afternoon, maybe she could understand it better. But it never made any sense, how or why what had happened to her could happen to someone. To a child. And yet it had.

She lifts the knife to eye level, looks at it in the moonlight. Yes, this is it, her mother's knife. Memory rushes back: the shocking richness of Deb's blood, and how much there was of it; Elsa's horror at what had happened and her urgent wish to reverse it.

40

Your hold, at sixteen, is firm around the handle of the knife. Your mother's best chef's knife, the one she favors and polishes and sharpens and puts away. The first one you find at hand when she enters the kitchen that afternoon after punching Tara in the back for refusing to start her homework. Tara, then twelve. Considerably older than when Deb started with you.

You'd thought, you'd believed, that she would never touch Tara.

But the sound of that bone-hard smack from the next room, Tara's sorrowful wail, the thump of your little sister running up the stairs, the way your mother sighs and shakes her head when she walks into the kitchen to make dinner, as if this is just another day.

It isn't.

It can't be.

Everything inside you racing to the surface when you pick up the knife and approach her.

The lush waterfall of blood from Deb's neck.

The way she looks across the room before falling—at the door opening, at Roy walking in, his jaw slack, eyes wide, sheet music spilling out of his bag as it drops off his shoulder—and tries for her husband's sympathy before crashing to the floor.

The way your father hurries to fix everything: clean the mess, hide the knife, invent the story of intruders. How he runs upstairs to comfort Tara and weave the first threads of the lie so that she won't have to know what her older sister did, how bad things just got: *A man broke in, a violent man, but he's gone now; Elsa was heroic, she scared him off, and now she's safe*. How he returns to the kitchen, where he contains you, shaking and terrified, in his arms. And holds you there for the rest of his life.

41

"Pizza delivery!" announces a man's disembodied, crackly voice through Elsa's apartment's intercom.

She presses the Talk button. "I didn't order any pizza."

"Elsa, it's me."

"Me?" But she can think of only one person who would have the nerve to show up uninvited.

"I'm not hungry," she lies, wondering if he actually *does* have pizza, because in fact she's very hungry and has nothing on hand for dinner.

"You don't have to eat. Please, buzz me in."

She pauses, then says, "One minute."

She takes her mother's scrubbed-clean chef's knife out of the dish drainer, dries it with a kitchen towel, and slips it into the drawer where she keeps her few cooking utensils. Something in the back of her mind, a warning, bleats for attention but she ignores it. It's been a long day, begun in the car to Vermont with Lex Cole, and it might as well end with him over a slice or two of pizza. She's tired of fighting him, and maybe he's right, maybe she could use a friend.

She buzzes him in, and he appears at her door holding a flat white box in one hand and a six-pack of beer in the other. "Sure you're not hungry?" he asks. "Or thirsty?"

"Well," she says, "I guess I am a little bit of both."

"I knew it." He walks past her and sets the pizza and beer down on her table.

"You know what I just realized?" she asks as she opens her cupboard and takes out two plates. "I don't know very much about you, and here you just show up at my place because you feel like it." She puts the plates on the table, pushes aside a stack of newspaper and unopened mail, and sits across from him. Twists the caps off two bottles and pours them each a frothy glass.

He raises the top of the pizza box, releasing a fragrant steam that makes her stomach growl. "You know about my parents, about Yelena, you've met my brother, you know where I went to school. Actually, you know a fair amount about me."

"About your past."

He lifts a cheese-oozing slice onto a plate and hands the plate to her. "Ask me anything you want. I have no secrets from you." The way he says it, it's like a dare. And she thinks: *You* should *have secrets, you need them to protect yourself, it isn't safe not to hold back the most important things.*

"Okay." She drinks deeply of her beer, cold, sharp. "Where do you live?"

"Queens—Ridgewood." Now a slice for himself.

The pizza is warm, not hot, and when she takes her first

bite, her hunger explodes. She chews, swallows, asks, "Single?"

"Boyfriend."

A reflexive half smile she instantly regrets. "Oh."

"That bother you?"

"Why would it? I just never really thought about it. What's his name?"

"Adam."

"Profession?"

"Coder by day, artist by night."

"What kind of artist?"

"Painter mostly, and also installations."

"So, do you live together—you and Adam?"

"No. Not yet. Maybe soon." He twists open a fresh beer and refills her glass. His, she notices, has barely been touched.

"That's nice." And she means it, deeply, so deeply, in fact, that she has to push away a blip of jealousy.

He asks, "What about you?"

"What about me?" Defensively. But this time, he persists.

"Boyfriend? Girlfriend? *They*friend?"

She laughs, but it's thin, discomfort having crept in. She says, "Obviously you and your brother talked about me, so you already know." About the permanence of her singlehood. About her tattoos that aren't tattoos. The second beer has gone to her head, made her feel cloudy, light. She knows she should stop now. She takes another long swallow.

"He really likes you, Elsa, and he wouldn't care about the…you know."

The cutting, that's what he wants to say. *The way you cut yourself to shreds.* What surprises her now is that she almost wants to hear him say it; for the first time, she wants to rip away the veil with someone outside her family. Tell him everything, the whole truth. But how could he possibly understand?

"You have a lot going on in your life right now"—he detours out of the heavy silence that followed his remark—"with your dad's health."

She nods. Sips her beer. Wonders what would happen if she rolled up her sleeve and showed him, actually showed him, her skin.

"And the case, it wasn't easy, to say the least. You were great, Elsa. I was really impressed. The way you cared about those girls, really threw yourself into it."

"So did you."

"It isn't the same." His eyes settle on her, and the map of her skin sizzles awake.

She thinks of her mother's knife sitting in her drawer.

Gets up.

Retrieves it.

Places it beside the pizza.

He looks at her, vaguely confused. "Want me to cut you a smaller slice?"

She lays her right arm on the table, flips it over, pushes up her sleeve, and shows him the pale, slashed underside of her ruined skin. "See this?"

He nods.

"I have a confession, and after I tell you, you can do whatever you want."

He reaches over and gently pulls her sleeve back down. "Don't."

"It disgusts you," she says.

"No. I've seen it before; Yelena never hid herself when we were at home."

But Elsa can't imagine anyone being so open and comfortable in her damaged skin, revealing herself casually. Was Yelena really that brave? Or did she give up caring? Or did she feel truly loved?

"It doesn't look nearly as bad as you think it does, Elsa."

Maybe, maybe not, she can't tell; to her, it looks monstrous. Her arm feels cold, naked, a thing of shame lying on the table between them. But she can't stop now; she has to finish what she started. She has never come this far before and she senses that if she holds back, she'll never try again. Roy is about to die. She cannot be alone with this for the rest of her life.

She says, "This is the knife that killed my mother." Almost speaking the precise truth: *I killed her*. She feels faint. And relieved. And terrified.

"Elsa." A flint in his voice, begging her to listen carefully. "Stop right there."

She gets it: he's *not* her friend, he's a cop, and she's an idiot …who just came very close to admitting to a murder.

"That was a long time ago," he says. "It's over. Let it lie."

Solid advice, but impossible. *Lie where?* she wants to ask. *Because my insides are as cut up as my outside, and my father is about to go, and I can't hold this knowledge alone. I can't.* She says, "How?" trusting the small, simple word not to betray her, but it does, oozing anxiety.

He reaches for her arm, for her skin, as if to touch it— and she almost lets him. She *wants* to be touched and thinks, suddenly, of how safe and welcome her father's embrace has always been and how soon she'll no longer have it. She looks at her watch, aware of how late it's getting, how she could still get up there to join Roy for a cup of tea. This detour, this pizza-dinner-dancing-around-the-edges-of-a-possible-friendship episode, has not only perilously softened her defenses but stolen valuable time.

She pulls down her sleeve. Pushes the knife beneath the mess of newspaper and mail. "Let's pretend," she says, "that I never showed it to you." The knife, she means, but the way he glances at her arm lets her know how broadly he interprets her request.

"I can't unknow you, Elsa. I don't want to." He picks up the knife—newspaper sliding off, mail scattering. At the sight of the blade held in front of her, sharp, brilliant, she jumps back decades into her mother's eyes and sees herself wielding it with keen intent: a terrified girl, more powerful than wise. And then her mind leaps across to the kitchen door where her father stands, gape-mouthed, watching, and lands in *his* eyes, into the quicksand of his helplessness that was always, always stronger than his love.

"It's heavier than it looks," Lex says, and she returns to the moment.

"You have no idea."

He folds the newspaper around the entire length of the knife and makes a neat rectangular package, which he tucks beneath his arm. Stands. Says, "Come on."

"Lex"—a fester of argument in her tone—"I can take care of that myself."

"I know you can." But he doesn't give it to her. "I can tell you're anxious to get back up to your dad. I'll drive; I hardly drank anything. We can make a quick detour to the Hudson River, play a little game of Frisbee—what do you say?" He makes a gesture as if to hurl the newspaper-wrapped knife, to rid her of her every burden.

"And then what?"

"I'll wait while you visit your father. Or, if you want, I'll take the train back to the city so you can spend the night."

"Someone will find it sooner or later, and *then* what?"

"Then nothing. No one's looking for this—no one. It's just a knife. You should see the crap they regularly dredge out of that river." Warmth tugs at the corners of his eyes, and he's right. She doesn't need or want this relic of the worst moment of her past, and there's no reason to act as if she isn't grateful for his help. He has worn her down, infiltrated her, made himself her confidant whether she's prepared for one or not.

She takes her bag from the back of the chair and tosses him her car keys.

He catches them with his right hand and with his left wrests free another slice of pizza for the road. "Ready?"

"No," she says, and leads him out the door.

ACKNOWLEDGMENTS

Weeks before my mother died, she said something casually in conversation that sparked what became this novel. First and foremost, I have to thank her for giving me this one last thing. She was my first-ever writing teacher; in her fourth-grade classroom, I joined my fellow students at her direction in creating tiny illustrated books. That was the moment that I fell in love with storytelling and bookmaking. As I grew up and wrote novels that found a place in the broader world, she helped me however she could, reading drafts and offering comments and also stepping in whenever I needed help juggling my own children along with a budding career. But as with most mother-daughter relationships, layers of history and argument tended to jostle for attention. The confluence of her loss and the meandering path this novel took as it found its story and voice will remain, for me, a time of personal and sometimes painful growth. She left too quickly and we never finished our conversation. Had she read this novel, the conversation would inevitably have deepened.

Others to be thanked include my brilliant and patient literary agent Dan Conaway, along with his assistant Taylor Templeton, at Writers House, where drafts were read and discussed until the novel gained its footing. Emily Giglie-rano, the talented editor at Mulholland Books who opened her wings and took in this project, nudged me forward, always with grace, until together we found the story's balance. Everyone at Mulholland Books and its parent, Little, Brown, have been wonderfully supportive, especially Josh Kendall, Reagan Arthur, Judy Clain, Sabrina Callahan, Pamela Brown, Nicky Guerreiro, Neil Heacox, Michael Noon, and Tracy Roe. And for bringing this to readers around the world, I'm lucky to have Maja Nikolic on my team at Writers House/London, where she put this novel into the hands of Ruth Tross at Hodder/Mulholland UK and back into the trusted hands of my longtime German editor Suenjie Redies at Rowohlt.

Many thanks to Supervisory Special Agent Scott Schelble of the FBI's Child Abduction Rapid Deployment Teams Unit and Angela Bell in the FBI's Office of Public Affairs, both of whom gave generously of their time in answering all my questions about how a missing-child investigation works.

My dear friend writer and editor Suellen Grealy read the novel in progress and was a great help with a trove of excellent suggestions and encouragement. And last but never least, the earliest and most steadfast reader of what must have seemed like endless drafts was, as always, my husband Oliver Lief, whose feedback was never less than incisive; somehow, over the years, he has found a way to give me both good news and bad news straightforwardly but with kindness.

ABOUT THE AUTHOR

Karen Ellis is a pseudonym of longtime crime fiction author Katia Lief, who is a member of the International Thriller Writers, Mystery Writers of America, Sisters in Crime, and the Authors Guild. She lives in Brooklyn.

MULHOLLAND BOOKS

You won't be able to put down these Mulholland books.

BLUEBIRD, BLUEBIRD *by Attica Locke*

RIGHTEOUS *by Joe Ide*

A MAP OF THE DARK *by Karen Ellis*

THE GIRL ON THE VELVET SWING *by Simon Baatz*

THE TAKE *by Christopher Reich*

DOWN THE RIVER UNTO THE SEA *by Walter Mosley*

GREEN SUN *by Kent Anderson*

Visit mulhollandbooks.com for
your daily suspense fix.